PRAISE FOR WES DEMOTT AND *THE FUND*!

"One of those rare novels that transcends its genre. This is far more than a great thriller!"
—Nelson DeMille, author of *Up Country*

"A suspenseful thriller that kept me turning the pages. Outstanding!"
—U.S. Senator Larry Craig (R-ID)

"A stylized, turn-on-a-dime crime story where the lines between love, murder and espionage are deftly blurred."
—*Publishers Weekly*

"A writer to be watched!"
—*Atlanta Journal-Constitution*

THE FINAL TEST

It was impossible to guess what might go wrong the next day, but if Baker's death looked like a murder and ended up in the news, I couldn't risk the desk clerk calling the police: "Silver Corvette with a long-haired driver? I had someone in my motel just like that." I parked a half-mile away in the lot of a bar on Route 3. The joint was rocking, so anyone seeing my car before I came to get it in the morning would suspect its owner had drunk too much and rode home with a friend. I grabbed the bag that held everything but my Goodwill clothes and walked back toward the motel.

The next day was Thursday, as good a day as any to kill Randall Baker. Despite what Parrish told me, I doubted that a clean assassination was necessary for graduation from Jaspers. The fact was, since I was the only Jasper candidate in my class who had never killed a man, they wanted to make sure I could really do it before sending me after someone who really counted. Or maybe they simply wanted to give me a taste of blood because I'd never really hurt anyone badly.

Either way, I didn't care. I was going to kill Baker.

HEAT SYNC

WES DeMOTT

LEISURE BOOKS NEW YORK CITY

A LEISURE BOOK®

June 2005

Published by

Dorchester Publishing Co., Inc.
200 Madison Avenue
New York, NY 10016

ISBN 0-8439-5545-7

Visit us on the web at www.dorchesterpub.com.

HEAT SYNC

"The end of the human race will be that it will eventually die of civilization."

—Ralph Waldo Emerson

BOOK ONE

BOOK ONE

Prologue

Jim Parrish stopped along a block of buildings bleached white by the sun. Their color matched the desert that surrounded the city like a barren moat, making it hard to get to this North African capital and even harder to leave—especially once the transportation was monitored and the roads were barricaded. He'd had to factor that desert carefully into his escape plans.

It was a hot day, well over a hundred degrees. Parrish sweated under his traditional flowing robe and headdress as he bartered for a silver bracelet he wanted for no one in particular, a kind of woman he had never known but wanted to meet someday. He didn't expect it would ever happen, but even a savage like Parrish had hope.

He spoke to the ragged street vendor in Arabic, a harsh language he'd learned years ago and practiced frequently. He couldn't wait for the day to come when he could forget it. The back-of-the-throat grindings and sudden glottal stops sounded far too brutal for such an intelligent culture. At the Defense Language Institute in Monterey it had been fun practicing to suddenly stop a word by emulating working-class Brits saying, "what-a-lot-of-little-bottles." It was no longer a joke, though. If he mispronounced a word or forgot a response, he could blow his mission. He should have just kept quiet, but Parrish always had to test himself under pressure.

The vendor rattled away at a pace too fast for Parrish to understand much beyond the fact that he was holding firm on the price, even though it was clear how badly he needed to sell something. As the impoverished tradesman extolled the craftsmanship of his work, his pride battled across his face in a pathetic war with the desperation of his situation. After holding the bracelet so that the sun glistened off and into Parrish's eyes, he picked up a dull ring of little value and polished it on his sleeve, admired it, and then offered it to sweeten the deal.

Parrish looked around slowly, barely listening by that point. The sirens were only a few blocks away and coming fast, so he paid the vendor his price. It was too high, but he respected the man's hard work and pride and didn't want to take any of it away. He put the bracelet on his wrist, straightened the long, loose white fabric of his *dishdashah*, and walked away from the grateful seller who shouted praises behind him and wished the peace of Allah upon him. Parrish gave the cheap ring to a little boy, who looked it over and then tossed it to the ground.

By the time he got into position at the corner, the sirens of the motorcade were less than a block away, screaming through the streets as if predatory and unstoppable. Cars sped out of the way or pulled to the curb and waited. Parrish looked over the roof of a junker down the street, nearer the sirens, and worried it might have blocked his path of trajectory. But he'd chained his bicycle to a sign next to the crosswalk, so there wasn't room for the old car to stop without blocking the cross street. On the package rack of the bicycle was a satchel containing an explosive device he'd constructed himself, none of the materials traceable to the United States.

The motorcade turned down his street, just as the intelligence report had predicted. As soon as the last of the advance security cars passed through the target area, Parrish clicked a remote transmitter to arm the device and turn on the light beam that aimed from the satchel and across the road, allowing the king's own limousine to trigger the explosion, detonating himself without even knowing it. Too many times in situations like these, an assassin would fire early or late and totally miss his target, but then the Red Army Faction perfected this method. They killed the head of Deutsche Bank with it when he'd said he was untouchable, proving it to be an effective and hard-to-prevent device for killing people.

Two or three seconds after arming the weapon, the king's level-four armored limousine broke the light beam, just like a customer walking into a store. But instead of sending a signal to a chime or bell, this broken light beam detonated twenty pounds of dynamite packed in a thick steel box in the satchel on the bike. On the side of the box facing the street was a five-pound copper lid, aimed directly along the light beam.

The blast instantly destroyed dozens of innocent

people and sent the copper lid hurtling toward the limo at 1,400 feet per second. The speed bent it into a wedge—a five-pound artillery round that slammed into the limousine, crushing the side of the car, spinning it around and exploding the fuel tanks. Car parts flew everywhere and rattled through the city street like shrapnel, cutting down a dozen more pedestrians as the escort vehicle immediately behind the king's slammed into the flaming limousine and exploded a few seconds later.

Parrish was the first man running toward the king, leading the crowd of Arabs that rushed the incinerating vehicle. It was definitely the king inside and not one of his doubles. His lifeless, burning body was wedged against the door, the gold medal of authority still hanging around his neck on a heavy chain.

Parrish backed away and sheathed the palmed knife he would have used to slash the king's throat had it been necessary. As bodyguards rushed from the other cars, Parrish straightened the *gutrah* on his head and moved back with the crowd, covering his face and jabbering away in panicky Arabic like everyone else, just another terrified man in the street.

This kind of killing was a throwback event, the grand old way of assassination at which Parrish was one of the best. The hope for a clean kill that would look like an accident had vanished with Cameron's capture and murder, so Colonel Maddigan had ordered Parrish to do something quick that would distribute the suspicion among dozens of politically unstable neighboring countries.

Parrish walked away and down the street, proud of his service to his country, of having just done something significant to protect her. If President Devereau was too tunnel-visioned to see any threats beyond terrorism, he was sure there would always be men like him who would watch America's back.

Staff Sergeant Jim Parrish was nothing more and nothing less than an American patriot.

One

"Thompson!" our instructor shouted as my team of SEAL candidates struggled along the beach of Coronado. "Drop the log and double-time to Commander Nance's office. That's an order, damn it."

"Only after we've reached our goal," I said, once again pissing off someone in authority. It was just my way back then, I guess. I never understood why I did things like that, but I could certainly have made some guesses. All my life I'd been a man of many theories, and although it might not apply on a chilly morning on a sandy beach, one of my favorites was that all men, including me, reveal a lot about themselves when a short-skirted woman slides out of a car or chair.

"Don't screw with me anymore, Thompson. I'm sick of it!"

Some men—but not my instructor, I was pretty sure—make a point of looking away, as if they don't care about such foolishness. These men are saints or, more likely, just too polite or scared to follow the natural instinct that's kept our species alive, and that's why I never trust them.

Other men are cowards, pure and simple, stealing a glance and then looking away.

"Damn you, Thompson!"

A few sneak a sheepish peek and then act like they're sorry, exploiting a woman's natural tendency to forgive anyone who apologizes, even if insincerely.

And then there have always been the few—like my highly decorated SEAL instructor, who at that very second looked ready to take my head off my shoulders—who take a steady, interested look up her skirt, which is what every damn one of them wants to do. These guys, in my opinion, have courage.

As for me, I'm twenty-eight, healthy, hetero, and a guy who looked away, stole a glance, and then looked away again.

I might also be a liar.

"Okay, Thompson, you've just earned a night in the water alone."

"Fine, but I'm still bore-sighted on my mission and won't leave my team."

Unfortunately for me, women in short skirts *never* seemed to be sliding out of cars or chairs when wondering what kind of man you were dealing with at Basic Underwater Demolition School. If I'd had any idea what was going to happen in the next few minutes, I might have hired just such a woman to go to Commander Nance's office with me and get out of a chair seductively. It might have saved me a lot of grief, but probably not.

The day had already been exceptionally tough, but easier in some ways because of the anger we all felt like a virus that spread over the base. I was wet and sandy from struggling under the log's weight, shivering on the beach as my instructor cursed a string of threats at me—always scary, but even scarier since the rumor of a SEAL being beaten and executed overseas. That almost made us glad to be abused, as if we were bound on both a personal and professional level to suffer with a tortured SEAL brother we never had a chance to meet and never would.

"Make it two nights in the ocean alone," my instructor screamed, as if I'd been the one to kill him. "Now get to Commander Nance's office before I make it three!"

We kept moving and I wouldn't quit, ignoring his threats as best I could as we plodded slowly through the small dunes of Southern California, a beach-width away from the cold Pacific, an uncivilized world away from the curious guests of the Hotel Del Coronado, struggling through unstable sand in brutal teamwork with a six-hundred-pound log on our shoulders. One hundred pounds per man. One hundred twenty if I left as ordered.

But I had no intention of leaving. I wanted to feel the pain. I wanted to make the sacrifice. I wanted to show more courage and loyalty to SEALs than any other man there, even the instructors.

"Thirty yards more," I said, using strength I needed for the load. "Give me five more minutes. We'll make it this time."

"You want me to make it a *week*?"

"Twenty-five stinking yards. Come on, guys, let's heave and leave."

"Okay, Thompson. That's it, a week it is."

"Twenty yards more." And then: "Make it two weeks."

My instructor kicked the sand and threw up his hands. He spun around and looked at the control officer, who ran over and toed across the sand in front of us.

"Here's your new goal, Thompson. Your team made it, total points, now drop the log."

The other men immediately followed his order, and I had to go along. The log rolled off our shoulders and the shifting weight took three exhausted men down with it. I doubled over but kept from falling. "You should have let us do it right," I said. "I wanted to do it right."

"You're a pain in the ass, Thompson. Now get out of here, double time. You've already earned a week of nights alone in the ocean."

I straightened up and managed a breath. "I earned two."

"Go!" He turned away from me.

I took off down the beach in my helmet, wet shorts, and T-shirt, with splinters in my shoulder and open blisters on my palms and fingers. My sweat and stink and speed attracted everyone's attention as I ran through the small base. I forced people to notice me, to see my honor and loyalty to SEALs. Faces came to jalousie windows, senior officers stopped as I passed on the sidewalk, enlisted men stepped onto the grass and saluted. I pushed against several months of cumulative pain to run like that, making my sacrifice for the tortured SEAL, paying my price for his death, weaving around the one-story buildings of Coronado Amphibious Base to a building near the main gate. I tripped at Commander Nance's office door, straightened instantly and knocked, then waited two seconds and entered.

I was out of breath but tried to hide it as I braced at attention while Nance and an Army colonel studied me from the side of the grim office. I stared at Commander Nance's wall of impressive plaques and commendations, bursts of red, white, and blue on a Navy-gray wall. My calf muscles spasmed and made me wish I'd had trousers to hide the show of weakness.

"I've lost a good man in Africa," the colonel said to Commander Nance while he stared at me. "I have a critical need to replace him."

"I know," said Nance. "Captain Pike called this morning. Cameron was in my training class at Camp Lejeune."

"Unlucky bastard."

"They torture him before the beheading?"

"God wouldn't recognize him."

"Jeez."

"No family, though, so that's good. And Jim Parrish was there to grab the slack, doing old-fashioned things in which he's so proficient. At least that worked out."

Nance looked spooked at the man's name—Parrish. He tried to smile but couldn't quite do it. "Jim Parrish. Jeez. Now, there's a guy I'd hate to tangle with. So what kind of fallout do you expect?"

"It'll be another reason to beef up the war on terrorism, to spend more money on asymmetrical threats—rich, angry men instead of powerful, angry nations. It won't matter one bit the killers made a crude attempt to make it look like terrorism."

I shivered in the cool room. The colonel noticed and shook his head in disappointment as my shoulders threw off the chill.

"This fellow is the best you've got?" He asked about me as if I wasn't there.

Commander Nance—Lurch to his peers, and there couldn't be many—strutted across the room to me. His six-foot-three frame went for six and a half in the colonel's presence, his volleyball-sized head straining a powerful neck stretched a little too proudly.

"Thompson . . ."

That was my name there. Not Henry or Hank or H.T., like my buddies back in Danville, Indiana, called me. There I was Thompson, Lieutenant J.G., junior grade.

None of us had a first name anymore. Made sense, too. An instructor would have had a tough time sounding vicious shouting, "We're training you to be SEALs, the deadliest small-force threat in the world. Killers! Survivors! Do you have any idea what that means, Hen-*ry?*"

"Sir."

"Thompson, this is Colonel Maddigan, from the Pentagon. He has new orders for you. Voluntary, just like here."

"Sir, new orders? I haven't graduated yet, sir."

That was it, what I knew had been coming. Only fifteen percent of BUDS applicants are accepted, and seventy-five percent of them leave before they graduate as SEALs. Cold has always been the biggest reason, the worst enemy. Cold water, cold weather, cold, cold, cold. They let you sit around and shiver for hours and then demanded your best.

I would never quit, but I wasn't going to graduate, either. The cold had won. The handful who could endure it spent hours trying to teach me ways to stop shaking, but I just couldn't do it. Maybe I just didn't have enough body fat, which always made me wonder if the problem could be solved with potato chips and ice cream.

"You've tried like hell, Thompson. We've all seen it. But you won't graduate. In your case it's just physiology, certainly nothing to be ashamed of. You've gone further than most. You've led your class in many aspects of the training, especially in stealth skills. Which is one of the reasons the colonel is here."

I didn't really hear his consolation speech. I kept staring at the SEALs trident on his uniform, accepting for the first time that I would never wear it. I tried to convince myself it was too big anyway.

I turned toward Maddigan. I was petrified wood from weeks of abuse, and it showed. Maddigan was a study in boredom, like a man playing high-stakes poker.

"Sorry about my appearance, sir."

Colonel Maddigan made a slow lap around me. He was scary, which surprised me because I'd always thought of the Pentagon as the military's corporate headquarters and the people who work there as soft. After all, how many barroom brawlers could there be at IBM's home office? Maddigan made me believe there might be a few.

"Lieutenant Thompson," he said, then stepped in front of me and frowned. He was about forty-five, maybe fifty, my height, five eleven, but much thicker around the chest. His face was cold but handsome.

His eyes searched me with an honest intensity and signaled the intellect encased in his rugged head, looking as gnarly and challenging as a coconut. A ragged scar, long healed but forever purple, dug away from his right eye and then severed a shallow grave in his cheek. When the horrible scar reached his jaw, it escaped under his uniform.

"Thompson, have you heard of the Joint Services Personal Warfare School?"

I searched for an acronym that might ring a bell. Almost everything in the military had one, and the trick was to figure it out before the time was up. JSPWS. Jeswas? Jospews?

"Well, have you?"

"Well, sir, I think I might have—"

"You haven't."

"You're right, sir. I haven't."

Maddigan smiled, bending the scar dribbling down his face and neck. He looked scarier smiling than frowning. IBM headquarters might be a kick-ass place after all.

"It's a loosely regulated force of the best people available. Any chance you fit into that category?"

"I try hard to be the best, sir."

"Good for you. I'm not impressed."

"Wouldn't impress me either."

Maddigan had his next words ready, but my comment made him do a double take before he spoke. "Your training up to now has been conventional, but Jaspers isn't traditional and not everyone fits. We're far more elite and effective than SEALs, at least in our narrow area of operation."

That pill stuck a little, so I checked Nance's reaction. He chuckled, which prompted Maddigan to say, "Commander Nance did a tour through my command before he came back to SEALs."

Nance picked up the story. "Thompson, the colonel collects people from all the services and intelligence communities, from the Border Patrol to the CIA and lots of folks in between. They're all trained to work independently. If you want my opinion, I think you'd do well at Jaspers."

Jaspers? Not fair. They hadn't used all the letters and they'd thrown in some that didn't belong. "Thank you, sir."

"You'll be promoted to full lieutenant upon graduation."

"Your confidence is appreciated, sir."

"And not much of the work involves swimming in near-freezing water. That's been your only setback here."

Maddigan seemed annoyed by the conversation. Nance shrugged an apology and Maddigan continued. "If you don't quit or flunk out, I promise you a turn at the front line of America's defense, out there on the fringe where you can make a difference. You want to make a difference?"

"Yes, sir."

"Willing to fight to do it?"

"Yes, sir."

"You sure? Lots of folks joined the service just for the training. They never really thought about killing when they signed up."

The guy just wouldn't take yes for an answer. "I'm here to fight, sir. I'm here to do what's necessary to protect my country."

Maddigan walked to the window and looked at the alley of grass between us and the barracks, where a squad of men were training with rubber practice knives. I stayed where I was and took another look at the trident on Commander Nance's uniform. Nance saw my disappointment and said softly, "Warriors, Thompson . . . patriots . . . they aren't defined by a hunk of metal. Never have been. I'm much prouder of what I did in Jaspers."

"Your life will change significantly if you take this assignment," Maddigan said with no emotion at all.

Wet and exhausted and stripped of the formalities of uniform, I felt dirty and filthy and underclass, more than a little combative and definitely cornered. So as usual, I tried to attack. "Apparently," I said as smugly as I could, "Cameron's life sure did."

"Who?"

"Cameron, sir."

"Never heard of the man."

"But you just told Commander Nance—"

"Come over here, Thompson."

I'd tried to throw Maddigan off his game but failed, so I walked over and stood uncomfortably beside him as we looked outside. Two men tangled in the grass, grunting against each other's power while the rest leaned against the wall and waited their turn as either sentry or attacker, to be taken by surprise or do the killing—a foot from behind to the knee, a hand over the mouth, head tilted back to expose the throat, and then a slash across it or a thrust into the brain.

"Take a look at those men out there. They're training to kill, right?"

18

"They're learning to be SEALs, sir. Killing is just part of that training."

"Then would you assume that Jaspers shares a similar regimen?"

"I suppose so, sir."

Maddigan's right hand rose to his face. As he scratched his chin he noticed his scar, and then ended up making idle little crosses along it. "Then you would be wrong. My people serve to kill, period. Jaspers exists for that reason and that reason alone. America's military is politically unfocused, leaving few of us ready and available to do the hard, dirty work. I think you want to be a killer, Thompson. For your own reasons, maybe, but a killer all the same."

Me a killer? The killing I'd done amounted to bugs and a few animals. But I was pretty sure I could kill a man. I wasn't even appalled by the idea. I probably should have been.

"I'm probably as capable as the next—"

"Look, I'll be honest with you. Jaspers isn't the best career move. No one from our community sits on promotional boards, and the Pentagon has trouble accounting for your time under my command. But my very proud, very elite group of people love the job."

"You're talking about patriotism. I understand."

Maddigan's brutal eyes stared into mine, then through them and past me, all the way to some foreign battlefield. At least that's how it seemed as I looked at the absent gaze on his sturdy face. His heavy brows seemed to strain against the weight of orders given, of lost lives and crying families, of loneliness, maybe even failure. Wrinkles crisscrossed the corners of his eyes like memorials to the weight of command.

"It goes beyond patriotism," he said with reverence, a quiet eulogy for Cameron, I figured, or some other tragedy he was reliving and regretting. His head was down as though he were telling a difficult truth.

"Goes beyond honor and duty and loyalty," he continued. "My men and women are fanatic about preserving this great nation. Jaspers gives them their chance. If you want that chance, it's yours." He gave me a halfhearted smile and touched my arm, like a father just noticing a surviving son. "Questions?"

"A hundred, sir."

"Any that won't wait?"

"No, sir."

"Yes or no? On the school."

What were my choices? Failure? Turn down Maddigan and get kicked out of SEALs? I would rather be a Jasper, if that's what they called themselves. Chances were they went by something more sinister and freight-laden, like *Operator*—a real SEAL. But Operator, Jasper, what the heck, Maddigan looked like someone I'd be proud to fight beside, even though I already sensed his fights weren't reported in the papers, at least not accurately.

"Okay," I said, knowing there was no option to stay at SEALs. "If it's all that, I'm in."

"Well done, son," said Maddigan. Then he handed me some papers, which I guessed were my orders, and shook my hand, which I guessed might break my fingers. "If you do as well there as you've done here, we've got some work waiting for you."

"Aye-aye, sir."

Maddigan smiled a little and his scar bent out of line again. I smiled a little, too, wishing I'd had a tougher problem with acne and a ravaged face that said "this guy means business." I was fairly certain that all my face said was "pretty nice guy, doesn't like cold water." Although nothing else came, I kept straining until it looked like Maddigan was going to burst out laughing.

"Told you he was your man," Nance said proudly.

Maddigan searched my face as if he'd never see me again. "Jaspers is pass/fail, Thompson. The price of failure can be steep, and the price of passing can be worse. Cameron passed and look what it got him, so I hope you're up to it. Catch an eastbound plane and report to Camp Lejeune tomorrow for initial training." Then he walked out.

"Congratulations" said Commander Nance. "You'll do fine there. It's been a pleasure having you under my command. I'm sure our paths will cross again. Dismissed."

"Thank you, sir."

I stepped outside into the dry Santa Ana wind that attacked from the desert. It had spawned another wildfire that overran the hills and shrouded them with the ash of burning trees. It was such a sad sight that I looked away, toward the ocean. I breathed deeply and considered the sudden change my career had taken.

In matters of the heart, wallet, and military I usually moved slowly, tumbling major decisions around to smooth the dangerous edges. I'd been that way since . . . well, I guess I'd always been that way. It was a family thing. Most of my relatives were farmers, and farmers are tedious decision-makers because the wrong crop can put them out of business.

My father was cautious like that, and it was his caution, his fear, that caused him to fail this country I love. I wasn't emotionally damaged by it or anything like that, but I recognized the influence it had on the person I was becoming.

Another one of my theories is that the taproot of our human experience is either nourished or poisoned by our insecurities, those gnawing little wounds and fears that drive us to despair or excellence depending, it seems, upon the timber of our particular personalities—hard, gnarly, soft, flexible, or whatever. I've always thought of myself as a fir: sturdy and serviceable, good for lots of things but celebrated for none and valued accordingly. That was always fine with me. I would have had trouble being an oak— hard, inflexible, and prized for its defiance at bending or yielding. My father was an oak, or at least he was when we last spoke, just before I left for the Navy and he left the U.S. Marshals. I was sure he'd always be an oak. Maybe turn into a gray oak someday, but always staying hard and unyielding.

Even as a fir, I was a little surprised I'd so quickly abandoned my dream of being a SEAL. If I'd made a mistake, Shannon would tell me. Thank God we were talking again. We almost split up over something stupid we did in New York, but that was mostly behind us, I hoped.

I went to the phone outside the base convenience store. It was a typical San Diego day: cool, beautiful, and peaceful except for the white-helmeted SEAL candidates running past me in wet uniforms and a noisy old Buick idling in front of the phone. I waited for the Buick to leave, spending the time thinking about what to tell Shannon.

We'd met two years ago when we were both new at the White House. I was part of the Navy's detail and she was one of the press secretary's assistants. Although she wrote a great press release and occasional speech, I think her job was a reward for the work she did with her mother on President Devereau's campaign. Or something to do with the long family ties that elevated Devereau to the status of a favorite uncle. Not that it showed to anyone else, of course. But she told me when they were alone, nothing about their relationship had changed with his inauguration. I believed her, too. I could hear it in her voice when they talked on the phone.

Anyway, when she lost a confidential memo I'd delivered, I took the hit and told her boss I'd lost it. That caught her attention. Heck, I had room in my file for a letter of reprimand. Just paper.

And besides, she was beautiful. Some Mediterranean ancestry allowed her to skip makeup other than lipstick, which was always subtle. She wore very little jewelry, and what she did wear, I gave her—a pearl necklace for special occasions, a decent gold watch, and a charm bracelet for every day. An idiot friend of mine suggested the charm bracelet, and so I gave it to her without considering her profession, never wondering if an assistant presidential press secretary might look frivolous on television with charms dangling off her wrist. I told her often that I wouldn't be hurt if she just wore it occasionally. She kissed me and said she loved it, and I never saw her without it.

I was just about to reach in and turn off the Buick when the guy finally came out of the store, a civilian security guard who made me wait while he stopped and lit a cigarette, threw down the match, and stuffed the pack into his shirt pocket. He smiled at me, but I didn't smile back. His car chugged away, and I dialed. It was a pain going through the White House switchboard.

"Henry."

Was I irritated a minute ago? If so, I lost it to the beautiful voice that called me Henry in a way that was fine with me. I'd been a million laughs to people I met who thought they were the first to put an *Oh* in front of my name and made me sound like a candy bar, as in "Oh. Henry. Hello. Ha-ha." That's why I preferred H.T.

"I'm glad you called, because I've missed you."

"Missed you, too. Guess what. I've been reassigned to the East Coast."

"That's great. It'll be nice having you closer to home."

Home had been a tough word for me for a few years now, but it sounded good coming from Shannon.

"You mean no one's taken my place?"

She laughed.

"No threats out on the horizon that would keep me from coming back?"

"Let me look around." She paused, and I heard her tell someone she'd be right with them. "Yes, handsome men in pursuit of me are everywhere, Henry."

"I know they're everywhere. I worry constantly."

"At least I'm honest with you. But relax for now. Your clothes aren't out on my porch."

"If you ever do that again, put my boxers on the bottom, okay? Don't hang them on the porch lights."

"Okay. Henry, I'm really sorry, but I've got a time bomb on my desk."

"Right." I hesitated and cringed, just a little. "Well, I just wanted to get your opinion on my new job."

"What new job?"

"I'm kind of moving on."

"Moving on? People in the service don't just move on. They're not a band of nomads."

"I think I've been promoted. It's an elite force, too."

"What are you doing? I thought you'd never leave SEALs."

"This just suits me better."

"What does? What's this new job called?"

"Can't tell you. It's secret."

"It's *what*?"

Shannon usually had little interest in the military. She thought of servicemen as blue-collar dull, kind of like policemen. She liked me in spite of my uniform, not because of it, but she sure sounded interested as she waited on the other end of the phone line. But not in a good way.

"If you beg, I might tell you a little."

"Sounds like you've already made up your mind."

"Look, Shannon, it happened pretty fast. Try to understand."

"No. I think you should become a SEAL first. That's what you wanted. I wasn't aware that anything had changed."

"Well, it's too late now. I'm sorry."

"Me, too. I thought we talked these things over."

"Don't be like that. Please."

"I'm not being anything. Look, I've got to get back to work. My boss is upset and I need to get in there."

"What's going on?"

"Oh, I'm sorry. Didn't I mention that it's secret?"

"You're not being nice."

"Well, I'm mad. You would be, too."

She hung up. I stared at the phone as though it had done something wrong, like it had turned against me somehow. I was tempted to slam it into the cradle, but I didn't want to act like a child.

I slammed it down anyway, then spun away and charged right into a man I didn't know was behind me. He dropped his change as he tried to step back, holding out his hands to catch me as I struggled for some balance.

"Sorry, Chief. My fault."

"Didn't mean to sneak up on you, Lieutenant. Your boss?"

"Girlfriend," I said as I chased down his money.

"That's what I meant."

I handed him his change and then wandered over to the fence that separated the base from the highway. I took a deep breath and a last look around.

Coronado wasn't really much more than the narrow tip of a huge sandbar, a barrier island attached to the mainland by a bridge to San Diego. Between the low seaside buildings it was a short and easy view from the highway to the beach.

Dreams of being a respected soldier brought me here and pushed me to my limit, down the beach and into the surf, desperate to board one of the rigid-hulled inflatable boats maintained across the road, and then dropped near an enemy I might get to engage. That same dream had me leaving Coronado in order to pursue it.

I went back to the phone and called the North Island Naval Air Station terminal. A flight to Cherry Point was scheduled to leave in the morning, and I intended to be on it. I would become a Jasper, although I would always think that Operator sounded better.

Two

The cargo plane I was on made a short stop at the Naval Air Station in Fallon, Nevada, and that was where Cameron, the SEAL murdered in Africa, got a face. At least I guessed it was Cameron. The Reno newspaper referred to him as "Mr. David Green, American businessman executed for alleged espionage activities." His undated photo was credited to David Green, Sr. and showed Cameron standing in front of some office windows with a business-school-sure-paid-off smile. But behind the smile, expensive suit, and perfect haircut, his gun-sight eyes showed that same unyielding toughness I learned to recognize and respect at SEALs and expected to see even more at Jaspers.

I unbuckled myself from the web jump seat and threaded my way through the C-130's belly. It was filled with wooden crates of helicopter rotors, and I wondered if one of them would ever be used on a chopper that carried me into battle. Then I remembered how vague Maddigan had been about what I'd be doing as a Jasper, and that made me doubt if my battles could ever involve anything as noisy as a helicopter. The farther I headed in the direction of Camp Lejeune, the more Maddigan's lack of clarity made me uneasy and validated Shannon's concern about Jaspers being something I wanted, something good for me.

At the front of the cargo bay I climbed up to the cockpit and got dirty looks from the flight crew, so I went back to my seat and sat down. I tried not to look at David Green's photo as I reread the article.

President Devereau expressed his sentiments in this statement: "This administration, this country, and its people have a long tradition of intolerance toward crimes against our citizens. This was an atrocity against one of our countrymen, and we will seek—no, we will demand—justice. But as with any criminal investigation, let's first find the facts and presume Mr. Green to be innocent of any espionage activities while remaining open to the answers found by our own investigation."

The statement sounded like Shannon wrote it, and I wondered if I was on her mind at the time. She could have been angry because I hadn't consulted her before I left the SEALs, or she could have just been missing me. She might have been wondering where I was headed and what I was going to do, never dreaming I'd be taking David Green's place, assuming I was right in believing he really was Cameron.

I decided it was best if she wasn't thinking of me at all, and that hurt a little. Not a new feeling where she was concerned, but the cause was entirely new.

For reasons rooted in our personalities, my relationship with Shannon was often tumultuous and constantly meandered across the centerline. I usually assumed we'd be like our folks and spend the rest of our lives together, but to be honest there were a few times when I never wanted to see her again. Both feelings felt right when I had them.

I was upset with her for making this into another problem for us, but I couldn't get mad because I was the one who caused it. I'd added the secrecy of Jaspers and Maddigan to our future without talking the decision over with her. I'm sure she would have talked over any promotion with me, sat up all night getting my best guesses on the good deals and bad deals of the new position, the responsibilities and glory of her new job, all the reasons she should take it or not. I should have talked to her about Jaspers, if only in an abstract sense. But I couldn't do anything about it, so I tried to relax, and wondered what was waiting for me at Personal Warfare School.

We landed at Cherry Point, and I stepped off the plane into the late-afternoon fever of a Carolina summer. Nothing moved but the heat off the tarmac. Down the flight line, hundreds of drab aircraft faded into the distance, then disappeared behind a shimmering mirage. In the other direction, corrugated steel hangars bordered acres of asphalt so hot there were black puddles in the low spots.

A Marine sergeant pulled up and leaped from his Hummer. He was flat-faced and short, with an upper body of freakish proportions. He grabbed my bag but asked me nothing, although he looked at my Navy uniform as though it were a clown suit, I guess because it wasn't green or camouflage or starched stiff. I knew his type from Coronado, men who comprehended their orders and followed them with no questions asked. Everything else was superfluous, and anyone less dedicated was to be overrun or discarded.

Humidity felt like watered-down gravity as we drove a little more than an hour to Camp Lejeune, past rural homes with skiffs in the driveways and a small town called New Bern. As the sun faded and the temperature dropped, it got easier to appreciate how pretty this part of North Carolina was. Everywhere I looked I saw treed riverbanks, marshes of reeds, and coastal water. Boys pushed jonboats along low-tide banks, wading through the pocked mud and tossing fiddler crabs into aluminum prams to be used as bait for later. Each bridge had a few fishermen with wire carts and several poles, leaning against the concrete guardrail and smoking slowly. Some of them glanced at our military vehicle and then raised their beer before taking a sip.

Bars and tattoo parlors guided us through Jacksonville as though they were channel markers, increasing in number right up to the main gate of Camp Lejeune. I was saluted into this world of shaved heads and perfect lawns and polished brass cannon casings, the dressings of any military base pulled tight to Marine standards. We drove several miles more, beyond the manicure and polish of command and support and into the areas of combat exercise. We stopped twice for migrations of Amtraks and air-cushioned landing craft that flooded like the tide over scrub-covered dunes, crossing the sand-blown road like the amphibious monsters they were. While we waited, the sergeant shouted above the noise that we were at

Courthouse Bay on the New River, which sounded to me like a resort, although I had my doubts.

"It's an old barrage balloon base," he said. "Engineers use most of it now, but only the good sections. Not where you're going. Heck, you'll probably love it here." He chuckled.

It was dark by the time we crossed through a woodsy swamp for the final five minutes of the trip. As far as I could see, the road over the swamp was the secret facility's only link to the rest of the base, the only thing that kept the Jasper area from being completely separate. It was almost as if Maddigan's area of operation was trying to secede from Camp Lejeune and, I'm guessing, its rules for conventional warfare. But that land-bridge road, which provided the only wheeled-vehicle access for men and matériel, was the stubborn necessity that made secession impossible.

I saw the lights of a few small buildings on the other side of the swamp, stuck here and there with no apparent forethought. The main base's precision and uniformity were in sharp contrast to the random appearance and increased isolation of the Jasper camp, and that contrast confirmed some of what I'd already guessed about Maddigan: his disdain for useless regulations and mistrust of authority, feelings he definitely would have hidden from me in Nance's office unless he wanted me to know.

The few other words I got from the sergeant informed me that there were no medical facilities or dependent housing on our little slice of heaven. No kitchens and no phones except for instructors. "Kind of third world," he said, and actually laughed at me as we squeaked to a stop in front of a Quonset hut.

"This is U.S. Special Operations Command, Joint Services Personal Warfare School, Initial Training Facility, Camp Lejeune, North Carolina. Welcome."

I got out of the Hummer and he drove off, leaving me with my gear on the sand and metal-plate road.

"And the cabana bar is where?" I asked the darkness that settled in around me.

"Over there," said a disembodied voice. "Next to the parasailing rides."

I turned as nine men stepped out of the shadows of the Quonset hut, the incandescent glow from the window making partial eclipses of their faces. I had no idea where they'd come from, because they weren't there a minute ago. Our headlights would have lit them up.

They wore an assortment of fatigues, but none had ranks or service insignias. At first glance, they looked like one of the championship teams pictured in my college gym, a bunch of clean-cut athletes ready to take on all comers.

"How about waterskiing? They got that, too?"

A couple of men laughed as one of them stepped out of the group and walked up to me. He was older than the others, his face small and narrow with big lips and a swollen nose that looked like it had been busted a few times. There was gray in his eyebrows and hair, but not much. He didn't seem to like my uniform either. I really wished I had a SEAL trident pinned to it.

"No," he said. "They don't. And they don't serve you breakfast in bed or wash your clothes or any of that other stuff you got in the *Navy*." He bit off

"Navy" as if it were a persimmon, and that made me want to tell him that my last C.O. could have beat up his C.O. or something like that. But I didn't, mainly because I knew this guy, at least guys like him—men with low thresholds for being attacked and tremendous skill at attacking. An admirable mix in war, but scary to live with in a barracks.

So I followed my dad's advice and tried to ignore him. I smiled and looked at the other men and acted as friendly as I could without looking like an idiot. I waited a few seconds, then a few seconds more, but no one seemed to want to be my friend. Nothing was said, so it was him and me. Darn.

"Really?" I said, forcing myself to accept his challenge. "We always got breakfast in bed in the Navy, so maybe you'll be nice enough to bring me coffee." I stared at the whole pack of them, picking up some differences now—hair length and color, tans, one of them black. Then I tipped the bill of my hat and walked through them into the barracks. There was a bunk at the back with an empty locker, so I unpacked my gear and climbed into the rack. I closed my eyes, but it was easy to hear eight pairs of boots tramp over to my bed and feel someone hovering over me.

"You're Thompson."

I didn't need to open my eyes. I recognized Big Mouth's voice. "I'm resting. Mind?"

"Not a bit. Rest all you want. It ain't like there's work to do."

I looked up at his little face with the swollen nose. "What work?"

"We've got a night helo-cast. Briefing in ten minutes; liftoff in fifteen. You might want to get ready, 'cause Captain Pike won't tolerate us being late."

"Navy captain? Or just a Marine captain? Some Army guy, maybe?" I was trying to give Big Mouth's service a slam, which would have been a heck of a lot easier if he had some identification on his uniform. I wanted to look around the barracks for clues but didn't dare take my eyes off him.

"Don't matter. Can't hide behind rank in Jaspers. Enemy ain't gonna treat an officer special if they catch him, so don't expect it here, *Lieutenant*." There was that persimmon again.

I swung my legs off the bed and threw myself erect. Big Mouth took a step back and squared up, which surprised me. Then he surprised me again by getting close. He was baiting me for a fight, but I was going to avoid it. I didn't feel like fighting anyway. He was obviously top dog here, and it was fine with me if he held on to that spot.

"Shoo," I said as I made an imaginary push with my hands. "Go away." Then I gave him my back and un-buttoned my shirt, watching a guy with slicked-back hair adjust his gear on the next bunk. He was younger than me, with bold brown eyes and hair longer than the rest of the group's. In his eyes I could see that Big Mouth was glaring at the back of my head but wasn't going to hit me. His eyes would have given me more warning. But I was ready all the same, until Big Mouth bumped my shoulder and walked away.

I had never been shot at and never shot at anyone, but I knew a few people who had done both, and they told me that when the conflict ends there's a huge level of leftover adrenaline in your system that gives you the shakes. Big Mouth hadn't exactly given me the shakes, but he'd caused an ugly impression of this place so soon after my arrival that my stomach was grinding the way I expected it would under fire. Much the same way it turned into knots when Shannon wound me up over another man.

"Man," I said to the guy across from me, trying not to sound as relieved as I felt. "What's his problem?"

The guy buckled his pack, then looked at me.

"You," he said, as if giving me the time and nothing more.

"Me?"

"Yup."

"Well, that didn't take long. What did I do?"

"You held him up."

"I just got here."

The man was all set to go, but sat on his bunk and looked at the wall while I stripped off my pants and hurried to get ready.

"It's his day," he said to the metal-and-rivet wall of my new home. "The way it's set up, at least what I've heard. We'll each take turns in command of the group. Today's his day, and you're late. But we had to wait for you or be marked down. Now we might miss the whole thing, and he's pissed. He loses points if the mission gets scrubbed."

"Oh."

"Don't let him bother you too much, though."

"I won't. A dog is a dog. Once I accept that, there's no reason to be bothered by his barking."

Big Mouth must have heard this, because he spun around and said, "*That* does it!" So once again I was reading the story of my life, seeing that I'd crossed the line and said one thing too many. He was clearly beyond his capacity for self-control. His elbows were out like wings. His hands were open and his head was forward as he accelerated toward me with one thing on his mind. Ice cream. I wished.

I pulled up my trunks and stepped into the aisle where there was more room. I couldn't believe I was going to fight this guy. He was a killer, I could tell, and I had no business . . . I scared myself thinking like that, so I tried to focus on his nose, rather than thinking of him as a killer with great training and a frightening record. Other men have broken that nose, so he *could* be beaten. I hoped.

"I warned you not to mess with me, Thompson."

"Hey, lay off, man. I'm green off the boat and don't need your static."

Anger has always been contagious, and Big Mouth's infected me with ravaging speed. My body flared, possessed by a frightening animal I'd rarely seen, an elusive creature that ignored evolution, a beast that rattled his cage and bent back the bars until he finally escaped.

The beast postured me against Big Mouth and lowered my center of gravity, spread my stance, angled my shoulders, and raised my hands toward that big ol' nose that gave me confidence.

"Outside, Thompson, I'm gonna—"

"Lay off!" I shouted over him. He looked surprised for a splinter of time.

"Outside!" He shoved me, but I was planted solid and wouldn't move. He stepped in to push me again, but a thousand synapses sparked in my brain, allowing me to track his hand with my eyes and calculate the speed, then snatch it out of the air, bend it up, and put pressure on the wrist before twisting him around and forcing him to the floor. My beast overpowered any reluctance in my nature and I stomped down hard, isolated his shoulder, and wrenched his arm toward the ceiling until the blade dislocated.

Big Mouth screamed, but only once.

I studied the other men, unable to predict what they might do, but committed and unwilling to back down if they all attacked. Although I couldn't hear anything, I noticed everything else that happened in my war zone. Every blink. Every movement. Every shifting stance.

The men stared at me as though I were a god or crazy.

Big Mouth didn't move, and no one else challenged me.

It was over. I waited five more seconds to be sure, and then dropped his hand to the floor. He grimaced but didn't make a sound.

Victory slowly diluted my adrenaline cocktail, purging the juice from my veins and the power from my arms. I had no idea if I was hurt, even though I couldn't imagine how.

Emotional sobriety set in. Then civility. And finally shame.

"And then there were nine," came a new voice from the end of the hut. I went back on defense for a second, but this was a quiet voice that lacked emotion. One of the men said, "Evening, Captain" with reverence, so I guessed it must be Pike. He was middle-aged but moved with the lithe agility of youth. His brown eyes were wide open—unblinking and searching—and his pinched lips were like a beak, his face a scowling owl. He was obviously not a scavenger. I would have bet right then that he ignored or abhorred the weak, always preferring to challenge the strong. His uniform was custom-tailored and smartly pressed. His cap was level, not cocked to the side or pushed forward or back. He walked with the tight precision of a machine.

I guessed Pike was nearly fifty, which probably made him a Navy captain. He walked through the hut and the other men stepped out of his way, watching him watch me. He stopped in front of me and put his hands in his pockets, then glanced at the big-nosed heap of a man on the floor. He couldn't have looked less interested. I couldn't have been less interested, except that I felt terrible for what I'd done.

"All right, now *you're* in command, Thompson. You've got a wounded trooper and a helo to catch. Do your job." He stepped over Big Mouth as he walked out.

I forced the fight behind me and moved on, wondering what I'd gotten myself into, where the helicopter might be picking us up, and what else I could have done to avoid that stupid fight.

"Who's my second?"

"Here." A large Scandinavian stepped forward, unfolding a map and flipping open a notebook.

"Where's the LZ?"

"Over the dunes," he said in a German accent as he jabbed his thumb over his shoulder. "That way."

"Briefing?"

"Same place."

"Mission?"

"A night cast into the ocean, then a swim and penetration of this area." He pointed at the map, at a jut of land down the coast. "We need to cap some religious extremist who has a training camp right about here. Then we bug out the way we went in. With luck."

"Gear?" I asked. "Name?"

"Ready." He looked puzzled and then smiled. "Rutger."

"I'm H.T. Are you German?"

"American, of course."

I reached down and tried to help up Big Mouth, but he slapped my hand away. A scream formed on his lips but didn't escape. He rolled onto his knees and stood up slowly, letting his good arm dangle like his dislocated one, I guess, so that he looked unhurt. I kept a close eye on him as I grabbed some gear.

"Saddle up, then. We'll take him with us. The chopper can drop him at the main base after dumping us."

I saw two men smile and heard the rest mutter.

"Move. It's time to be all that we can be." I was fighting my way back to normal, corralling my beast, locking the cage and mending the bars. I heard the black guy chuckle from the other end of the room, a snickering little laugh like my kid brother.

"It's not just a job," I said. "It's an adventure."

"That's the one," someone shouted. I was glad there was another Navy guy there. "Anyone remember the Air Force motto?"

Slicked-back hair cleared his throat and sang, "Way down there. Way down there. We're safe up here while the fight is way down there."

Everyone laughed except Big Mouth, who resisted all attempts to help him. He would make it on his own, I was sure, hating me for every step he took toward a mission in which he wouldn't participate. He was finished here, and it was a shame. I should have done something different.

I put on the first fatigues I dug out of my seabag, left my boot laces untied, then joined the men at the rear of the hut, hoisting the pack onto my back and checking the straps of the flippers. I would adjust the mask and check the Stoner automatic weapon while in flight.

We double-timed to the landing zone—or as close to double time as we could with Big Mouth doing his best to keep up, hobbling along in the dark, using his left hand to keep his right arm from swinging. We met Captain Pike in a wooded area just short of a clearing. As we ran up, he checked his watch and searched the night sky with his eyes.

"You're late," he said. "You'll have to go without a briefing. No intelligence reports except this: Stay in the safe corridors of travel marked on the map." He turned his back and looked toward the glow of lights and noise over the dunes. A chopper came thump-thump-thumping from the same direction, and I suspected that no matter what time we'd got to the briefing it would have been too late. Pike had probably ordered the chopper to hover on the other side of the dunes, and then radioed the pilot when he saw us coming. This was different from the training I was used to, and I was interested in the way it made me feel. I was barely keeping up.

Pike turned back and hollered as the helicopter pounded its way toward us. "Adapt to your circumstances. Don't get caught. Don't get killed. Don't fail. Thompson!"

"Sir."

"Rip those markings off your uniform. Everyone in this command is nonofficial."

"Yes, sir." I noticed again that I was the only one with any insignias. "On the flight, sir."

The black, unmarked chopper flared as the pilot went nose-up. I signaled my men to move out, then stayed behind with Big Mouth, staring at him, waiting for him to board while the rotor wash snapped at our uniforms. To look at this tough sucker, it was hard to remember he was hurt. I was amazed and a little nervous about ordering him around, but I was about to do it anyway. Then Pike nodded for me to leave and Big Mouth, well, almost smiled. That made me wonder how much of this had been staged. Had Big Mouth been there to test me? He sure seemed chummy with Pike as I headed out, standing at ease beside him, the hand of his good arm searching his pockets for cigarettes.

I was the last one on board. A guy next to me—I was anxious to learn some names—took out a knife and cut off my name and the U.S. Navy label from my chest and the tag from behind my neck. Then he removed my collar devices and handed everything over to the pilot, a civilian in blue jeans with blond hair curling out from under his aviator's helmet.

I opened my orders as we cleared the beach, flying low across the choppy Atlantic. All the men sitting in the open door on my side of the chopper seemed relaxed as they casually rubbed in their camouflage grease. It was dark, and we were about to jump into a turbulent ocean and swim three miles to the beach, find and kill a man in enemy territory, and then get away. Even practicing this stuff should make people pucker, but none of the men seemed scared. Two of them smiled at each other, their white teeth flashing from their green-painted faces.

I wondered about families and wives and hometowns but sensed that these men were too tough and singular to put much stock in such things. They were anxious for the mission, whereas I was thinking about Shannon and what she was doing, wondering if she was mad enough to date someone else. I hoped she was too busy. But if she somehow connected me to Cameron's death, she'd be even madder if she knew where I was.

"Thirty seconds," the pilot both shouted and signaled.

Our packs were small, but big enough to hurt if we jumped into the water with them. So we propped them between our feet, attached to a cord shackled to a carabiner on our harnesses.

"Jump!"

We kicked off the packs. A second later, the cords pulled us out. We hit the water, a wave slapped me in the face, and the chopper kept going. I couldn't hear anyone over the breaking waves and wind, but I signaled toward the beach and we started swimming. It was three miles to the beach and we were playing beat-the-clock. Sunrise would happen whether or not we'd finished.

I was scared of failing and scared of what I'd gotten into. I wished I'd had a chance to see Shannon on the way there. I should have gone through Washington and made a quick stop by the White House with some carryout, maybe. Instead, I was on my way to kill a man. In practice.

At least tonight.

Three

We swam to the beach with our packs and weapons supported by air bladders and chemical light sticks trailing behind so we'd have a chance of being seen by any boats running out for a night of fishing. I was struggling to keep my head high enough above the water to see my men and my compass as four-foot waves increased the chances of my waterlogged uniform dragging me to the bottom. At the top of each swell I looked around for weak swimmers, hoping I wouldn't have to attempt a rescue out there. I was always a strong swimmer, but I doubted I could have saved anyone that night. I was almost certain it would have been impossible.

I shepherded the group most of the way toward shore, swimming back once to untangle Rutger from the rope of a crab pot. At the surf line I had them stay beyond the breakers while I swam ahead to check the beach for defenses. The black guy with my kid brother's laugh came with me. He was a fast swimmer like me.

A wave turned me sideways as it threw me onto the beach and forced me to keep my weapon close to my body in an up-and-down position so I wouldn't lose it. I refused to give it up to the water as the wave rolled me over and over, although I wanted to let go and use my arms to stop. I finally straightened out and crawled through the surf on my belly, aiming my weapon toward the beach, hoping to avoid detection while the waves crashed on my back and filled my nose and eyes with stinging salt water, the sand sluicing up my shirt and down my pants—a typical experience back at Coronado.

I slithered the hundred yards or so to the dunes and sea oats, moving slowly with my weapon ready, expecting anything from concussion grenades to a live-fire ambush and trip-wire defenses. Finding none of them up to that point, I signaled for the others and counted heads as the ocean spit them out. They crawled toward the dunes like crocodiles, then spread out and covered all approaches as if they'd done this all their lives. I was excited.

I nodded at the black man while I caught my breath and chased water around in my ear. He was already breathing easily. "You're a good swimmer," I said. "What's your name?"

He rose slowly and peered over the dune at the swamp two hundred yards inland. All the while, he looked like boredom might kill him. His large eyes clicked this way and that, moving constantly in some kind of ritual he learned God knows where. His thick lids were nearly closed, and when he yawned a gold front tooth suddenly made me worry about reflections and wonder about military regulations. Then he electrified himself onto his knees, whipped his weapon around, and took dead aim on Rutger, who had sneaked up to us with the map.

"Dwayne," the black guy said, digging sand out of the corner of his eye as he wiggled back around and made a show of ignoring Rutger. He proned out on his side and looked across the swamp for the enemy.

"You're kidding. About the name?"

He squinted at me and then chuckled. "Dad's idea of a joke, I think. Nice redneck name for a black guy."

"It's not a joke to aim at me," Rutger said. "Try to be cool, man. Remember, I'm on your side."

"My blind side," Dwayne mumbled. Then: "Don't ever do that again" with perfect clarity.

"All right, that's enough. Rutger, let me see the map."

He handed it to me and held a red light so I could see, all the while keeping an eye on Dwayne.

"Okay, here's the deal," I said. "We have to navigate two miles inland to get to this guy. The swamp up ahead marks our safe corridor of travel, twenty feet inside the north and south banks. It's nice and wide, so don't let anyone wander out of it. I see plenty of cypress trees and vegetation to use as cover and concealment. Rutger will take two men and move along the north side of the swamp. Dwayne, you do the same on the south side. I'll take the middle. Let's move."

As they crawled away in silence, I signaled for the men covering the beach to move forward. A half-moon was dragging itself out of the water, but it was still dark. Darkness was our ally. Our enemy was the man we came to kill.

To kill a man.

What a concept. I could still hear Maddigan saying Jaspers existed for that reason and that reason only. The implication was clear, even to a country rube like me. Jaspers was never intended to be a deterrent force, and it certainly wasn't a policing force. Jaspers—unless I was way off the mark—was in the business of assassinations. I wasn't about to ask and doubted that anyone would have confirmed it, but that's sure how it felt.

As we moved out, I found myself wondering what that meant to me.

I was a little surprised I wasn't put off by the idea. Although I might have wished otherwise, I've always been honest enough to admit that the kinder and gentler way I liked to see myself—along with the rest of mankind—was pretty much a joke, nothing more than a comforting pretense in civility when times were good. It was a fun-house image of the actual far less-evolved version of ourselves that will kill as first nature for another thousand years, the adrenaline-poisoned viper that's been striking at perceived threats since we first learned to puncture each other with sharp objects. Pretending to be civilized felt nice and I was glad we were trying, but I never confused effort with success.

I'd been killing people since I was a kid. I couldn't even begin to count the number of friends I shot playing cops and robbers, or cowboys and Indians or war. Could never imagine the number of hours I spent imitating James Bond—although my license to kill expired when Mom called me home for dinner. Whether I was catching fish at the pay-lake or poisoning rats in the barn, killing had always been an instinct and would always be one. All it would ever take to prove that theory right was a serious threat against my family or future. I never pretended otherwise.

In my case I killed without a threat, but I ate the fish, and the rats were pests so I knew those kills were justified. I could look back on them with pride for providing meals and protecting grain and livestock from destruction and disease. Noble causes that earned me praise from my father, back when he still understood the term.

Assassinating a man—killing another human being who didn't know you were an enemy—that had to be different. Or did it?

I slithered down the dune until the bushes and weeds grew tall enough for us to get off our stomachs. From there we walked in a low crouch until we hit the swamp. I grabbed a branch and squatted down, then slid off the edge and into the brackish water, holding my Stoner above my head as I sunk to the middle of my chest. I glanced back through the tangle of roots and overgrowth to make sure my men were following me, and then I started wading. After forty minutes, I reached a spot where the swamp was wide and clear, and took a minute to check the north and south teams to make sure we were advancing together.

The guys north of me were a little ahead, low and holding their position. I showed them my palm and then checked on Dwayne's team. They were moving a little slower through tougher terrain. The moon was over their shoulders, so they were easy to see. Dwayne signaled for us to hold and wait for them, and I passed it along to my men and the other team.

Then I looked back and noticed the guy humping the machine gun. He must have been sinking under The Saw's weight, so he'd crawled out of the water to walk in the danger zone along the swamp's edge. He was on solid ground twenty feet or more outside our operational corridor.

Dwayne saw him, too. He cussed loud and then made a dash for him, splashing beyond the edge of our safe corridor. He'd just shouted orders to the machine gunner when I heard the devils coming.

Two Marine helicopters popped over the trees and roared down on us, bright in the moonlight, their 30mm chain guns firing steadily over our heads with a 70mm rocket thrown in once in a while. I looked for the machine gunner but couldn't see him through the effervescing water that jumped up from the steel barrage. The Apache pilots jinked their way through the trees, blasting away like they were having one heck of a good time, their night-vision gear making them excellent marksmen, their gunfire making my ears ring as projectiles stitched the water and dirt along the exact edge of our corridor. Dwayne turned back and ran like crazy toward the safety of the swamp, his arms swinging in big arcs, his torso twisting, his pumping knees pushing a frothy wave as his entire face begged me to do something.

"Keep moving! No, wait . . . Dwayne! Get down, get down!"

Just as he dove for the water, a Hydra 70 rocket hit him in the back and blew his chest to pieces. A crimson spray added brilliance to the exploding mud and water as his trousers alone finished the wobbly dive.

Oh God.

My breathing and heart stopped. So did the ringing in my ears. I'd never known anything like that silence, even as a cannon from one of the choppers flashed a few more times. I saw it fire and saw the rounds slam into the water, but I was in a dream and didn't hear them. I stared at the foaming water where Dwayne had stood a second ago, waiting for the dream to end so Dwayne could rise out of the swamp. I wondered why he'd gone after the machine gunner instead of just yelling, and why the pilot had been so careless, gunning Dwayne down in a swamp that offered no place to hide. I hoped the machine gunner would suffer forever for what he'd done.

But underneath it all I heard myself asking if it was my fault, worrying whether it would be me, and not the pilot, who would suffer most. A man was dead. An American soldier. That it might be my fault was horrifying.

But I didn't send him after the machine gunner. I didn't know about the Apaches. I didn't do anything wrong.

Nevertheless, a man under my command was dead, and the arguments of my mind were incapable of overpowering the wretched feeling that sank from my heart to my stomach.

I kept watching and couldn't take my eyes off the spot. Then the machine gunner jumped up from where he'd scratched into the dirt and ran toward me. He was screaming, his mouth stretched open and his eyes full of terror, but I couldn't quite hear him either. I remember thinking he was praying as he ran.

Gradually, my ears started to ring again and then throb with pressure. I grabbed my head to hold it together while the machine gunner ran up and yelled in my face. I heard him then but still didn't understand his words.

I thought about Dwayne's gold tooth.

I no longer wanted to be there. I knew I didn't want to die there. I wished I were home.

I grabbed the emergency radio and tried to transmit, but the words coming out of my pinched throat were squeaks. I unkeyed the mike and tried again, practiced saying "hello, hello, hello" to no one until I was sure the words would come, and then I tried again.

"Weasel Blue to Weasel Red. We've got a casualty on the ground! *Scrub!* Repeat, scrub your air attack."

I aimed my Stoner at the lead Apache, ready to shoot if he opened up again, vaguely aware that at that moment I was perfectly ready to kill another human if it became necessary. It would have been justified in order to protect the rest of my men.

"Roger that, Weasel Red," said one of the pilots. "Confirm one man down. We saw him too late. Putting a light on him now."

One Apache shone a spotlight into the swamp. The other landed on the ground and idled, its rotor making slow, noisy laps. I suddenly missed Dwayne, and at the same time I hated him. I was both proud and ashamed of his actions, flushed with contradictory emotions I'd never known before over a man I'd just met.

I cautiously approached the bottom half of Dwayne's body, which floated in tannin water near a swamp oak. I stared at it for most of a minute as the rotor-blown water made the legs dance like a silly clown. When I could stand it no longer, I slung my weapon over my shoulder and grabbed his waistband. It was loose, thank God, making it easy to keep my fingers out of his body cavity. I tried not to desecrate him further as I bobbed him upright and his left foot floated to the surface.

I wanted to send his family as much of him as possible, so I scooped up anything that was still attached, wrapping entrails and intestine around my arm like spaghetti, jerking it from the mouths of a swarm of small fish that cut quick lines on the surface of the water. I carried the bloody half-carcass to the helicopter, pushed Dwayne in, and then walked over to the machine gunner. He watched me coming for him and offered no resistance as I hit him in the face so hard we both fell down and stayed there.

The Apaches flew away, but I didn't watch them. When I finally did look up, I was surprised to see that the other men hadn't deviated from their orders. They hadn't moved an inch and weren't really watching what was going on with Dwayne. They were down and defensive, ready to fight, grimly aware that these things happen, even in training, and they couldn't allow it to distract them from the mission.

Pike's calm and direct voice came over the radio. "Weasel Red to Weasel Blue. You've allowed your mission to be compromised. There'll be no extraction. Get back as best you can. Good luck."

I didn't bother to answer. I wanted to ask if he knew a man had just died there, but I was sure he did. I sat there until Rutger came over.

"It wasn't your fault. Let's go."

"Man, did you see it? He was here and then he was gone. Just like that."

Rutger cradled his weapon in his crossed arms. "I saw it. Just like that. Let's go. Deal with it later."

He looked at me, then away, then back again. He did that twice with increasing impatience, as if thinking about taking over my command. I forced myself to stand up, guessing that Rutger had seen men die before. Even as a part of me longed for the emotional distance he managed, another part of me hoped it never got that easy.

I told the machine gunner to stay behind and go back to the beach and wait. It's never been good leadership to separate one man from a squad, but I did it anyway and it wasn't a problem for me. A new place had opened up inside me, a formerly undiscovered room where I now stored my disinterest in his life right next to the loss of Dwayne's. The room, although small, seemed to have lots of space, like a comfortable bunker that had never been used— sanitary and clean with a heavy lock on the door. As he shuffled away like the loser he was, I couldn't close the door fast enough. Once I had the door locked, I stood waist deep in the swamp and scrubbed Dwayne's tissue off my uniform.

I forced myself to concentrate on the map, which took an enormous effort. Rutger continued to watch me as I loaded the camp coordinates into the GPS without a word and signaled the men to follow me. We walked all night, mostly in silence, slogging along in the boggy margin between forest and swamp, half expecting another ambush and moving carefully just in case, too aware that we really could die here, listening hard for helos or clicks or movement up ahead.

Dawn lightened our burden by putting Dwayne's death into *yesterday,* something from the past and therefore easier to deal with, even possible to talk about. I tried not to recognize voices as a couple of guys cussed the pilots. Someone else directed every epithet he knew at the machine gunner, making me glad he wasn't with us. I didn't care where he was, either. If he had been there, I would have hit him again.

I heard someone say that I was to blame and I wondered, had I done a poor job of leading, of giving instructions? Was it my fault in any sense other than I was in command? I finally settled into the conclusion that yes, I think so, although I really didn't know what else I should have done.

Hunger became a welcome distraction from the death behind us, possessing our minds and making us a little crazy. We looked for snakes or rabbits but saw none, thought about survival techniques and made jokes. A few of my half-starved men told stories of cannibalism as a way of recognizing Dwayne's ghost among us, trying to show that he didn't really scare us, even if he did.

We walked the entire day and late into the night. It was almost midnight when we approached our camp on the New River. No guards were posted along our approach, but still we slipped in with the stealth of burglars, not wanting to be embarrassed if our base had been overrun by pretend enemy forces who weren't hungry and exhausted. It would have been hard to care less.

On some level, though, underlying my pain and shame and fear, I was proud of what I'd endured in the swamp, even though I'd lost a man doing it.

Maybe *because* I'd lost a man. Pride and self-respect are the blue-blooded offspring of the kind of filthy, dirty hardships I'd just experienced, making me more of a war fighter, a warrior. Nations survived and conquered other nations because of the skills and hardness of men like me. Some men died in the process, cut down or blown up in soggy paddies or muddy trenches or scorching deserts. The men who didn't die got to live with the glory.

At Officer Candidate School they told us that a soldier's sacrifice is not just on the battlefield. I heard it there. I learned it in the swamp. We must be willing to sacrifice daily, whether dying in a deserted region of coastal Carolina or standing watch in the Arabian Sea. I'd always been in awe of people who chose careers in the military, further amazed that most did it because they wanted to, not because they needed a job.

The men with me complained all through last night, all of today, and late into the evening, but I knew they too were proud. Complaining was just a way to celebrate the accomplishment, a chance to brag without bragging, as in, "I can't believe they'd shoot at us, then keep us on the move for twenty-four hours with nothing but the water we carried. Man, it ain't right. Humans weren't made to endure this abuse."

But we did endure the abuse, all the way to our little hut. It would sound funny to say we were glad to be *home*, but we were, cleaning our weapons when Captain Pike wandered in. No one snapped to attention. I announced, "Attention on deck," but no one moved. Then Pike stepped in front of me.

"Skip the formalities, Thompson. Rank around

here just indicates the chain of command. Colonel Maddigan is the overall boss. I'm next. Got it?"

"Yes, sir. Habit."

He cocked his head as though unsure I was listening.

"Gentlemen," he said with a scowl on his face. "If you didn't know it before, you damned sure know it now. The military is a risky occupation. In the last fifteen years, up to and including our current losses in Iraq, more servicemen have died in training than in all combat operations since 1969. Tonight was just another unfortunate example. It happens. It will continue to happen. It's part of the bargain. Thompson."

"Here."

Pike took a hard, one-second glance around the room, then came back to me.

"Outside."

We stepped out into the camp. Mercury vapor lights made sporadic halos on the ground, but mostly the camp was dark. Dull yellow light came from a few of the small wooden buildings. A truck rumbled down the dirt road and cut toward the swamp.

"You failed, Thompson."

"If you say so. But you rigged the game. We didn't set off any warnings. We avoided perimeter defenses that would have given us away. We engaged no enemy. I don't think we failed. With all due respect, sir, you knew exactly where we were and then you cheated. You gave those pilots their orders to shoot at Dwayne. You got him killed by manipulating us into an impossible scenario."

"It always is."

"What?"

"That kind of mission is always impossible. You

can't engage a national leader or a well-guarded zealot with a small team of men. It's too hard to get close. There's no way to bring a small team to bear on guys like that."

"Then what was the point?"

"To evaluate you. The other men too, but you were the one in command. Tomorrow it's someone else's turn in the barrel. You did an acceptable job. I debriefed the pilots, so I know it wasn't your fault you lost a man. Do you see my point, though, about the futility of a small team?"

"I think so."

"One man might have made it through unnoticed, or an air strike or cruise missile could have probably taken out your target. A small force works well for the kind of work the SEALs do, but it's either too much or not enough for what we do here. Understand?"

"Yes, I've got it."

"Good."

Then he walked away. No other comments about Dwayne. It was a long march home, and I was too tired to push. Pike probably planned on dealing with it later. Seemed to be the general strategy.

Back inside the Quonset hut, the men had broken out some food and warmed it with heat tabs. The weapons, mostly light assault rifles, were cleaned and stored. Someone had cleaned my Stoner. I guessed it was Ernest, the guy with slicked-back hair and perfect teeth from the next bunk. I gave my weapon a quick inspection—after all, it was mine—then replaced it in the rack.

I ate enough to fill my shrunken stomach and then showered before bed. The water wasn't hot, but my bunk was, steamy and damp from the coastal humidity. The last man standing snapped off the lights. I was on top of the sheets like everyone else, unable to remember ever being so exhausted, even after all those weeks at Basic Underwater Demolition.

A mosquito buzzed around my face, but I was too tired to swat him. Compared to my other recent pains—Dwayne's death, my hunger, thirst, heat, scratches, and chiggers—a mosquito could almost have been a fun thing.

A soldier three racks down started to snore, which might have induced sleep or insomnia. I was sure it made someone think about murder. The mosquito buzzed, more soldiers snored, and a tactical jet wound up its turbines in the distance. I was more lonely than I was tired.

Nights were the worst part of the service. I was in an isolated camp, living on top of people I hardly knew and missing Shannon, the woman I loved. I would have given just about anything for her to hug me right then.

Dwayne's death made me want Shannon differently than I ever had before. Tonight I needed her cool hand stroking my head, her light fingers tracing along my eyelids as I retreated into the protective sound of her voice, hiding in her arms from whatever truths or demons lurked in the darkness of the night. I reached across my bunk for her but found only loneliness. Our extended separation transformed the distance into an enemy that used propaganda against the love it opposed. What did I think she was doing tonight? Who was she with? How much fun was she having with them?

Shannon enjoyed sex a lot, and when we made love she sometimes told me about the men who flirted with her, the telling made even more passionate by her half-second gasps my pounding caused. Jealousy—one of the natural predators that stalk the world of relationships—made those words sad and hurtful. I asked her to stop teasing other men, but she said it was something she enjoyed, so I learned to convert my jealousy to passion, making love to the woman every other man wanted. Her stories would always wrench my guts, sure, and I occasionally complained that she led men a little too far, but it was a pain-versus-pleasure kind of deal, and the pleasure was slightly more intense than the pain. Usually. At any rate, it slew a relationship's other major predator—boredom—so that was something, I guess.

I was a fairly innocent farm boy back then, but even I could see that for all her sophistication and heritage Shannon was a rebel, intent on proving that smart people needed to create their own morality in their private world, whatever worked for them and the people they loved. She was fond of saying that accepted sexual norms were nothing more than "witheringly Puritanical ethics lumbered upon us by people who wouldn't know fun if it bit 'em in the ass." Which, of course, was part of the reason she teased.

It was always fun going along with her, though, rebelling against the rigidity of my youth and the hypocrisy of morality at which, like courage, my father pretended. Besides, I believed Shannon when she said she was faithful to me, even though she usually followed that pledge with a teasing smile and a guilty glance. She gave herself a lot of sexual latitude, so I was never quite sure.

Deep down, though, I never doubted that I could rely on her when I was far away. At least that was where I put my faith in the light of day, when I could reassure myself with her record of honesty and my memories of our happiness—riding our bikes along the canal, sailing the Chesapeake, curling up on the couch with some wine, popcorn, and a video. But tonight as the mosquito fattened himself in the murky light of this metal building, those good memories seemed to retreat and the distance bred suspicions that tempted me toward leaving Shannon, even though I knew I would never forget her.

I searched for a cool spot on the sheets to lay my hot legs but couldn't find one. More men were snoring, but I wasn't going to get any sleep. I was just trying to get through the night the best I could, knowing that the woman I loved was far away, single, a little pissed off, and available to a better man who might be out having dinner with her. I might have been losing her that very moment.

Lonely nights were the only times I missed my parents and missed being part of a family. Even though I was the one who turned my back on them, I had no choice, really. But I always knew I'd do better with Shannon than they did with me. If I ever disappointed her, I wouldn't let her leave me over it. A man can't let his family go, not under any circumstances. He can't let them get too far out of the safe corridors of travel. If he does, he will never get them back, at least not in the same condition as when they left.

I rolled onto my side and searched through the window for first light. My sheets were wet, my legs ached, and my muscles twitched. Off in the near distance a strange noise intrigued me, so I tossed my legs off the bed, dressed in a fresh utility uniform, and carried my boots silently outside into the night. The noise came again—like a moth toasting on a bug zapper—from the other side of the low, frame buildings. I glanced back at the Quonset hut, but no one followed me.

Another crisping click and then a flash of light bounced off the buildings. I ran toward the sound and around the closest building, then ducked into a recess and looked to see where the flash had come from. A couple hundred yards away something moved, abstract in a shroud of moonlight and masked by a fog that settled on the ground. There was a smell in the air I couldn't quite identify, something like burning hair. I backed into the breezeway of the white lapsided building, frightened. I was close to an electrified field of some kind, maybe too close, I didn't know. There weren't any warning signs.

I stared at the field as a large deer wobbled to its feet and set off dozens of lasers that blasted out of the perimeter darkness. The deer tried to run from the onslaught but fell in a heap. It didn't move again.

I had no idea how close I was to being a target myself. I pressed my back closer to the wall, wondering why Maddigan believed we needed this kind of protection. I felt trapped, and that made me wonder if the lethal field was there to imprison rather than protect me, its purpose far more sinister than the chainlink fence at Coronado.

As I crept away with my back scraping along the siding, I felt afraid of not only the field but of what it was and what it represented—a separation between me and the legitimate warriors on other parts of the base. Although only a chain-link fence separated the Marines of Camp Lejeune from the civilians of Jacksonville, Maddigan separated the Jaspers from the rest of Camp Lejeune with deadly force. I was sure Maddigan had his reasons. I hoped I would agree with them when I learned what they were.

I slinked back to the Quonset hut and climbed into bed, second-guessing my decision to come here, wondering if I'd gone too far already, and if so, if was I trapped. Would Maddigan allow me to leave? Was his idea of an elite force in line with any legal definition? If not, how far could I go along? Would being a Jasper make me a good or bad soldier?

Then I wondered if an Apache from Camp Lejeune might fly over the field someday and kill me the same way it killed Dwayne.

Four

"Wake up, Thompson."

"What?"

"Wake up," Ernest said again. "Pike wants us outside. Damn, you're a sound sleeper." He pushed his hair straight back and followed the other men out.

"Gentlemen," Pike said as I joined the others in front of our Quonset hut. "Come with me."

He walked away and we followed, men yawning and kicking stones and rubbing our eyes as if bored or still asleep. I tucked in my shirt, alert as a prairie dog because I knew where we were going. I just didn't know why the place existed, why an open field on a secure military base was laced with lasers.

As I walked along thinking about the deer's final struggle, I remembered a car accident from when I was a kid, where a guy wrapped his car around a tree. The deer last night acted like that pitiful driver who snagged and gashed against the compacted wreckage, his legs and pelvis pinned against the tangle of steel and sheet metal, his bloody left hand scratching and fighting for a miracle. His car was crushed so completely, there wasn't even a gap in the wreckage where my dad could reach in and compress his wounds.

But the driver wasn't terrified; at least he didn't look that way to me. He was scared, sure, but what I remember most was his determination and desperation, tugging on his own legs, trying to get them free as the fractured bones tore through his trousers and wedged against the crumbled dash. He endured incredible pain for a chance to rejoin the living and be outside the car with me and my dad.

Dad was a brave man back then, waving me away as gasoline soaked the ground and wicked up his pants. He ignored the risk of explosion and talked calmly to the driver as destiny crept up on him, stroking the guy's hair and asking him what words he had for his family, making whatever promises the guy needed to hear, telling him about heaven in a way that made even me want to go there.

In the end, my dad held the driver's bloody hand between his and prayed until the man gave up and sobbed his own eulogy, charging the air with unbearable sadness as he stared at me and cried his own son's name again and again. Then he stopped crying and almost seemed to stop breathing as he calmed down, arched his back in pain, and smiled at me through his tears and died.

Until Dwayne, he was the only person I'd ever seen die. Both of them stared at me when they left, putting unwanted memories on my shoulders to carry around for who knew how long.

I closed the door on Dwayne last night while staring at the deer, accepting that both Dwayne and the deer were dead but much less certain why. I never expected to forget either one, but in an attempt to chase off both their ghosts I looked at the sun and then at the camp around me. It looked different in the daylight, actually kind of pretty. The ground was low-country and level, nearly sea level. Pine trees, five hundred yards away, surrounded the camp on three sides. Unlike the wide, beautiful conifers out West, these pines were tall, straight, and skinny, and stood in stark contrast to the occasional live oak with spreading branches.

Behind me was the New River, maybe a hundred yards wide with an uninhabited point of land as the other shore. Far off in the opposite direction I could just make out a razor-wire-topped fence, defining the border between us and the combat engineers' training area. I was surprised that Maddigan had allowed kudzu to overgrow it, almost as an act of defiance to the manicure and order of Camp Lejeune. Other than that fence, there was nothing between here and the trees but the field.

One-story buildings—white lap-sided rectangles connected by breezeways—reminded me of the ones at Boy Scout camp. Small, varnished pieces of pine numbered each building, and the numbering was simple by military standards. The building we were approaching was the one I leaned against the night before, Building 13. Our Quonset hut was Building 11. I didn't see any buildings over 20.

No one talked as we strolled along like a herd of cats, our uniforms the only evidence that we were military men, our casual gait compelling evidence of exactly the opposite. Again I wondered if all of us were soldiers. Two guys—Ernest with the slicked-back hair and his buddy Nicholas—swapped grins like they'd sneaked into a ballpark. Their hair was too long and they had thick sideburns. The bottoms of their trousers hadn't been bloused or tied, so the strings hung out and dragged along the ground like kids' shoelaces. I'd heard of civilians participating in armed forces training before, I'd just never seen it happen. At least not until then.

Pike slowed, and we did the same. I moved to Building 13 and leaned against the wall as Pike began to speak.

"I want you men to know this field is here, want to prevent a repeat of yesterday's tragedy in the swamp. I don't want to lose another man, so respect this area. Learn from it, but stay out. It's a dangerous place."

The other men looked across the field expecting, I think, to see hordes of barbarians with swords in their teeth. Instead, four soldiers were bending down behind an old deuce-and-a-half at the far edge of the field just inside the tree line, making a show of tossing the electrocuted deer into the back of their truck. I slipped back into a shady corridor between the two halves of the building, leaned against the wall, and closed my eyes.

"Pay attention to the captain!"

My eyes popped open as I flinched away from the wall and looked around the breezeway. There was no one near me. Then the same voice shouted from my other side: "Pay attention!"

70

I snapped around in time to see a man walking away, already a long way out of my striking range. He wore fatigue pants and a black golf shirt. I couldn't see his face, but at that moment I would have believed he didn't have one, that he was a ghost and nothing more. I thought he might have been Big Mouth, back from the hospital and ready for round two, but he was the wrong build. This guy was about the same height but too lean, about five feet ten, one hundred and fifty, fifty-five pounds. Whoever he was, he was intimidating, for sure. He was close enough to push his breath onto my cheek, yet gone before I could react. That kind of stealth gave me the creeps. I was taking notes.

No one else seemed to notice him except Ernest, who waited until the guy walked away from the building before he wandered over, hands dug deep in his pockets.

"Perish," he said. At least, that was what it sounded like.

"What?"

"That's his name. Parrish. Scary mother, huh?"

I'd heard the name before but couldn't place it. Maybe when my heart rate leveled off.

"Where did he come from?"

"Don't know. He's here, he's there, he's everywhere." He straightened up and struck a superhero pose. "He's a phantom."

"Damn near wet my pants. No kidding."

"Don't feel bad. He got me like that, too."

"How long have you been here, Ernest?"

"Call me Elvis. Most of three days."

"I go by H.T. What's up with the field?"

Elvis glanced at the air around us, I guess to see if Parrish was hiding in it. Then we both looked over at the field. The soldiers were swinging the deer back and forth to build momentum, eventually releasing it and letting it fly. It hit the bed of the truck with a thud, I bet, although I was too far away to hear. The soldiers drove away, and I looked back at Pike. I would have checked on Parrish, too, except he'd totally disappeared. That couldn't be good.

"I heard a rumor," he said. "The field has something to do with the mantra around here that it's almost impossible to get close to a target."

"*Gentlemen,*" Pike said, glaring at us. "I'm glad to have you here for this initial phase of Jasper training. You will only be here six weeks, so don't get used to my smiling face."

Pike did smile, and his scowl faded, altering the tough message his face had been sending. Then he quit and the original message returned. I took notes on Pike, too.

"This is an accelerated weeding-out process, gentlemen. I'm here to make you quit. If you don't learn to hate me, I'm not doing my job. Along with a bag full of other hardships, you will also be tortured. I can pretty much guarantee that you *will* regret coming. If any of you are quitters I'll find out, and then shame on you.

"So I'm going to ask that any quitters leave now. Even if quitting is nothing more than a distant thought, I'd like you to act on it. There'll be no penalty. In fact, I'll give you a glowing evaluation and help you get any other duty you want. Why? Because I need men with absolute resolve, men who desperately want to be here and aren't just sticking around for their careers."

He turned around and gave us a few minutes to think it over. No one spoke. I thought about everything in the world except quitting. I knew how dangerous it was to give a toehold to that weakness.

Pike turned back around. I think he was glad we all stayed, although he looked a little surprised.

"Good. Now, for those of you who make it through, you're going to be given a rare gift. You above all others will be the ones to protect this nation, the men most likely to keep America safe in an increasingly hostile world. Questions?"

I couldn't quite get past his torture comment, and while I wouldn't quit over it, my mind was still stuck back there. I mean, torture can take many forms, and since I hadn't seen any medical facilities here I assumed the pain would be subtler than broken bones.

Pike rose onto his toes and repeated himself. "Questions?"

I raised my hand without thinking. I didn't really have a question, but I wanted to show I wasn't scared speechless. I didn't want to sound combative either, so I tried to remember where I'd crossed the line with Big Mouth. I'd never been good at learning boundaries.

"Thompson."

He remembered my name. Great.

I started to speak, but then Pike looked to his side

and gave a small signal. I waited as Parrish strolled from behind Building 13 and joined him, staring at me with menacing black eyes. His face was casually malicious, like a snake. His gray hair was short on the sides and gone on top, exposing a leather scalp stained by a small birthmark, a poorly defined rose—at least that's what it looked like from where I stood.

"Just a follow-up question about torture, Captain. Have women ever been through this training?"

"Three, Thompson."

"Were they pretty? I mean, were they pretty when they got here *and* when they left?"

There was some laughter, which sounded nice because so far life at Camp Lejeune had been deadly serious.

"Thompson, if you're trying to guess how hard it's going to be here, don't use those women as a scale. I would never want to engage any of them in personal combat."

"Especially if they weren't pretty."

Pike laughed with the others, but it didn't sound genuine. Parrish stood at parade rest beside and slightly behind the captain.

"You've got a good sense of humor, Thompson. I heard about you from Colonel Maddigan and your last X.O. Humor's a good thing. Trouble is, your instructor, Master Sergeant Parrish, doesn't have a sense of humor. In fact, I've never seen him smile, except once at a most inappropriate time."

Parrish stepped forward, and Pike turned slightly to see him. "Have you ever made a joke, Sergeant Parrish?"

"No, sir."

"Come on, Jim, not once?"

Jim Parrish. Now I remembered. Back in Commander Nance's office in Coronado, Maddigan said Parrish was there to pick up the slack in Africa after Cameron's murder. Nance had shown fearful respect at the sound of Parrish's name, shocking me that anything could scare Commander Nance. But seeing the way Parrish carried himself, I understood.

"No, sir," Parrish said. "I may have chuckled three or four times. Actually laughed once. But jokes? No, sir, never."

Pike rubbed his chin as Parrish stepped back. "That's what I thought. Well, Sergeant, perhaps Thompson can teach you a thing or two about humor while you teach him personal warfare."

"Yes, sir," muttered Parrish.

I decided to roll the dice again, trying to get even with Parrish for the scare he'd given me a few minutes earlier. "I don't know, Captain. Could be hopeless. I'll give it my best shot, though."

Pike blinked like he'd been night-blinded. He looked at Parrish, who stared at me. I stared back until I had to forfeit and look away.

"All right, gentlemen," Pike continued, "let me tell you why we're looking at this field." He signaled to someone behind me, and a crackle of electricity lifted the hair on my arms. Pike and Parrish took two steps away from the field, as though they suddenly realized they were standing too close.

"See that small mound of dirt out there?"

My eyes followed his finger and saw, well, a small mound of dirt.

"Parrish designed this field's protection grid and buried a German Luger under that mound. He says it's impossible to penetrate the field and retrieve it." Pike turned to Parrish. "The Luger is in perfect condition, isn't it, Parrish?"

"Perfect, sir."

"And it's worth quite a bit of money?"

"About twenty thousand dollars. It was Hermann Göring's personal side arm, stamped at the factory with his name and rank. To me it's priceless. But it's safe under that mound and protected from the elements."

"What if someone managed to get it? Why would you risk losing it?"

Parrish stepped in front of Pike and cleared his throat.

"Men, Captain Pike asked me to simulate defenses you might encounter in a real situation, based on my experiences all over the globe. I offered my Luger as proof that what I designed was impenetrable.

"Some of you are probably thinking you could shut off the power and reduce the threat. You could. But the switches are secured and booby-trapped, so even if you did manage to throw them, there are still plenty of threats that will maim or kill you. Stay out of this field. If you enter it, fall as soon as you're hit. Try to ignore the injuries you'll get on the ground and call for help. Do not try to run, or you'll die in seconds."

"But if they retrieve the Luger," Pike said, more as a tease than a question, "it's theirs?"

"Yes, sir. It's theirs." He stepped back, and Pike stepped forward.

"We're out in the sticks, gentlemen. There will be more elaborate challenges as you progress to the advanced school in Virginia. We just use what we've got around here. So study the defenses. Analyze them. Much of what you might encounter *out there* is in the field or protecting it from a distance. Use it as a mental challenge. Try to solve the puzzle. But stay out of it."

I already had a pistol and had no intention of frying my testicles for another one. I was barely listening, daydreaming instead, diluting the dark loneliness of last night with the bright light of morning. I thought of Shannon.

We were sailing the Chesapeake somewhere near Tangier Island. I was handling the tiller, nearly lost in the rare feeling that everything was just as it should be. Shannon sunned herself, leaning back in a red two-piece that stretched across her firm body. It was almost as if we were a family.

I once doubted I'd ever want to feel that way again. Since leaving home, I suspected that a worthwhile marriage—and the feelings of family I associated with it—was just another fraud my father perpetrated on me. After he let us down, I questioned every value and commitment he taught me, marriage included.

"Hey, Thompson, we're dismissed."

"What?"

Elvis walked away with the others while Pike and Parrish watched me. I turned and followed Elvis to a small canteen, little more than a room with cans of food and a few basic appliances, including a refrigerator with cold milk. I poured a big glass of the stuff.

The machine gunner who got Dwayne killed quit after the chopper picked him up on the beach, so there were eight of us left. I felt like I knew every man, sort of, having shared the challenges and misery of the mission with them. Elvis and his buddy, Nicholas—a big Italian guy who could have been a pro wrestler named The Pulverizing Paesano or something like that—were talking to three men who wouldn't have fit in anywhere but the armed forces: high and tight haircuts, pressed fatigues, and eager, watching eyes. There were subtle differences between them, for sure, but any of them would have looked pretty snappy in one of those Marine commercials. Elvis and Nicholas, on the other hand, could have been insurance salesmen or gym instructors.

"Yeah, I was in Iraq for most of '04," said one of the soldiers as I walked over, his eyes catching mine for a second. I was surprised again by his heavy New York accent, like the cabbies and gangsters in movies. His light complexion, blond hair, and—I don't know, freshness—made me think he was from the South. I had no idea which one of the services he was in, because we were all wearing the same basic uniform and there were no markings.

"It was a blast," he said. "At least at the beginning. Before that I was a Pathfinder against bin Laden, laser-guiding bombs into the mouths of caves in

Afghanistan. But it wasn't nearly as much fun. We killed people personally when we invaded Iraq, man. Just the way we're supposed to in war. Took 'em on and kicked their ass. Hell of an adventure for a while."

He stopped and looked disappointed. "Before long I was slopping paint on walls and basically doing mop-up bullshit, which wasn't at all why I joined in the first place. Other guys managed to get into the line of fire—mostly when they didn't expect it—but what I was doing really sucked. When I got the chance to come here, man, I jumped at it. I stripped off some Iraqi gear for souvenirs and brought it along. Show you some time."

Elvis and Nicholas and I just listened. Then Nicholas wandered off and I turned to talk to Elvis.

"What's your story?"

"Me? No story to tell. Nicholas is the guy."

I looked to see his friend at the other end of the room, lumbering around like a bear. The hair on his back was so thick, it crawled out of his T-shirt and up his neck.

"Meaning?"

"Just stay close to him and on his good side. When things get dicey, he's the guy to be with. He's a quick study of threats. Saved my life twice."

"Twice?"

"Well, not exactly. He saved my life once in combat, and once I pissed him off and he didn't kill me. So I call it twice."

"Your lucky day. Where did this happen?"

"Can't tell you. Over there." He jerked his thumb

toward Europe, maybe the Middle East. I couldn't be sure, because he didn't aim that carefully.

"Here's a friendly warning, Thompson—never pet a burning dog. It's obvious you like to tangle with authority, but give Parrish a little extra room. Talk is he's killed twenty-one men. Thirteen in combat and eight on individual missions."

"Really?"

"He's been Maddigan's go-to guy for years. What I heard, anyway."

"What else?"

"Not much. Pike told us to stay away from him until he made his own introduction."

"You mean this morning, that speech about his Luger?"

"Beats me," he said. "Guess so. He didn't talk at all the other day."

"Did that sound like an introduction to you?" I snapped to parade rest and threw out my chest, trying to convince anyone listening that Parrish still didn't scare me. "My name is Jim Parrish," I said. "I can kill you with my tongue. I can kill you with my big toe. If you step into my field, you'll die a thousand and one deaths. Questions?"

I jumped as warm breath hit my neck and I heard Parrish's soft but menacing voice.

"I say something funny earlier?"

Parrish was right there behind me, proving my dad's wisdom that the best way to find someone was to say something behind his back.

"Well, did I?"

He stared at me with those cold black eyes. It must

have dawned on Elvis that he wasn't a part of this, because he slinked away.

"I wouldn't call it funny," I said. "But I could help you punch it up a little."

"Don't bother. Your advice would be wasted."

"You're probably right."

"You're the smart-ass, aren't you?"

I wanted to say no, that I was an officer in the United States Navy and therefore due the respect of my rank. But for all I knew, Parrish was the Marine Corps commandant just pretending to be a sergeant, so I played it cool.

"I'm Lieutenant Henry Thompson. I assume you've read my service jacket. Does it say anything about me being a smart-ass?"

"Yes."

"*Really?* Then I guess I have to own up to it. Anything else you'd like to know? Maybe how to lighten up a little?"

I looked around. The other men could not have watched Parrish and me any harder if we'd been dancing together.

"Are you going to make my job difficult?" He asked it with sincerity, as if he just wanted to know what he was up against.

"I'm here to do my best, Sergeant. Has nothing to do with you."

I knew I was pushing, so I watched Parrish carefully, struck again by how small he was. Not small really, but just regular. He carried himself like a man who knew he was invincible.

He took my elbow and led me away gently, direct-

ing me away from the other men and the safety of
their numbers. I glanced back, and they laughed
noiselessly and waved like little girls. Parrish and I
stepped outside, which had me remembering high
school dances and fists suddenly swung at my face, so
I was ready to leap. But Parrish walked about twenty
feet from the canteen and sat down on a log where
the yard stopped and the road began.

"Sit down, Thompson. Please."

I sat, about eighteen inches away from him.

Parrish scooped up a handful of sand and let it
filter through his fingers. I noticed that half his
thumb and the entire trigger finger of his right
hand were missing. He studied the sand carefully,
as if going over the exact steps required to turn
beach sand into an explosive or poison or who
knew what.

"I tried to keep you out of Jaspers, Thompson."

"I'm not really interested in what you *tried* to do." I
watched for his hands to come for my throat, but he
didn't react, almost as if he didn't hear me.

"I'll tell you why, because I want you to know. I'm a
straight-ahead kind of guy. If I'm troubled, you'll
know it."

"Great." I scooped up a handful of sand and did my
best to ridicule him, but the sand escaped in sweaty
clumps. Parrish noticed.

"Captain Pike and I are supposed to have final approval of who comes here and who doesn't. I re-
jected you. Nothing personal, but I read that crap in
your service jacket about your natural tendency toward leadership. Frankly, there's no place for that
here."

"No place for leadership in the military, Parrish?" Since we were being cozy, I figured I could call him by name.

He stared between his knees at the ground. "No, not here. We don't want you to become dependent on anyone or for anyone to become dependent on you, which is more likely."

He looked at me. I couldn't think of a thing to say to those dead eyes.

"We teach an individual skill here at Jaspers, which is why I have to split up those two civilians you're so chummy with, Elvis and Nicholas. No leaders." He leaned back and looked at the sky, using his hands to prop himself up on the log. "I'm not one, either, so it's not a competitive thing. I'll do my job, you do yours. Don't be the guy everyone turns to for help. That's your style, but leave it behind. Questions?"

You bet. "If you're supposed to have the final say and you didn't want me, then why am I here?"

"This whole facility is under the command of Colonel Maddigan, who answers to a four-star at MacDill. You've met Colonel Maddigan?"

"Yes. An interesting guy."

Parrish didn't quite smile, but he did do something that came close. I just didn't know what it meant.

"Interesting? I've never heard him described quite that way."

"Why am I here?" I asked again, still pushing.

"I zeroed you, but Colonel Maddigan called and asked me to reconsider. I did, but even though I didn't change my mind, he sent you anyway. I'm a soldier who follows orders, and since I trust Colonel Maddigan more than any man alive, I'll assume he has something special in mind for you, some mission that requires a guy with your background or personality." I know he wanted to laugh like he was sure it couldn't be my personality, but he didn't. "If the colonel wants you that badly, it's good enough for me."

"So there we have it."

"Just don't make my life difficult."

"I'll try. Not to, I mean."

He cocked his head and squinted at me, his eyes like black marbles. I bet he thought he'd wasted his time as he stood up and walked away, leaving me sitting on the log, thinking.

Since my arrival at Camp Lejeune, I'd seen a man slaughtered by his own military. I'd aimed at an Apache helicopter, ready to shoot it down and kill an American pilot. And I'd just given lip to the man whose name scared the hell out of Commander Nance. It took a few minutes of sitting on the log before I felt strong enough to take on whatever was coming next.

As I sat there, an F/A-18 Super Hornet screamed overhead and lobbed practice bombs toward rifle fire a couple of miles away, way on the other side of the electrified field. The plane was sharp and clean, with USMC and American flags painted under the wings and on one of the tails. I was sure the pilot knew exactly what he was doing and why he was there, that he truly believed he was participating in an honorable profession, training for war and ready to follow that path as far as necessary to protect his country, ready to kill for that noblest of all causes.

After a minute or two, I found that I missed having my name and rank on my uniform, and the U.S. Navy patches and tags they cut off that first night.

Five

I lived every second of the next five weeks in fear. Pike more than lived up to his word and made me hate him intensely, although I didn't just single him out. I learned to hate every single instructor there, if for no other reason than the nearly debilitative fear they made me admit to myself.

Elvis and I helped each other survive. We felt like prisoners of war illegally sharing food or water, and we were every bit as careful not to be caught. Teaming up or helping someone else had been declared a violation, punishable by another round of torture I wasn't sure I would survive.

Elvis was terrified because he'd gotten off easy so far, and that convinced him that when his time came it would be far worse than it was for the rest of us. I tried to help him stay strong, although I believed he was right.

"You'll get through whatever they do to you, Elvis."

"I don't know about that," he said as he soaked another towel for my back. "Maybe I'll break down and cry like a girl, who knows?"

"You're unbreakable. Come on, believe in yourself."

"Sure."

"There's only one more week, and if they wait until the last minute, heck, it'll only take a minute. Wouldn't that make you the luckiest man here?"

He spread the hot towel over my back and it made my shoulders feel better. He'd been changing them every ten minutes, trying to get me healed for our first weekend off since arrival.

I wanted to go out with the others and celebrate that my turn was over—unless they decided to take me again as they had some of the men. But I wouldn't allow myself to let up, not for a single second. Long ago I'd hardened to the challenge of this place, put my head down and focused on the goal and nothing else. Until I crossed the land bridge over the swamp and walked out the main gate of Camp Lejeune, I wasn't about to slack off. If I allowed any weakness to show, it could inspire them to torture me again.

To be honest, I was amazed they actually tortured me in the first place, an experience of fear and absolute vulnerability I would never forget. They grabbed me out of the shower when I least expected it, took me somewhere dark, cold, and noisy, then set into making me suffer. Although they hurt me enough to ache for weeks, the physical ordeal wasn't unbearably painful. Mentally, though, it was nothing short of terrifying. Two guys quit—if carried out on a stretcher or put in the brig could be considered quitting. The injured man, Rutger the Scandinavian, cracked his head when he hit the cell floor too hard. The other one was the picture-perfect soldier with the thick Bronx accent. He went stark raving loony, attacked Captain Pike, and was hauled away so suddenly that all the stuff he stripped off Iraqi soldiers was still in his locker. There was no chance he would ever come back for it.

Little was expected from the rest of us as domination and fear infected every cell and fiber of our minds and morale. Each of us prayed constantly that some other Jasper candidate would be the next one to suffer. We had traded heroics and self-respect for the hope of survival, of getting out of there whole and only marginally mad or disfigured. All of us were each other's enemy, although Elvis and I had somehow formed an alliance that engendered more hatred from the others than we would have got separately.

Even though I swore to myself I would never consider it, I found myself contributing my share to the talk around the water cooler, so to speak. Things like "I don't want to be one of those who never makes it out of here" or "Do you believe guys are really tortured to death here?" As the weeks piled up, the questions were spoken less often than the comments, probably because no one really wanted to know the answer—or already did.

The instructors' threats made us believe our lives were at risk to the point we were certain of it. The men we'd entrusted with our training became vicious, evil captors who convinced us we could die at their hands, that they were determined to cull out weaklings who would fail in battle. They told us, of course, that no one ever knew why their victims died because that was the foundation of Jaspers' training— untraceable ways of killing.

The waiting was terrible, dwelling on the devices and methods they threatened to use on me, the same ones any of us might encounter in real situations around the world. When my turn finally came, it started the longest ten hours of my life. I was kept awake by fear and threats, and cold, naked, bound and blindfolded, poked and prodded and showered with ice water, lifted off the ground by a rope that strained my protected wrists and wrenched my shoulders as I shivered.

"What's your father's name?" asked the man in the darkness behind me. He was Cuban, I think. I'd seen him before and recognized the voice. I remembered him as dark and pocked and mean-looking. I called him Fidel, but only to myself.

I barely heard his voice. I had stopped paying attention hours ago.

He slapped the top of my bare thighs with a piece of bamboo. He started with the bottoms of my feet about four hours ago, working his way up to my knees as my dented shins swelled. Now he was almost to my groin, the tip of the bamboo rod slamming into me just inches from my exposed and dangling genitals. I didn't want him to crush them, but that's what he was promising to do unless I gave him the answer that would make him stop.

But I wasn't even going to think about answering. I'd decided early on that nothing was going to come out of my mouth except blood or spit or a warm sticky mixture of both.

"Your father's name, Thompson," he said as he shifted again to a friendly tone, acting like he couldn't understand my reluctance. "I already know it's Howard. I just want to hear it from you. Answer this one question and maybe you can go."

I closed my eyes and told myself for the hundredth time that I wouldn't open my mouth. Not that night. Not if it killed me. Not even to scream.

He kicked away the stool I was standing on and I dropped two feet. My arms felt like they came out of their sockets and my muscles twitched wildly from the strain.

"Tell me your father's name or I'm going to kill you!"

I focused on Shannon, who was ahead of me now on our skiing vacation in Vermont. It was my first time on skis, so she took it easy while I tried to keep up, my arms making big circles as my ski tips crossed. She stopped, and I fell near her. She helped me up and hugged me.

I'd been thinking of her for hours, finding fragments of the trip I thought I'd lost, bits of conversation, tossed snowball, meals ordered, touches, giggles, snuggles. I undervalued all of them at the time, but here, scared and very nearly broken, I wondered how I ever failed to appreciate them. I had lots of other memories about her I was saving for later. It was still early. I hadn't yet come to grips with my own limits.

When would I break and start talking?

My biggest problem was that Fidel asked only innocent questions that I didn't see the harm in answering. What could it hurt to reveal my hometown or date of birth, especially when I knew he already had the information? But I'd read enough about interrogation to know you could never allow yourself to start answering questions, even easy ones. It would just be giving the enemy a tool, an advantage over you. Besides, once you started talking it would be too hard to stop.

Fidel put me back on the ladder and asked for my father's name again. But by then I was exhausted and knew I couldn't hold out much longer. I'd already endured more than I thought I could take, and so I decided to do something to change the dynamics. I jumped off the ladder. I don't mean I just fell forward, either. I jumped as high as I could. It surprised Fidel so much, he leaped forward and broke my fall, maybe saving me from serious injuries.

He ordered the others to cut me down and then lowered me to the ground. As he was holding me, I caught a glance at his eyes and thought I saw respect, although I couldn't be sure. If it wasn't respect, maybe I'd convinced him I was unbreakable or an idiot, perhaps both. He untied my arms and feet, looked them over for serious cuts, and then handed me my uniform. "Go back to the other men," he said nervously. "You pass. If you say a word about what happened here, you'll be back."

I wanted to stare at him to show victory or to celebrate survival, to restake my claim on my own self-respect, but I couldn't get my eyes off the floor. I was naked and dirty and exhausted, trembling with fear and shivering so badly from the cold it made the chilly Pacific seem like a spa. At that instant, it was much harder to hold back my tears than it was to keep my mouth closed while Fidel tortured me.

I shuffled into the Quonset hut, barely moving but

trying my best to look fine. Each man looked at me for a signal that it would be all right for him, or that maybe it was worse for me. They thought I would tell them what happened. The time they'd spent with me had convinced them I'd give details, even to them, my enemies. At the minimum, they expected me to wink or make a joke.

But I stared at my bunk as I wandered toward it and never looked at anyone. I would be okay. I just needed some time. I tried to act like I'd joke about it, maybe after a few days, but I already knew I wouldn't.

A couple weeks earlier, Elvis's buddy Nicholas was grabbed in the middle of the night and no one had seen him since. The rumors said he died, that he resisted too much as the instructors stepped up the pain and fear until finally his heart gave out. I didn't want to believe that Parrish or Fidel or the others had killed him, even by accident, but how would I know? That little camp in the beautiful low-country of North Carolina was more horrifying than any movie or monster I could conjure up in my mind.

I guess in a way I was lucky. As bad as the torture was, it wasn't as hurtful as when I called Shannon just before they strung me up—naked, blindfolded, and shivering. It was part of the ritual of torture—a last phone call to a loved one in case we didn't survive.

"I've got something to tell you," she said. She still sounded a little mad about my leaving SEALs. Something was sure bugging her.

"Look, Shannon, I've just got a minute and wanted—"

"Steve is in town and wants to take me out."

One of my captors said, "Thirty seconds."

"That guy from the bar in New York? Terrific. Did you call him or did he call you?"

"Does it matter?"

"Look, we've been over this."

"I know. Hey, we *talked* about this."

"Well, you can't go."

"What?"

"You heard me. You can't go."

"And since when do you have control over what I do? Besides, I only said he asked me out."

"Are you going?"

"I don't know yet. I wasn't going to, but I'm thinking about it now."

"Fine. I've got to go."

This time I hung up first. There was no way she could call me back. I was so pissed off, I turned to the man who held the rope around my neck and said, "Do something scary, jerk-off. You're boring me." He cured that by jolting my chest with a cattle prod.

Shannon and I didn't exactly have a perfect relationship, largely because of all the things she needed to work out for herself, things that she said had very little to do with me. I wanted much more from her but was willing to settle for best friend. Occasionally, I felt like little more than her lover, stuck in a relational no-man's-land, which was exactly where all our problems lurked. Since we weren't engaged, she was free. Since she was free, she could date. By some perversely complicated female logic, she said it had nothing to do with the way she felt about me.

Jaspers got that weekend off, and although I'd already decided not to celebrate my survival, I had thought about flying to Washington and surprising

Shannon. But I couldn't with Steve in the picture, because I had to let her make her own choice about what to do. I was tempted to go back and keep them separated by force, but what good was a relationship with someone you couldn't trust or who was trustworthy only if she feared you might show up and surprise her? I knew the right way to behave, but I still felt like I was in high school, wanting to watch my girlfriend's house to see if she went out with someone else. I was supposed to have outgrown that sort of thing, but age hadn't diluted the urge. My stomach ground and my chest hurt, and I thought once again about the airlines, a rental car, and how long it would take to get there.

Elvis put one last towel on my back and then sat on his bunk next to mine. He looked like someone facing open-heart surgery. I'd tried to help him, selfishly hoping it would make me forget what Shannon was doing.

"I feel better now," I said. "Thanks."

"I still haven't heard from Nicholas."

Elvis thought Nicholas was his responsibility. He shouldn't have had to worry as a trainee at a United States military installation, but he did. I worried about Nicholas, too, but tried not to let it show.

"He's fine," I said. "He probably advanced to another class. Or maybe he got sick and was set back. Don't worry. I doubt they hurt him."

"The rumors are probably a load of crap."

"Most likely." I said this and hoped it would hide my memory, the time I sat on a log with Parrish and heard him say he'd break up Nicholas and Elvis.

"So," he said, forcing enthusiasm into his words, "you feeling good enough to go out? My sisters are in town. You'd like them. Especially Molly. Might be your only chance to meet them."

I sat up, and the towel fell off before I could reach it. I tested my shoulders to prove I wasn't badly hurt. "No, thanks."

"I figured. You're not much for going out, are you?"

I rotated my arms. Everything worked, but painfully. "You'll want to spend time alone with them. I'd be a third . . . fourth wheel."

"That makes a lot of sense."

I laughed, and it hurt my ribs. "Not the smartest thing I ever said."

"So what are you going to do?"

"Read, maybe. I just want to stay in bed."

"Guess I don't blame you."

"You go on. Have fun."

Elvis walked to the door and looked back. He was having trouble leaving me behind. We'd watched out for each other too long.

"Go."

He left. I closed my eyes and went back to Shannon, who was getting dressed and ready for her date with Steve. I'd seen her do this a hundred times, so I knew what was happening. She'd already picked the dress to wear, and my bet was on one of the man-killers that was cut low or hemmed short or both. It was about seven-thirty, so she was sitting at her makeup table in matching bra and panties, painting her toenails and preening herself, doing all the subtle things that made a pretty woman an irresistible one. She'd given careful consideration to her choice of underwear—a bra, probably purple or black, that matched silk panties even though she preferred cotton. I could see her clearly, and as I watched like a voyeur I wished she would wear those ugly cotton briefs I hated so much. But she didn't, and that tormented me right down to my socks.

Shannon and I never lacked for an interesting sex life. It was the most exciting thing in my life when it was happening around me, but threatening from this great a distance. If President Devereau knew some of what we'd done in our sexual playground, he would have given us both a lecture or, more likely, told her father. Devereau was kind of pissy about things like that. Even though Shannon was only a low-level staffer who happened to be a family friend, he was legendary for being a prude and intolerant of what he considered aberrant sexual behavior—which I pretty much interpreted as anything with the lights on.

We'd been very careful. It made sense for anyone willing to experiment a bit to be careful no matter who you were, but that basic rule went double if your boss was a fanatic about morality—a hypocrisy of society we impose on ourselves, as Shannon says.

One of our favorite games was to go out separately to a crowded bar and pretend to be alone while we watched each other flirt. Sometimes we'd even compete to see who got a sexual offer first. Of course, I was always at a huge disadvantage, being male. Men stopped talking midsentence when Shannon entered the room, but I had to rely on wit and liquor and charm. She generally spotted me an hour and fifty bucks to spend on drinks.

We never accepted any of the offers, but it was fun to get them. Last time out, a beautiful woman saw me the second I walked in the door and rushed up to me. She said she knew me and was excited to see me again, although it was obviously a lie. I think I set a new record that night, getting picked up within ten seconds of entering the bar.

Shannon saw the whole thing. Determined to one-up me, she squeezed into a group of several men at the bar under the pretense of ordering a drink that the guys bought for her, of course. She toyed with them and teased them long enough to get half a dozen offers to "go someplace else." So there we were, Shannon at the bar surrounded by men adoring her body, and me in the nearest booth with a woman who was ready to leave with me.

As I said, we never did anything with these people. It was just a game we played, a way to prove to each other that we were desirable. On some level desirability equates with control, so in a very real sense it was a power struggle between us.

It may sound crazy, but I liked watching her drive other men crazy as she leaned this way and that and sat down in a way that revealed a flash of underwear to men who were already hardwired to look up her skirt.

A few days before I left for SEALs training in Coronado, we caught the shuttle to New York to go barhopping. We ended up in an expensive bar in the financial district, the kind of place that catered to Wall Street types and the women who sought them. Not a place where women would be after me, but Shannon liked it; so there we were, keeping our distance, when a guy asked her to shoot pool in the back. She went and I followed, trailing a few feet behind several of his friends. Shannon was wearing a short beige skirt and a sheer off-white blouse over a beige bra. She was definitely walking the tightrope between beautiful and sleazy.

There was one other guy in the pool room when we got there. If Shannon hadn't been with me, I probably would have asked him to shoot some stick, because he didn't look overly impressed with himself like the others. He practiced the same careful attention to detail, but his clothes and appearance were relaxed. He didn't seem to be showing off for anyone.

But Shannon *was* there, so I sat down and tried to see her new friend as she might, to see if she was really interested in him. The guy who'd invited her back wore the kind of suit I saw all the time in men's magazines, something I'd never wear even if I could afford it, which of course I couldn't. He was about Shannon's height, and I guess he was good-looking, although I had no clue how women defined that.

Anyway, the guy bought her another drink, and since she knew I was there to protect her, she drank it and asked for another. It wasn't long before he was standing behind her, pressing into her, trying to teach her how to shoot pool. This guy acted like the cock-of-the-walk, toying with the hem of her skirt and even lifting it once so his friends could see her panties. She just let it happen, even to the point of bending over the table and looking back to see the men staring up her dress. Then she looked to see how I was doing.

I could have thrown her onto the pool table and taken her right there.

Well, I watched until this guy started making crude

comments, pushing too hard as the alcohol kicked in. I had just started toward him when I heard Shannon say, "Thanks for the drink and the game. I hope you don't think I'm rude, but I know that man over there and want to talk to him." She nodded in what I thought was my direction. I lifted my drink toward her and at the same time gave him a look to show he'd been beaten, hoping the look would be enough to move him along.

The guy turned polite again and kissed her cheek, then walked away with his friends, leaving Shannon and me and the guy in the corner who was playing pool when we first went back. I wanted desperately to take her back to the hotel after staring at her panties as she tormented all the men in the room. But just then the other guy walked over and whispered something to her. I still don't know what he said, but Shannon must have liked it, because she motioned me to stay away. She sat down with him and immediately laughed at something else he said, both of them smiling and having a good time for about ten minutes until she did something she'd never done before. She pointed me out, then whispered to him and giggled. He nodded and then walked over with a slightly confused look. He invited me to join them before going to the bar to get me another drink.

"What's going on?" I asked as I sat down beside her.

She moved her hips and crossed her legs tightly. She always got wildly sexual on these evenings out, and this was the longest she'd lasted without jumping my bones. I had no idea what to expect from her at this point.

"He's very nice," she said. "I like him."

"Great, I'm sure he is. Hey, you know what? I'm dying to take you back to the hotel. Can we go now?"

"I want him."

"What?"

"I want him," she said again, looking more than a little possessed.

"But what about me?"

"I want you, too."

Like a dumbstruck idiot I sat there confused and silent, analyzing her comment as if it were a physics question. I was about to hold out my hands and explain that life was full of choices, but you only got to pick one. Then it dawned on me what she was thinking.

"Oh."

She giggled some more. At least she was having fun.

"You mean both of us? At the same time?"

"Yes," she said. Then she shivered with excitement. "Oh please, Henry. Lots of women want to do this, just one time to know what it's like, to see how they do. All men want two women, right? Why shouldn't a woman want two men? It doesn't mean anything. Just curiosity."

I pondered it for a minute, remembering hundreds of my own fantasies with two women or, more accurately, my fantasy of two women replayed hundreds of times. But this was Shannon's fantasy, not mine. A dozen stupid questions and at least that many naive comments swirled through my mind, and I tried to pick the best of them to ask before he came back with my drink. I was confused by my emotions, thinking that maybe I could go through with it, reminding myself that we would all be consenting adults. But then I reduced the philosophical and emotional arguments to a simple "Naah. I don't think so."

She crossed her arms and wanted to pout, but instead she came up with a plan for winning, the way she always did when she really wanted to convince me. "You don't understand, Henry. It's important for us to do this. I want, one time before we . . . well, while we're still crazy and dating, to have two men. I don't want to be ninety years old and wondering what it would have been like. But I won't do it unless you're one of the men. You've got to be okay with it, so please try to understand. If you can't, just trust me on this one."

I'm not sure what I felt, but I think I was happy. I mean, she's surely had chances to do this without me, and it sounded like this might satisfy something that was keeping our relationship from moving forward. So I went back and ran through all the arguments again. Let's see: We don't know this guy, which by tomorrow will be a big bonus. I'm sure Shannon will insist on safe sex, so not much worry there. I'll be with her if he turns out to be weird, although in truth he does seem like a nice guy. . . . What was I saying?

"No. Let's get out of here before he gets back."

She slowly wiggled her bottom around on her seat, and I knew what she was doing to herself. I've never been the brightest coin in the collection plate, but I did know that when she locked her legs that tightly and squeezed them together, well, let's just say I was envious of what she could do in public and I couldn't.

"P-l-e-a-s-e, Henry. For me." She smiled and bit her lip. Her eyes were big, and she was only an "okay, Shannon, I'm in" from going to a sexual place I had to admit held interest for me, even if it was just to see how she handled it.

I would probably have gone along with anything at that point. I'd tried coming up with good reasons to stop her, but now I was leaking onto my trousers and looking for the door, so I was pretty helpless to do anything but concede. She had me and she knew it.

"Oh, thank you, Henry. I've always said I'd do this before—"

She stopped as the guy walked back with drinks.

"Before what?"

She didn't have time to answer.

"Steve, this is my boyfriend, Henry."

"Hi, Henry." He tried to shake my hand, but he was holding my drink and his drink and had to set one of them down first. It was an awkward moment, but funny to Shannon.

"Hey, Steve. Thanks for the drink."

"No problem. Shannon tells me you guys are really tight. I'm flattered to be included."

Flattered to be included? For some reason, I found that funny and kind of pictured him ordering drinks and rehearsing it. *Flattered* to be included. Flattered to be *included*. Flattered *to be* included.

As for me, I wanted to use my opening statement to let him know this was all news to me, that I hadn't come here looking for a man to join us. But Shannon cut me off by rising into Steve and kissing him firmly on the mouth, one of her hands pressed against his chest and her other hand—I couldn't believe I was seeing this—reaching for his crotch. I was worried that someone might see us back there from the main bar, but more worried that I might explode. If you've never seen a woman who loves you kissing another man like that, you're in for a lot of pain and, okay, I'll confess, a weird, unexpected thrill. Sort of the same craziness that attracted me to scary movies and roller coasters, I guess, which made me wonder if that was part of Shannon's attraction. She was crazy enough to keep me from ever getting bored with her.

Anyway, we went back to the hotel and Shannon dealt me yet another surprise while my new best friend Steve parked his car.

"I want you to wait at the lobby bar, Henry."

"Like hell!"

Okay, a little too loud maybe. But I was so jazzed, I could have leaped fifty feet—from a lotus position.

"I'm a little nervous. Give me a chance to learn my way around this guy, okay? It won't take long, and I'll be more relaxed when you join us."

"But—"

"You know I don't care about him. I care about you. This is probably the only time we'll ever do this, Henry, and I don't want you remembering me as being . . . no good."

The only time? Well, there was some good news. "Shannon, I think you're the most—"

She put her finger over my mouth. "Shh. Here he comes. I'll call you in a few minutes."

My old pal Steve walked up and looked puzzled until Shannon took his hand and led him to the elevator. I followed as they got in and turned around. We stared at each other. As the doors closed, I couldn't think of a thing to say except "Have fun," and I sure as hell wasn't going to say that.

I sat at the bar for about eighteen minutes and nine

seconds, more or less, staring at the bartender's phone and cursing it for not ringing, pretty secure about my size but still a little uncertain, wondering who would be better and more satisfying to Shannon. Creepy things like that. I generated a strategy, which was simply that if Steve took heads and I took tails or vice versa, we'd never have to see or touch each other.

At the first sound of the ringer, I jumped up so fast I surprised the barman, who almost didn't answer it in time. I was about to dive over the bar myself when he finally connected my anxiety to the ringing phone.

"You Thompson?"

"Yes! Yes."

"Some woman's looking for you." He offered me the phone. As I took it, I thought about something clever to say, about who'd be listening, and what I was about to do.

I didn't say anything. I couldn't. I tried like hell, but I just couldn't make my voice overpower the screaming truth that this was a line I could not cross. I handed back the phone and decided I'd had enough and went to catch a plane back home. I got to the departure gate early and slept until Shannon woke me three hours later.

"You didn't come," she teased, smiling seductively as she sat beside me.

"Not funny."

"Not even a little?"

"Leave me alone, Shannon. I went along with your idea, so I'll take the blame and we'll be fine. But give me some time, okay?"

"You're making too much out of this."

Wes DeMott

I looked her over. Nothing about her was different from before we met Steve. Nothing visible, anyway.

I closed my eyes and acted like I wanted to sleep. "Been meaning to tell you, Shannon. I'm leaving in ten days for Coronado. I got accepted to SEALs."

I glanced over and saw her looking out the window back at the city, as if hurt and confused. "Good for you," she said as her head dropped and her voice went soft. All the fun and seductiveness was gone. I knew she was sad. To be honest, that was my intent.

"It's what you wanted," she said, and then gave me a brave smile, like a child accepting an unfair punishment from a parent they adore.

She walked away and I didn't see her again. I planned to apologize on the plane, but she must have taken a different flight home. I admit I didn't look very hard for her before I left.

Now Steve was once again in our relationship, and it was time for her to hurt me back. As I sat there rotating my shoulders, I felt jealous, insecure even, although I hated applying that word to myself.

Wounded and scared in a barracks all alone and tempted to wallow in a mess I couldn't change, I looked for anything to force my focus away. My first thought was of Jaspers and how isolated I was at this remote camp, and how much more isolated I was from the rest of the military.

Isolation was the panic that had been gripping my guts since I left home, the enemy I constantly had to guard against. Although I left Indiana determined to lose myself in a world of strangers, there were times I could barely stand it, times I probably would have quit and gone home if not for my ace in the hole—

106

Shannon. Without her I would have been totally alone in this world, an outcast by my own election.

In the dark and loneliness of my Quonset hut I admitted to missing my family, although not in any particular way. Mostly I just missed the feeling of having a family, of believing that I could count on them for good words and strong support regardless of whatever allegations or circumstances attacked me. But whenever I thought back and tried to find specific examples to celebrate, I couldn't. I never needed to wonder why, and it was probably fair for me to take all the blame. After all, I was the one who turned my back and walked away from them.

My problem was that I wasn't strong enough to maintain that emotional distance, but neither was I enough of a loner to be a Jasper. I finally understood that. Parrish was right when he tried to keep me out, spot-on accurate in his assessment of me. So why did Maddigan force him to take me? How and when did I pop up on his radar screen? I wasn't an old hand at the way the services worked, but I couldn't imagine colonels out scouting the troops, searching for good prospects to fill their ranks. But maybe they did?

And then it occurred to me that if I didn't belong there, maybe no one did. Maybe all Jaspers felt out of place but stayed for the opportunity, eventually adapting enough to appear at home and comfortable—although I never saw anyone there who was at peace or anywhere near it. Perhaps that was the goal of Jaspers, to keep us tormented and emotionally isolated from humanity in order to prepare us for an inhumane job, using torture and secrecy and deadly agendas that humans were never intended to learn in preparation for times that God never intended to happen. Mankind creates those situations so often—war springs to mind most quickly—that it justifies Jaspers' existence. That much I knew for sure.

I accepted that as the reason I was there. Being honest with myself, I guessed that was what I wanted—war, and all the destruction and pain and carnage that horrible word implied. If it was personal warfare, even better. A one-on-one fight would be a decent way to keep my country safe and prove myself courageous. I would know I won it alone, killing my enemy in a noble effort, earning the kind of respect Nance showed for Parrish, doing the one courageous thing my father failed to do when he'd been called upon to kill another man.

I would miss the uniformity and camaraderie of SEALs, but in truth those guys might never see a war or get a chance to kill anyone, so Jaspers was my best chance. I was willing to pay the price of clarity, living in the unfamiliar territory between right and wrong where Jaspers did their work. Although I did not want to do wrong, neither would I insist on seeing what I did as the right thing. At least at the time I didn't think so.

As I lay in bed worried about Shannon and Jaspers, I heard the electrified crackle of what had come to be called Parrish's Field of Fun and Frolic. Another dumb animal had stumbled into the area, sacrificing itself to remind us there was never a time or place to relax, that protections and defenses always existed around important people and, in this case, Hermann Göring's Luger.

Shannon was sitting in her bra and panties, getting

ready for her date with Steve. I was agonizing over what she might do, so I had no choice but to escape. It took only a minute for me to decide, and then I was on my feet, dressed in a camouflage uniform and outside.

The camp was quiet and almost dark, the sun having just set. Pond frogs belched in the swamp and dragonflies chased mosquitoes in and out of the mercury vapor lights. No one was on the grounds. The camp was a small place, really; therefore, it was easy to notice any movements at all. But there weren't any.

I went to the supply hut for what I thought I might need based on several weeks of observations fueled by curiosity, a pretty good understanding of myself, and an expectation that a night like this would eventually come.

We had some pretty slick toys, but I couldn't carry them, so I took only the essentials: camouflage paint for my hands and face, mirrors, night-vision gear, a big knife for digging, and insect repellent. My odds were terrible, so I stuck a rescue whistle into my pocket. Just outside the door were some thin metal rods with tiny flags that we used to lay out pretend training situations. I grabbed a handful of them, too.

I'd spent a lot of time analyzing the field and the guy who designed it, so I expected the easiest approaches to be more dangerous than the hardest. I'd walked the perimeter and located several lasers and infrared sensors and felt I had a decent chance of slipping through the first hundred yards or so. After that, who knew?

Absolutely the ugliest part of the Jaspers camp was the diseased swamp that separated the main road from Parrish's field. During this past week I'd seen a badger in this filthy water, watching carefully, I figured, for the water moccasins that seemed to love the place. We weren't allowed to kill the snakes unless they got into our Quonset hut, so those poisonous neighbors were nearly as abundant as the mosquitoes that bred in the swamp.

I crept to the instructors' barracks, which were right beside the field with a great view when it was possible to see. I was thankful there weren't any floodlights aimed at the field as I crouched on the ground and applied the camouflage paint and bug juice, the good old army stuff in the little green bottle. I used the whole bottle but had another one in my pocket, certain I was going to need it. I slipped the night-vision gear into a waterproof bag and then glanced through the window. Parrish was sitting right there, reading with his back to me. I moved on.

The water was gross sludge, about four feet deep right off the shore. Moving slowly and paying attention, I pushed the infected surface apart with my chest as my feet searched the muddy bottom for level footing. I took a long stick to poke around in front of me, and I wasn't three feet from shore when it touched something stretched across the bottom. It was a wire or monofilament line, and it was there for trespassers. As a kid I'd studied everything about the war in Vietnam and would always remember how the Vietcong strung underwater wires at stream crossings. They attached the wire to a stake on one side and a grenade on the other, the grenade's pin missing but the spoon held in place by a can that was nailed to something. When a soldier moved through the stream, he'd catch the wire and pull the grenade out of the tin can, and then *boom!*

I had no idea what that wire was attached to but didn't expect a grenade. Maybe a siren, though. Or a concussion charge. Or maybe it ran all the way to Parrish's big toe.

I stepped carefully over the wire, knowing I'd been lucky to feel it while moving that fast, a pace far too quick for the conditions. I wanted out of the water before some poisonous snake bit me, but more than that I wanted to get close to Parrish's pistol before I failed. I had to slow down.

I was fairly certain there weren't any motion sensors over the swamp, because animals would have set them off. But they might have been aimed higher off the water, so I crouched until my nose just barely cleared the scum, my mouth tightly closed so that the bacteria, insect eggs, and water bugs didn't wash down my throat.

It took me an hour to cross the small swamp, moving three feet a minute, a good rate considering the circumstances. If I kept that pace, I'd get back to the swamp before sunup. I finally got to the other side, struggled onto the bank, and rested on the ground, facedown.

Something crawled inside my trousers, but I couldn't do much about it without knowing where I could move to avoid the lasers. I pulled the night-vision goggles out of the plastic bag and put them on, turned the switch, and looked at the tiny green television screens in front of each eye. Dozens of lasers became instantly visible through the intensifying lenses, crisscrossing the field at one-foot intervals starting about a foot off the ground, probably so rabbits could pass through. I suspected there were other types of lasers I couldn't see. I also bet Parrish had buried pressure switches in the low grass and maybe a mantrap or two, so I probed the area in front of me with my knife, all the while trying to ignore being eaten alive by something in my uniform.

The ground was hard, which meant any dirt that had been disturbed should be easy to find. Five feet out of the swamp that's exactly what I found. I slipped my knife into that spot and located a pressure switch. I marked it with a flag and moved forward.

Mosquitoes buzzed all around me and bit me like never before. I never knew they could penetrate a thick uniform. All the repellent must have washed off in the swamp, and I couldn't reapply it without rising into the laser two inches over my body, so I endured the bites and dragged myself across the ground until I realized with a little panic that the bites weren't mosquitoes. I was covered with fire ants, their bites like injections of burning gasoline as they attacked furiously. There was still repellent on my face, thank God, and that kept most of them out of my eyes, but they were all over inside my uniform and biting everywhere. I wanted to scream, to jump up and run away, strip down and brush them off, but I couldn't. I could barely endure them as I forced myself to ignore everything except my mission.

I moved away from the ant colony of warriors pouring out by the thousands. I expected to find more of them as I crawled past poisonous and thorny plants, and who knew what else waited up ahead.

Ten yards and thirty minutes later I heard a rattling on my left, like BBs being poured onto a tambourine. The goggles had poor peripheral vision, so I snapped my head sideways to see, even though I'd already identified the noise.

"Oh, God. Oh God, oh God, oh God!"

A big diamondback was ready to strike, not two feet from my face. He was eight feet long maybe, although it was hard to tell because he'd coiled up like a cowpie. His dark head was up and weaved from side to side as his tongue licked the air between us. His tail rattled like my old Camaro, and I'd never felt so helpless and vulnerable in my life before. I was his if he wanted me. Flawed instincts told me to jump to my feet, but fear and determination kept me where I was, surrendered to this lethal sentry.

"Oh, God. Nice snake. Nice snake."

The rattler kept weaving and licking, his head nearly as big as my hand. I was stiff as lumber, proned out in front of him. I turned my knife in my hand, hoping to kill the snake when its fangs injected me, maybe cutting down on the amount of venom he pumped into me. It was a stupid plan, but all I could think of doing.

"Shoo."

Rattle, rattle, rattle. His head weaved left and I wanted to move right. But I didn't move a muscle. I'm not sure I could have.

"Shoo. Go away."

Rattle.

"Oh, God!"

Rattle, rattle.

We stared at each other for a three-hour minute as

he displayed his absolute power over me. I stayed motionless on my belly, eye to eye and inches away until he finally got bored, uncoiled, and slipped away with the bulge of whatever he'd just eaten swelling his middle.

I was so relieved that I let my face drop into the dirt.

"Ouch!" I'd forgotten about the goggles, which stuck out about six inches and smacked the ground, smashing my face and probably giving me raccoon eyes. "Damn!"

I pulled them off and rested in the low grass. The ants had been vicious; and lots of them were still crawling around in my trousers. The snake scared me senseless, and my face hurt from the goggles. I allowed a couple minutes to feel sorry for myself.

There. Enough.

Moving slow was harder with all the fear I felt. I sped up to about four feet a minute, maybe five or six when I was doing well. My legs were already swelling, but at least the ants had retreated after running off the invader of their domain. I planted flags along my route, bending them low to the ground so Parrish wouldn't notice them in the moonlight.

The mound of dirt that protected the Luger was a million miles away. I had to concentrate or I'd get caught or hurt. I didn't really think I'd get killed, having decided that the deer was a charade for our benefit, perhaps let loose in the field after being injected with one of the lethal serums they talked so much about. There were probably enough electrical defenses in the field to stun me, but I doubted I would die. I wasn't sure, though.

It was hard to keep focused on what I was doing. I

was here because I needed a distraction from Shannon, but this field barely managed the task. My hand moved slowly forward, probing the ground with the knife as my eyes watched for snakes. My wet uniform chafed at a thousand insect bites as muscles cramped in rebellion against my prone position.

Still, the majority of my agony came from my heart, from Shannon sitting in her bra and panties getting ready for her date with Steve. It was going to hurt, but I couldn't do a damn thing to stop it.

Six

Parrish's Field of Fun and Frolic turned out to be neither, although it *was* tricky and painful, intimidating and tormenting. The simple challenges were the worst, like the rows of sharpened gutter spikes stuck through steel plates. They were buried in the ground I crossed an hour ago, and since I couldn't go around them—and rising to clear them would have set off motion detectors and lasers—I crawled painfully across them, protecting my palms with two flat rocks as the spikes shredded my uniform and dug shallow furrows down my chest and legs.

When I finally approached the mound that protected the Luger, I almost gave up. It wasn't a mound of dirt at all, but rather another fire-ant hill about two feet high and three feet in diameter. From my first two yards out of the swamp, that's what I suspected, but it would have been nice to be wrong. The goggles revealed a crisscross of lasers so close to the top of the anthill I wondered if the ants got zapped by them.

I thought about the stings from just outside the

swamp and wondered if bites to the exposed meat where my skin had been shredded would be much more painful. I knew I couldn't allow myself to think like that for long, so I rolled carefully onto my back—ever so careful to avoid the lasers—and poured repellent from the second bottle on my body. It burned like hell in my cuts and gouges, and I hoped it would burn for several more minutes, perhaps disguising some of the pain of the bites to come.

I rolled back over and poured the repellent on my knife, hoping it would keep the little buggers from crawling up the handle, and then poured a perimeter around me to discourage some of the midget menaces as I rooted around in the dirt. There were so many ants that the ground appeared to move, so I tried not to look at the ground, trying instead to focus my concentration on the job I'd chosen to do.

I slowly inserted my knife into the mound and thousands, perhaps millions, of ants poured out and came straight for me. I couldn't help but admire their valiance and aggression as I nicked something hard, buried almost a foot deep. I was worried there was another pressure switch, which would leave me no option but to dig gently into the hill of ants with my hands. They already swarmed all over me, covering my arms and hands as they worked their way to my face. I blocked off the pain but couldn't ignore how woozy and faint I was getting. I had to hurry.

As I had feared, the pistol was resting on a preset tension plate in a thick plastic pouch. Removing it was slow and tedious work that would have been challenging enough without the angry fire ants swarming on me. I kept telling myself to grab it and run, to claim partial victory for getting as far as I did, but that wasn't the point of Jaspers. The point they kept beating into our heads was that you had to get in and get out undetected. So I took my time, concentrating on the tension plate, pushing ants and dirt onto one side as I slid the Luger off the other while the ants attacked me without mercy.

I got it. No alarms, no lasers, and no explosions. I stuck the Luger in my waistband and moved away, retracing my route, quickly following my little flags over the spikes and through the ground thorns on my belly until I hit the swamp. I could hurry, because I knew that the only tripwire was near the other bank. I was running out of time but had a chance to make up some of it.

I crawled out of the swamp and hobbled toward the hut, watching for Parrish or any other early risers. I stopped in some shadows and removed the Luger from its wrappings. It was covered in grease, so I wiped the weapon on my uniform and slipped into our dark hut about an hour before dawn. I quietly opened the door to my locker and stuck the Luger inside. I was living with high-wired guys, so moving around without waking them was almost as challenging as Parrish's field but far less dangerous. I bet some of them were awake and watching, but in the tradition and paranoia of that place, none would ask where I'd been or what I'd done.

I crept to the bathroom and showered off the mud, blood, and stink from my shredded uniform. As I stripped out of it, I took care not to look at my welts and wounds. They probably weren't that bad. At least I wasn't bitten by poisonous snakes. I hoped to get an hour's sleep and then put on some antibiotic ointment. My face and hands were in better shape than my body because of the bug juice, so I hoped to convince everyone I was attacked by wasps. That would be my story, as they say, and I was going to stick to it even if it wasn't really believable.

The important thing was that Shannon was home from her date with Steve, unless she went back to his hotel and spent the night. Would she do that? Had I given her enough of a reason to be so careless with our relationship?

I was in my rack when dawn's first light hit like an advancing army, highlighting trees and terrain the sun would soon strike intensely. I hurt and burned and itched like crazy as I waited for Parrish or Pike to stroll in and get us up. Even though it was still early and we were supposed to have the day off, it wouldn't have surprised me if they came banging in there to keep us off balance, exploiting the hangovers some of the men had from last night's liberty. I almost got up and dressed anyway, knowing I'd be moving slowly and wanting to look as good as I could. But I didn't. I was too exhausted, although I did worry about having to fall out at a minute's notice.

A few men stirred awake. I tried to guess what they were thinking as they lay there with the gray gloom of the metal building reminding them this couldn't be home. Were they wondering if they'd be tortured today? Were they worried they'd fail and be shipped out? Or were they adapting, getting on board with the program of killing without a declared war?

And if they were, why wasn't I? I didn't really feel like a misfit, but I didn't feel like I belonged here, either. Men like Parrish belonged here. And Colonel Maddigan was in charge, so of course he belonged. But Maddigan's idea of protecting this country was different from mine, his patriotism more abstract in its nature, his actions, perhaps—although I'm not sure—less commendable. His results might be good, but I was already concerned about the price, and that concern churned at the edge of my humanity, out where early warnings signaled that I might be doing the wrong thing at Jaspers. I had to wonder: At what price did Jaspers become worthwhile? I didn't know, and that uncertainty, that ignorance, made me think about quitting.

Other than my family, I'd never quit anything before. I'd pursued goals until long after friends told me to quit, but frankly, it never crossed my mind until last night in the field. I'd almost settled for half of a victory—getting the Luger but not getting away.

All through my youth my dad taught me that getting something worthwhile meant you couldn't quit before you got there, that you had to tackle challenges with a last-man-standing determination. He was a good father when I was a boy and a great example when I was a young man, but around the time I became an adult he disappointed both my country and me, prompting yet another theory that the taproot of our human experience was nourished or poisoned by our insecurities, those gnawing little wounds and fears that drove us to despair or excellence. My dad's terrible failing was without a doubt the event that drove me toward excellence. I wanted to keep that in mind as I tried to narrow the questions I needed answered before I went any further in Maddigan's program: Was being a Jasper worthwhile? Did Jaspers' goals justify what they did to obtain them? Were they protecting America by sidestepping the law, or were they eroding the system they were ostensibly trying to preserve? Were they neutering the electorate they said they were protecting by ignoring the rules and mocking its standards?

I didn't really know, so I tried another tack, which was to think about those very same questions from years ahead when I was eighty or ninety years old. I was sure I'd want to look back on my life with pride that I'd done what was right, positive I wouldn't want to feel dirty and ashamed. But lurking between those easy extremes was one unsettling option: What if I had to do something shameful that was right for my country?

Tough question, so I shifted once more and tried to think like the Asians, who made their political decisions based on the effects they would have on their country a hundred years down the line. American politicians only worried how their decisions played on the six-o'clock news. That was probably why Jaspers existed in the first place.

I decided to trust the Asian way and stay with Jaspers, focusing on long-term goals, fully aware of how quitting would look in my service jacket. I loved the Navy and wanted nothing less than a career and a captain's eagle. That was my goal, but I hadn't finished SEALs, so quitting Jaspers couldn't be a good move. The military was half the size it used to be and promotions were that much harder to get. I wouldn't get too many gigs in my file before I got passed over, and then I'd be done.

I was too tired to think about it anymore, and that was the other reason I decided just to go along. I closed my eyes again and desperately hoped they'd let us sleep in, as promised. My skin was on fire and my body cooked in the fresh uniform I'd put on so I wouldn't bloody the sheets. My eyes felt like they'd never open again. My last thought before falling asleep was about snakes.

Sleep has always been a blessing to me, much like a memory lapse that followed a painful loss. My mind would find somewhere else to go, somewhere pleasant to hide. I loved sleep and was usually good at it, nodding off instantly and waking up reluctantly. Some of the guys in the hut slept as if they were getting shock treatments, twitching and jumping and snapping erect in their bunks, but I didn't do that. I closed my eyes and went dead. I did snore—at least that's what Shannon told me.

But everything was different that morning. My body crapped out and my mind took advantage of my exhaustion, forcing me to do things I wouldn't normally do and dragging me places I would never have gone on my own.

I was back home in Danville, Indiana, and I was about ten, maybe eleven. My dad and I were standing on the gravel driveway and he was showing me the badge he'd brought home from wherever he'd been for a long time, some school where he learned to be a marshal. I was a kid, so of course I thought of Marshal Matt Dillon on *Gunsmoke*. I was proud my dad carried a marshal's badge and thought he even looked a little like Matt Dillon—tall and lean with a long face and a big lower jaw, but with the quick blue eyes and small mouth of an analyst or inventor—someone who watched carefully, looked deeply, and thought clearly before speaking or acting.

I wanted him to pin the badge on his shirt, just under the edge of his coat so he could ease his lapel back and let his badge frighten bad guys into surrender. But he wouldn't do it. He carried it in a leather case. He said times had changed, that bad guys didn't let you walk up to them like Matt Dillon. They ran from you, he said, or shot at you from a distance. Then he laughed, messed with my hair, and said, "Luckily, most are pretty bad shots. Don't worry."

Heck, I wasn't worried because that was my dad. He could do anything, beat anyone, and win any fight. I'd never actually seen him fight and had never even heard of him being in one, but he was the kind of guy you knew would win.

Although he didn't pin the badge on his shirt, he did let me shoot his gun, a Smith & Wesson revolver with neat wood grips and something my dad called a bull barrel. It was so heavy, it took both my hands to steady it. I shot at our barn and missed it. I wasn't actually sure I missed, but Dad laughed and told me not to worry, that it took practice to hit anything with a handgun. He promised to make me a good shot, apparently convinced that because I didn't drop the gun I could eventually learn to shoot it. As I stood there beside him, I realized he was taller than I remembered from before he went to marshal school. His stature made me bigger, too. And a little bit smaller.

He started going away a lot. He liked the trips and came home proud, feeling good in a way I didn't quite understand. But it made me happy for him, almost envious. He was sure of what he was doing, sure he was doing well.

Then, when I was just about to graduate from college and go into the Navy, my dad left and a few days later another marshal came to our house. He held up his badge in the porch light, said his name was Reynolds, and asked to speak to my mother. The guy was a little younger than Dad and soft-looking, like he'd spent years wrestling budgets instead of felons.

He sat at the kitchen table without saying a word as Mom made coffee, which she sloshed unsteadily into cups. While she did that, I noticed Reynolds's manicured fingernails and had trouble believing he was a marshal. He was small and thin, maybe five eight and one-forty, with brown hair perfectly combed and lacquered. His blue eyes were small and intense but not squinty. There was a mole in the middle of his left cheek. We didn't like each other, but I wasn't quite sure why.

He started to sip his coffee but didn't. He set down the cup and straightened in his chair. "There's been a shooting, Mrs. Thompson—"

"Oh, my God! Howard?" Mom's hands flew to her mouth as if trying to catch those words.

Reynolds snapped forward, as if ready to jump up to help Mom. I was there first, my hand on her shoulder. I glared at Reynolds until he sat back down.

"Your husband's okay, Mrs. Thompson," he said, staring at me. "Wasn't hurt at all."

I didn't move other than to look at Mom. I watched her go from panic to relief in a second. Then she headed to some middle ground, straightening, focusing, and challenging Reynolds. I looked at his face and saw why, saw clearly that he had more to say.

"What aren't you telling me, Mr. Reynolds? Tell me the rest." I'd never heard her sound so cold.

Reynolds looked at the ceiling for the words, found them slowly, and then leveled his eyes at Mom.

"His partner's dead."

One hand went back to her mouth. "Oh no, not Matt."

I glared at Reynolds. I was about to demand that—

"Killed with your husband's gun." He puckered his lips as if he were going to spit.

"What? But . . . Howard didn't shoot him, did he? Was there a mistake? What happened?"

I leaned over and slapped the table hard. Reynolds and my mother jumped. I got close to Reynolds's face. "Stop screwing around and tell us!"

Reynolds ignored my mom now. He seemed madder at me, or maybe he was mad at my dad or Matt's death.

"You want the facts?" he said to me. "Fine. I'll tell you. The facts, *sir*, are that your *father* . . ." He paused, closed his eyes, and took a breath. It didn't help him much; he was still mad. "A prisoner overpowered your father in the Chicago airport. Took his gun and shot Matt in the face from six inches away. Then he made your father get down on his knees and uncuff him. The felon got away before airport security could get there. Your dad—"

"You're a liar!" I wanted to jump up and run to my room like a little boy or pound my fists against his chest. Reynolds stood up against my allegation. I stood as tall as I could.

"Is that right? You want to hear the rest of it? Want to know the whole truth?"

"We do," Mom said. She was now beside me, her arms around me loosely.

"Your dad," he continued, talking only to me, moving his lips but not his teeth, "grabbed Matt's gun and could have shot the guy as he ran through the crowd. But he didn't. He let Matt's killer get away."

"My dad's not a coward!"

He turned toward the door and took a step back. "Watch the news, kid. It was caught on a surveillance camera. I came to tell you before the world sees it on television." He nodded to my mom. "Ma'am." Then he walked out. I didn't hear anything else until I realized my mom was in the family room, crying.

Two days later, my dad got home. He had refused to return to Indianapolis without Matt's body, and by the time he did I'd seen the video a dozen times on TV. The local newspaper ran still pictures from it, frame by frame like the Zapruder film of Kennedy's assassination, and I taped the series of photos to my mirror. Although there were no pleading tears in my father's eyes as he looked up at his gun in the felon's hand, that didn't keep me from seeing them there.

Dad got home late and talked to Mom for hours. I was beat from helping a neighbor disc a field so I didn't get out of bed. He left me alone, and they went to bed just after three in the morning.

When I got up the next morning, he was walking around the farm and I doubt he'd slept much at all.

He had on the same clothes as the night before, but his blond hair was uncombed and flat where it had pressed against the pillow. I was studying for exams but felt no option but to go outside and confront him. My hands were in my pockets. The sun was incubating spring and the air tasted of damp hay and fertilizer. It was the first time I realized I was taller than my father.

He looked like he hadn't slept much at all since the shooting. His face was loose and sagging like a hound's, his blue eyes tinted with red, and his mixed-color stubble shadowing his jaw and cheeks.

We walked for five minutes without speaking. Then he commented on the farm's condition, the years the fields had been fallow, the frustration and disappointment his dad would feel if he knew his son had let the family farm go to hell.

He looked over at the barn, empty except for some horses my sister stabled for a friend. "Remember when you shot the barn?"

I was confused as I looked where he did, the two of us walking like old men to a funeral. It took a second for me to clear my throat and speak. "Shot at it, you mean."

"That's right. You missed, didn't you?"

"Yes, sir."

"It's hard to hit anything with a handgun."

"Yes, sir."

Dad kept staring at the barn, intense in his observations until he stopped and let his gaze drop to the ground in front of it. They stayed there as he said, "So, are you ready for Officer Candidate School?"

"Yes, sir."

"Excited?"

"Yes."

"Good. I'm sure you'll do well there."

"Thanks."

"I'm quitting the marshals, Henry. Coming back to farming."

I was stunned. Dad hated farming and only held on to the place because it was family land. He always figured family land to be special, even though Indiana was nothing but farmland.

"I'm going to start by getting the barn in order. Rebuild the loft and stalls, then shore up the joists, replace the siding your brother shot up trying to kill the rats, and give the whole thing a new coat of paint."

I looked back at the barn and could almost see him up on scaffolding, hammering and painting and getting it in shape. I took another step toward manhood by keeping my mouth shut, almost. I swallowed the question I wanted to ask and the demand for an explanation I clearly deserved.

"What will you plant?"

"Corn, probably," he said as he rubbed his palm across his lips. "Maybe soybeans. What do you think?"

I wasn't stupid about farms. I'd spent plenty of summers working the farms of neighbors and relatives, fixing machinery and driving combines, dragging a variety of attachments behind their tractors, and listening to them worry about surviving. So sure, I had an opinion.

"I think it's a mistake to quit the marshals."

He looked surprised, but it was the truth, and since I was growing up all of a sudden and talking man to man with my dad, I felt he deserved the truth. But having said it, I expected to hear his reasons, all of them well thought out, why he was sure of his actions.

"You could be right," he said, then picked up a stone from the gravel yard and hurled it at the metal silo. He missed, which he rarely did, then laced his fingers behind his head and looked at the sky with closed eyes. "But the facts are that Matt is dead and I feel responsible. A murderer is on the loose and he'll probably kill more people. Those deaths will be my fault, too."

I stared at the side of his head. "Dad, I've got to ask. Why didn't you shoot him? I mean . . . you had the chance."

His jaw locked. Muscles pulled the sags out of his face as he glared at me.

"You could tell that from the video, huh? When you weren't looking at crowd level, weren't distracted by the gun's ringing in your ears, and your eyes weren't full of Matt's blood?"

"I guess the video is from a higher angle, all right. But it's just . . . well, it looks like you were afraid."

"I *was* afraid, Henry. The airport was crowded and I was afraid I'd kill a civilian. I thought it better to hold off than kill an innocent person. Maybe that was a mistake." He took a step away from me. "Maybe being a marshal was a mistake. I just don't know anymore."

I looked at him, knowing exactly what I was supposed to say and wanting to say that mistakes happen, that people screw up, that sometimes things just go badly wrong. That really was what I wanted to say, and exactly what I would have said to my younger brother if it were his problem. My dad needed me to say it to him, I think, and I should have.

But as I stared at his hunched-over frame, what tried to force its way out of my mouth surprised me. A lifetime of face-your-fears lectures tried to hurl their way back at him. I wanted desperately to condemn him for failing to maintain control of his prisoner and his gun, for doing nothing while Matt was murdered, for being afraid to shoot as the guy ran away. I wanted to ask him why, after dinning it into me that you never gave in to fear, he had gone onto his knees, for God's sake, and begged like a baby in front of a criminal and the whole world.

But I didn't say any of it. I didn't have to. When my father turned around, I saw he'd read my mind and that he knew he was a failure to us both. In that guilt-laden second, everything changed between us. I wasn't sure how, and I guess I wasn't ready to find out.

Confusion kept me from saying anything else. He stood there silently staring at me, I think, as I walked away and back to the house. I went to my room and packed my things, gave my mother a kiss, and then got into my car and left. I rented a motel room with the money I'd saved for a trip home on my first leave and stuck around Indianapolis long enough to graduate, then reported to OCS at the earliest date they allowed. As I took the oath to defend my country, I also made a silent promise to be better than my father when my time came to kill.

Someone coughed in the Quonset hut and woke me up. I was sweaty but feeling better now about being a Jasper, almost glad for the absence of oversight and accountability that could easily have kept me from my goal. Colonel Maddigan was going to give me my chance to be noble and strong and better. When my time came I *would* pull the trigger. If I could put the guy who shot Matt and humiliated my dad at the other end of my front sight when that moment came, life would be just about perfect.

Seven

I shifted on my bed and kicked off my sheet, not caring if someone saw that I'd slept in my uniform. It was too early to get up, but my swelling, bleeding body made it hard to stay still. I was itching like crazy, and that made me think about Parrish's Luger. It should have been safe in my locker, but then again they might search the place to find it and I didn't want anyone to know I had it.

A small building by the canteen served as a storage room for damaged equipment, so I got up and stuffed the Luger in a bag and wandered over for something to eat. No one was around, so I slipped into the storage room and put the Luger in a barrel of dusty scraps just as the whistle called us to assembly. So much for their promise of a day off.

I took my time, hoping to be the last one to the instructors' barracks in front of Parrish's field. Captain Pike was already talking when I joined the ragtag ranks. I looked out at the field and saw my little flags. They led from the swamp to the mound, mapping a route over hidden, near-deadly obstacles the other Jaspers candidates could only imagine.

"Good morning, Mr. Thompson. Nice of you to join us."

"Thank you. Beautiful morning, don't you think?"

"You don't look too well, Mr. Thompson. Is everything all right?"

My body was so itchy and sore that it took all of my strength to keep my hands from raking it. But I wouldn't scratch now that Pike, Parrish, and all the other men were looking at me.

"Feeling great, Captain. Don't know what you mean."

He cut his eyes to Parrish, who fell out of ranks and walked over to me. He stopped about eight inches away and stuck his face into mine. His eyes looked enormous, the irises and pupils the same black color.

"What happened to you?"

"When?" Well, he wasn't specific.

"When you got all of those bites and wounds."

"Oh. I thought maybe you were asking about when I was a kid playing doctor with the girl next door and—"

"What happened? Tell me."

I was truly surprised by Parrish. I thought he'd be furious that someone beat him at his game and took his vintage Luger in perfect condition. But if he was angry he wasn't showing it, so I started to wonder if the pistol was a fake. Or maybe he was that much of a professional. He kept staring at my face, orbiting around me to see the bites from all angles, looking . . . well, to be honest, I thought he looked a little worried about me.

"Bees," I said.

"Bees?"

"Or wasps. I can't be sure." I hated to lie, I really did. But I will admit it was kind of fun.

"Wasps?"

"Wasps or bees. Could have been hornets, I suppose."

"Hornets?"

"Yellow jackets, maybe."

Everyone but Parrish laughed. He was impossible to read.

"Let's assume they were bees," he said. "Where did you get stung?"

"Well, mostly they stung my face. A few got me on the butt. I can show you if you'd like."

Parrish strained a very small grin onto his face. In truth, there wasn't a lot else he could do. The other men laughed, and Captain Pike turned toward Parrish's field because I bet he was laughing, too.

"Okay, Thompson," Parrish said as he kept trying to smile. "Sorry I was vague. Where *were* you when the bees—"

"Or wasps," I added.

Parrish's smile was as tight as a fat woman's panty hose, but I had to give him credit, he was a professional.

"Right. Bees or wasps."

I resisted the urge to add hornets and yellow jackets.

"Where were you when they stung you?"

"I was out walking about two o'clock this morning. I had to take a leak, so I went a little way into the woods. Just my luck, as I started flowing, the ground started buzzing. They swarmed out and got me, zap, just like that."

"Is that right?"

Elvis made his way through the small crowd, which couldn't have been easy since the other guys were clustered like hemorrhoids around Parrish and me.

"That's right," Elvis said. "There were hundreds of 'em. Ground bees. I was about ten feet away from H.T. They buzzed like a band of kazoos coming my way."

Parrish didn't even look at Elvis. "Is that a fact? Did you get stung, too?"

Elvis started unbuttoning his uniform trousers. "Sure did. Like Thompson, I was taking a leak and got a hell of a dinger right here on my—"

"Okay, gentlemen," Captain Pike said. "That's enough about bees and wasps and what have you." He waited for Parrish to disengage the words he was ready to fire, then continued. "None of you seem to have noticed from this distance, but if you look closely you'll see that the mound that contained Sergeant Parrish's Luger is destroyed. I would like to know who did it."

Parrish took one last glance at me and said, "You'd better get to the dispensary" in a quiet voice. Then he turned and walked back to Pike. All the trainees looked at the field and suddenly realized why we were there and what was going on. I could tell they wanted to turn back and look at me, but they didn't. Some started to turn my way, but no one did, even though they knew there was nothing to lose. They were all sure I did it.

We stood silent for a minute, maybe two. Captain Pike scanned the field a few times, then turned and put his hands on his hips.

"Congratulations are in order, gentlemen. One of you has infiltrated a very difficult area with extremely challenging obstacles. We've obviously overrated our ability to keep a Luger safe, or a man, if this had been the real world. Whoever did this can help us do better. So who was it?"

No one spoke. The other Jaspers stared at the field. I watched Parrish, who stared right back at me as though we were two men in a boxing ring waiting for round one to begin.

"Well," Pike said, "whoever it was has my respect and Parrish's Luger. Congratulations. If you want to meet with me in private, I'll be in my office. Dismissed. Enjoy your day off."

We fell out with the same lack of precision that was the hallmark there, kind of like a dropped watermelon or an atom splitting. Two men rushed closer to Parrish's field for a better look, then one spun around and hurried back to bed while another split for the canteen. I didn't move, and neither did Elvis or Parrish or Pike. We all stared at the field. It did look impossible, and in the reassuring light of day I could not comprehend any circumstances that would make me enter that field even a few feet. Thinking how I dragged my bloodied body across it made my legs a little weak.

Elvis stuck his hands in his pockets and turned to face me. "So, big night last night? Enjoy your rest?" He smiled.

"What? Oh, yeah, sure did. How was your evening?"

"Decent. Small-town entertainment, you know. Nothing much, but sure nice to see my sisters again."

"Thanks for backing up my story."

"Sure, no problem." He shook his head as if I was pathetic. "Bees? Man, you're a funny guy. You look like shit, though. You'd better get some medicine. I'm going back to sleep. I'd just climbed into bed when you came in."

He wandered off. I wanted to sit down and stare at the field some more. I was very nearly overcome with the same feeling I had after we humped our way back from our mission with Dwayne, a sense of accomplishment from having done something extraordinary. Only this time no one died. I amazed myself for the first time in my life and wanted to savor the feeling.

But spending more time there would only prove them right and confirm that I had done what couldn't be done. I knew it didn't really matter, but I wanted to keep them guessing. They would never have understood my reasons for going out there.

I didn't want to go to the base dispensary, so I walked out the front gate and hitchhiked to the main base, then caught a bus to the Jacksonville emergency room where several doctors and nurses came by to see the damage to my body. It was all pretty superficial, but there was a lot of it and that interested them. I told them the same story I told Parrish, and they gave me some shots and topical medications. It didn't help the pain much, but I did smell interesting.

I'd put off calling Shannon but figured it was about time. If she had stayed out late with Steve, she probably slept in. If she was in early, she probably went out for breakfast and would be home now. I used a calling card in the hospital lobby.

"Hello?"

I tried to decide if she sounded sleepy or mad.

"Hi, Shannon, it's H.T. Sorry I hung up on you before."

"Do you have any idea how frustrating that is when it's impossible to call back?"

"Yes."

"Don't do that to me again."

"How was your date?"

Neither of us spoke for ten seconds.

"So what have you been doing, Henry?"

"Not much."

"Are they keeping you busy at your *secret* school?"

"Not really. It's pretty basic stuff, actually. Tell me about your date with Steve."

She made a coy, guilty-sounding laugh, a poor imitation of the one she does when we get along. "I don't know what you're talking about."

"Is he still there?"

"Who?"

"You went out with Steve, didn't you?"

"Henry," she said, a little angry. "I don't know what's gotten into you, but I'm not having this conversation. We'll talk when you get back here. I don't think there's anything for you to worry about."

"Did you come home last night?"

"Of course I did."

"Did you go home with him first?"

"I'm not doing this. You have no right to ask me these questions."

"I think I do. Ask me anything, Shannon. *You've* got the right."

"I just did. I asked about your school, and you blew me off."

"That's different."

"No, it's not. That's what you always say, that it's always different for you. You're the one who chose to skulk around doing God knows what, and now—"

"Hey, Shannon, this is my job. Some of it's secret. You're the same with your job. You don't tell me everything you do."

"How can you say that? I write press releases and sound bites. The whole world knows what I do. Anyway, I told you we'll talk when you get here. You shouldn't worry. You think I'm out to hurt you, but you need to stop thinking that way."

"I've got to go."

"Don't hang up on me! When will you be back in D.C.?"

"Don't know. Got to go."

I held my breath, hoping she'd say something loving. She sighed instead. It was frustration, mostly, with some hurt and anger mixed in. I knew her well enough to understand her sighs, and I was pretty sure this one sounded different. She was hiding some guilt over last night.

"Good-bye, Henry. I'm telling you not to worry."

"Tell me what you did and I'll stop worrying."

"He called and asked me out. It was nothing."

"I know you like this guy, Shannon, so I have trouble believing that. Good-bye."

I hung up. I wasn't really hanging up on her, because she'd already said good-bye. I was just ending the conversation so we could do what she wanted, discuss it in person whenever we saw each other again.

That was crap and I knew it. The truth was that I

was hurt and mad and her stonewalling only made me madder. I could imagine what she did even if she wouldn't tell me. I guess it was possible she didn't do anything, but not likely. People tend to live down to my lowest expectations of them. Sometimes they even manage to disappoint me beyond that.

The good news was that my body hardly hurt anymore.

Eight

I caught the five-o'clock bus back to Camp Lejeune and hitched a ride to Courthouse Bay. I walked the rest of the way to the Jasper compound, even though my chafing clothes made my ant bites sting. It was late afternoon, evening really, and I tried to ignore my bites by appreciating the beauty of North Carolina, making myself focus on good things. The sky was clear and blue, a much softer shade than I remembered from home. There was a bit of haze on the western horizon backlit by the sun. I was actually a little cool, a reaction to the medicine, perhaps. The quiet stillness, my aches and pains, and the early-fall air reminded me of harvesting time back home and my pride in having done a hard day's work.

Sergeant Parrish was standing on the dike that served as a road to the Jasper facility. A temporary bridge spanned the small swamp, and the power grid for the field was off while Pike and Fidel and another man charted my progress on clipboards. Parrish stared at the filthy swamp with his precious field beyond it, my little flags providing him a connect-the-dots pattern of how I did it. If I'd been professional, I wouldn't have left them. Parrish wouldn't have left them, I was sure, and I doubted if Pike or Maddigan would have either. But I had.

Parrish had his arms folded across his chest, his head tilted with his stare fixed on the field, probably analyzing it for the hundredth time that day. I walked toward him knowing he was going to say something spiteful because I'd taken his Luger, making a joke of his ability to protect anything. So I tried to get into a snappy frame of mind and have a good riposte ready, although I was tired and sore and pretty much out of gas. I walked right up to him, but I really wanted to pass behind him unnoticed.

"Thompson," he said without looking away from the field. "Got a minute?"

"Sure. What's up?"

Parrish swiveled his body toward me, but his head stayed aimed at the field for a moment, as if getting the last information he needed. A sunburn blended into the red birthmark on his scalp.

"I'm wrong sometimes, Thompson. If I was wrong about you, my error."

"You think I got your Luger?"

"Look, you can have your little glory, boy, but I'd like it back."

"I don't have it."

He bit his lip and looked at the field. He seemed to be searching it for the words he needed, and after most of a minute he said, "Look, Thompson, I love this country like a devoted son. Whoever went to this extreme to prove their dedication gets my respect.

Even if it's you. So I'm *asking* you to sell my Luger back."

"Can't help you. Don't have it."

"Fine," Parrish said. He closed his eyes for a second and then opened them and *really* looked at me. Last night's rattlesnake might have been his brother or cousin. "Dangerous to mock me, boy."

"The world's a dangerous place," I said, and tried to step toward him. But when my feet moved they took a step back on their own, as if they had better sense than I did and wouldn't let me do something so stupid. Parrish followed me, moving closer than anyone would ever want. I glanced at the field and saw Pike running toward us. Parrish leaned into me and I almost fell backward into the water.

"No guarantee you'll leave here, hotshot. Sell me my Luger. I won't ask again."

"Sergeant Parrish!" Pike shouted as he came huffing over the planks that crossed the swamp.

"Sir," said Parrish, his voice as stiff as his stare. "Just about to extend your invitation to Mr. Thompson."

"Stand easy, Sergeant."

Parrish kept leaning and staring.

"I *said* stand easy."

I added "Hard of hearing?" for extra measure, and Parrish discreetly punched my chest with his elbow as he turned away. Pike didn't notice, but I sure did. I didn't react, but I couldn't breathe for a minute. Parrish angled off, moved a few feet away with his back to us, and looked at the field.

"Thompson," Pike said after watching Parrish for several seconds, "how about joining us for dinner tonight? To celebrate your *not* having Parrish's Luger."

He jerked his head toward Parrish. "He's happy to cover your tab. Aren't you, Sergeant Parrish?"

The back of Parrish's neck stiffened. "Absolutely, sir."

I wanted to catch up on sleep, but after hearing that I had to go.

"What time?"

"We'll wait for you. Come to Parrish's barracks when you're ready."

"Give me a chance to change."

"Nothing fancy. Just a bar down the road."

"Thirty minutes, then."

I bumped Parrish as I passed, wanting him to know that I was a dog, damn it, just like him, so he shouldn't be surprised when I barked. The sooner he understood it, the better.

I expected him to bark too. He flinched and his feet scraped the lime rock road, but I watched his shadow as I walked away and it didn't move. I guessed he'd wait until later to attack, when Pike wasn't around. For some reason I found myself remembering Nicholas, another guy Parrish didn't want in Jaspers. Whatever happened to him?

I went back to the hut and showered, then rubbed stinging cream onto my wounds. The deepest gouges bled. I waited for them to stop and then got dressed. I didn't shave, because it would have been impossible without shredding open the sores on my face.

I left the Quonset hut and retrieved the Luger, stuck it in a bag, and headed to Parrish's barracks. Parrish and Pike were inside. I didn't knock.

"Good evening, Captain Pike. Sergeant Parrish."

"Evening," said Pike. He looked comfortable in

khaki slacks, loafers, and a blue polo shirt. The clothes softened his scowl. "Come in, Henry."

So now I was Henry. And your first name is . . . ?

Parrish didn't speak as he poured wine for the three of us. He was dressed in black jeans and a white cotton golf shirt that was neatly pressed. He wore black cowboy boots, but he didn't look Western.

"Thank you," I said as Parrish gave me a glass but acted like he didn't hear.

Pike raised his glass. "To Lieutenant Henry Thompson, U.S. Navy and Jaspers candidate extraordinaire." Parrish barely sipped his wine.

Now it was my turn. This was my celebration, I realized slowly, but I wanted to change the focus. "To the men and women—even if they weren't pretty when they got out of here—who proudly call themselves Jaspers."

Pike and Parrish glanced at each other. I held my glass out there and eventually they both clinked it, but the look they shared told me their next toast might be to comrades who paid the ultimate price.

The last time I saw that look was during my first night in Coronado at the North Point Naval Air Station club. I figured I'd have one last drink before reporting to SEALs and ended up at the bar with a bunch of carrier pilots. I'd never realized how many aviator buddies those guys lost, not just to war but to mechanical problems and poorly coordinated flight deck operations, things that just went wrong in the normal course of defying good sense—hurtling an aircraft toward a moving, pitching flight deck in the thick of night on a black ocean. Even after being shot at with antiaircraft guns and missiles, the scariest part of combat was catching a wire and getting the plane safely onboard the ship at night. "Please God," they told me they prayed, "give me another safe night trap."

I had no idea what was in store for me as a Jasper or what claimed the most lives of graduates from this school, but I had no doubt there was a Jaspers equivalent to night landings on a carrier. Having experienced some of the torture techniques the instructors picked up around the world, I suspected some Jaspers died in manacles, abused by sadists in the bowels of some government prison until they talked, or didn't but died anyway. I know for a fact that Cameron did.

I was too melancholy over Shannon to go down that road, so I held out the paper bag with the Luger.

Parrish aimed a finger at my nose. "You said you didn't have it." He snatched the pistol, turned toward his desk, and made a save-face laugh. "I'll write you a check," he said. Then he mumbled something I couldn't quite make out. Pike looked for my reaction.

"Don't bother," I said, and boy, did that stop Parrish in his tracks. He turned back while Pike straightened a little. I watched them carefully, wondering how they were going to react. "I don't want your money. I'd rather know what happened to Nicholas. Elvis is worried about him. The pistol for the truth."

Parrish held the package as if it were his baby who'd been kidnapped. He wanted to keep holding it, keep it safe. It was obvious he didn't want someone taking it away again, but he surprised me by tossing the package onto the table. "Keep it."

He refilled our glasses, picked up his, and looked like he hated me more than ever.

Pike was staring at me, so I asked him, "What's the big deal? You didn't really kill him, did you?"

Pike muscled up, just a little.

"No, of course not. He was . . ." Pike pinched those beakish lips and looked at Parrish, but Parrish looked away. "He was a United States serviceman under my command. He was my responsibility. I would never have allowed something to happen to him."

Then Pike tipped his glass toward Parrish. "Anyway, Sergeant Parrish knows the story better than I do. You should get the information from him, understand?"

I tried to show that I did understand, that I remembered my talk with Parrish about his plan to separate Elvis from Nicholas.

"Take the Luger, Sergeant. I never wanted it anyway. I was bored last night and needed something to do."

Parrish wouldn't even look at it. "I don't take things I don't deserve. I'll pay for it, hotshot. No other way."

Pike cut in. "Oh hell, Jim, just take the pistol and forget about it."

"No, sir."

Pike slammed his fist on the table. "Take the damned pistol! That's an order."

Parrish gave Pike a hateful look that drove Pike to his feet, then picked up the pistol and padlocked it in his locker. I wished I could have taken it and returned it without anyone knowing. This Jaspers facility, like the rest of the military, operates on reputation, and I'd tarnished Parrish's. I felt his anger the entire ride to the bar. I'd been spoiling for a fight with him, but I'd wanted it to be private.

The County Line was a big place with a dining area

at one end and a dance floor at the other. Pool tables, off to the side, reminded me of my night in New York with Shannon. The memory usually excited and tormented me, but with Steve back in the picture it just tormented.

Parrish avoided sitting with me by making an excuse about an old girlfriend. He went to the bar and talked to her. They were about ten feet away, so I could almost hear what they said and their laughter. The waitress came over and flinched when she looked at my face. Pike ordered two beers. After she left, Pike said, "Try not to worry about Nicholas."

"Okay," I said while the jukebox played "If I'd killed you when I wanted I'd be out by now," or something like that. "Your reason for saying that?"

"Okay. Let's assume you were given a job to do, and after you'd shipped out Elvis asked me where you were. Jaspers always operates covertly and need-to-know, so what would I tell him?"

"Nothing."

"That's why I can't get into details." He raised his glass like he was toasting my ability to understand. "To the murky world in which we live."

I wasn't happy with the sound of "always operates covertly" and "murky." I preferred SEALs where I *might* work covertly, but other times I might be right out there making the enemy painfully aware of my presence. I had a week before the next phase and the final commitment to Jaspers, so I figured I might call Commander Nance about going back to Coronado.

"Is that what happened with Nicholas, or are you just stroking me?"

"You decide. I'm just giving you what-ifs." He paused. "By the way, be careful with Parrish."

"Because he's fragile?"

"Jeez, why are you like that, Henry?"

"H.T."

"Fine. H.T. What pushes you to do the things you do?"

"You mean the pistol?"

"I mean everything. The pistol, your willingness to come here in the first place, your refusal to back down from anyone, your lame attempts at humor when someone's in your face. Things like that. What makes you do them?"

Lame attempts at humor?

"I could ask you the same question. Why are you here, doing a job where you'll never get any recognition? After all, if your work is noticed by anyone, it kind of means you've screwed up, right?"

Pike started to drink but didn't. "I had a C.O. once, name of Bolger. He always used to say, 'At some point, usually on a dark night in some country you never heard of, you have to be ready to stick a rifle through a bush and blow somebody in two.' You understand that, don't you?"

"I do," I said. "It's the simplest element of war. Doesn't explain why you're here, though. Or why there's so much secrecy."

"Several years ago, Parrish and I waded ashore in Somalia. Maddigan was a newly minted lieutenant colonel back then, but well respected and very much in charge. We were an advance force ready to fight the enemy. Know what we found?"

"Reporters?"

"Bingo. Reporters and cameramen. They made it a stupid, embarrassing situation by sticking cameras in our faces. Maddigan was so frustrated, he was ready to pound his nuts flat. When he returned stateside, he convinced some of the more tuned-in military and political leaders that it was absolutely necessary that many elements of war be conducted in secret. Even though he got his way, America is going to lose the next big war it fights. Maybe not the little skirmishes along the way, but a big war. You agree?"

"No."

"Then you're kidding yourself. In justifying Iraq, the White House forced our military to refocus completely on new goals that assume every war from now on will be against terrorism—which generally means war against rich, angry men and not nations. The president even took to calling Korea a war on terrorism, as if it suddenly changed from the conventional border patrols we'd been doing for fifty years."

"So what?" I said. "War is war. It doesn't matter what you call it."

"That's where you're wrong. Names matter enormously. This 'all wars are against terrorism' mind-set has all the services gearing up to fight nebulous targets, throwing everything we've got at unseen bogeymen, and abandoning the symmetrical strategies of 'tank for a tank and a ship for a ship' warfare of the past—which is the very arena in which we've always been invincible."

"But terrorism is the current threat, so we have no choice but to fight it."

"Don't misunderstand me, Thompson, we do need to fight terrorism. But with all the irrational fear they spewed out as set pieces of the last presidential campaign, terrorism became the only thing our services were tasked to fight, and it remains that way today. Add ten years to that kind of narrow mind-set and then tell me how the hell we're going to defend ourselves against China. What if they decide to attack us the old-fashioned way, pouring a million troopers over our California beaches the way we did in Normandy? Or Russia, once Putin sweeps away what little is left of their democratic experiment and goes back to communism."

He said all of this with an authority I wanted to question but didn't. He had his hands clenched as he stared at me. When he saw that I wasn't going to engage, he eased back into a tone that matched his civilian clothes.

"Anyway," he said, sounding slightly apologetic, "all I really wanted to say is, I told Colonel Maddigan what you've done here, and that you've proven yourself ready for the final Jaspers school in Northern Virginia. I'll let you wait until you get there to hear the follow-up to the lecture I just started. Parrish disagrees about your being ready, but Colonel Maddigan authorized me to send you up there early. You can clear your head and nurse your body so you'll be fresh when the school starts."

The waitress walked past, and I asked for another drink. She nodded without looking at my face.

"No, thanks, Captain. I'll go up with my class."

"We consider you graduated. The advanced school

doesn't start for a week. We'll carry you on our rolls, but you can have some fun, visit your girlfriend . . . what's her name?"

"Shannon."

"That's right. I'm sure she'd love to see you. Separations are hard on families, even emerging ones like yours."

I was surprised he knew about her. I guess it came up in my background check. I wondered if Steve's name came up, too. If it didn't, it probably would now.

"I'll stay here. Thanks anyway."

"There's no need. Besides, it might be good for you and Parrish to be apart for a while. He's a sore loser. And dangerous, I'm afraid."

"I'd rather—"

"You'll go early." His quiet but direct order shattered the mood. He knew it and leaned back in his chair as if determined to keep the peace. "That's a nice thing about Jaspers that can benefit you. Short chain of command. Fast decisions. No politics. Makes it easy to do what's right to protect our country from enemies."

"That's what we all want to do."

"I like to think so, but how do you protect it from apathy and stupidity?"

"I don't know."

"You have to be resourceful, even ruthless. Make every decision accurately, with survival as the only goal."

"Cameron didn't survive."

"Wasn't ruthless enough. Simple as that. You know the story?"

"Just what I've read in the papers."

"Oh," he said, and then looked at his beer. It was empty. "We're a lazy, self-involved citizenry, Thompson. Led by a government none of us really trusts anymore, going in a direction no one seems able to control. Add to that the emerging belief that the way we've been using our military has diminished our security, not enhanced it. All we've done with that firepower is make new enemies we didn't have before by getting dragged into the conflicts of weaker countries, places we had no business sticking our nose."

"And Jaspers is the answer? Something you're doing here is going to save us from all that?"

"Of course not. If we're completely successful here, Jaspers will be a tiny stopgap, a way to get some of the most essential work done so this country lasts a few more decades and maybe, just maybe, gets itself straightened out."

"We're that far out of whack?"

"We won't be here in forty years."

"What?"

"America. We'll cease to exist if we don't make some radical changes."

"I don't believe that."

"Fine. Don't. You have lots of company. Everyone thinks we're at the pinnacle of the power pyramid because we're somehow destined to be there, that we'll always be there no matter what. But think about it, Henry. History is full of former most-powerful nations, like Italy, China, Great Britain, and Spain. The Soviet Union is a recent and shocking example of a superpower that no longer exists as a nation. The land is still there, and in my opinion the threat they pose is certainly reemerging, but our old enemy has a bunch of different flags flying over the various countries. How'd you like to see a Chinese or Korean flag snapping in the breeze over the government buildings in Indiana?"

"That's the future you see, Captain?"

"It's not a future I want to see, but hell, we're making it easy on our real enemies, the countries—I'm not talking about a few hate-filled terrorists—but the countries who want to take us over. Remember how Reagan won the Cold War?"

I felt like he was whipsawing me through recent military history, but there was definitely a thread running through his thoughts. The more I understood it, the more it frightened me.

"We outspent them militarily," I said, more as a guess than anything.

"You've got it backwards. What we actually did was use the threats of stealth technology and Star Wars to force them to spend far more on defense than we did. It eventually bankrupted their entire economy. Now the terrorists are doing the same thing to us and no one in Washington even seems to notice."

"We have no choice but to protect ourselves, Captain."

"It's an axiom of security that if you try to protect everything, you end up protecting nothing. Look around. The terrorists have us seeing bogeymen everywhere, and we're knee-jerking as fast as possible to spend billions trying to defend our ports, trains, planes, power plants, water supplies, borders, financial institutions, *and* fight a costly war in Iraq. They're enjoying the hell out of this, and they'll never give up the fight in Iraq, because that's yet another place we're spending billions of dollars we don't have. Hell, we're condemned men over there, chained to our oars and rowing in place until we rot. So add all that together and you pretty quickly realize that terrorists weaken our country every single day they keep us engaged over there or afraid over here. At some point—I'm talking about sometime in our lifetimes—the cost of all that is going to catch up to us. It could even force us to devalue our currency, which is something else we've seen other countries do but somehow think will never happen to us. A dollar might be worth a dime or a quarter, but a loaf of bread will still be two bucks. Americans don't think it can happen, and that arrogance is exactly what makes it so possible. Know what's funny?"

"Nothing you've said so far."

"Agreed. This really isn't either, but it's ironic, if not funny, that the terrorists don't ever have to attack us again to win this war. They're smart men, and I think they're doing exactly the same thing Reagan did to the Soviet Union, making us spend ourselves to insolvency. Nothing but the mere possibility of an attack inspires us to spend every last dime we have to avoid it, pushing ourselves so far into debt that one sad day in the future we'll have no choice but to trade our sovereignty and resources for financial relief. So why should they risk an attack, other than an occasional shot over the bow to keep us worried?"

I was angry at what he said, but mostly I was angry that it made so much sense. "Well, hell, Captain, if that's what's going to happen, let's just pack our bags and move to Switzerland."

"I'm not suggesting that. Make no mistake about it.

Our days as the world's leader are numbered, regardless of what we do. It just works that way. But I'm confident we can extend and perhaps add a hundred years or more to this great experiment if we just protect what we have."

"What will our enemies do in the meantime?"

"The bigger question is this: Who are our enemies? China? Korea? Iraq? Iran? Libya? Russia? Or maybe more subtle threats like Burma, Somalia, Syria, Sudan? Even Vietnam and Saudi Arabia. It's a pretty impressive list of choices, so who would you pick?"

"Maybe all of them."

"Or none of them."

"What?"

"They'll only be our enemies if they think we can be beaten. And right now, with all of our national attention focused on a few crazed extremists, we can be. You watch cartoons as a kid?"

"Still do."

"Me too. Try to picture America's military as one of those superheroes when they're in trouble. You've seen it a dozen times, the strong, invincible, flying hero—notice they almost always fly—allows something to happen that makes him weak and nearly helpless. That's what's happened to America as we focus so dangerously on protecting ourselves from madmen. We have to start looking beyond that, both politically and militarily, because soon we're going to be like a weakling wearing an inflatable muscle suit. From a distance we might appear to be strong, but we won't be, and other nations will find out, so our list of enemies will grow every day. Do you think Korea,

Iran, and Brazil would be proceeding so arrogantly with nuclear programs if they didn't know we already had our hands full in Iraq? I doubt it. The solution is for us to be strong again, to be unbeatable. Until then, you and I and the other Jaspers need to do what we we're trained to do. Be resourceful and ruthless. Make every decision accurately with the survival of our great nation as our only goal."

"Yes, sir."

"Sorry if it sounded like a lecture. Been at this a long time."

"It must feel good to have your experience, your clarity."

"Give it a little time, Henry. You'll get your Chamberlain's Charge, as I call it. After that, you'll never be the same."

Pike held his gaze on me for a second, then shouted over the bar noise to call Parrish to the table. Parrish ignored him at first, then kissed the young woman at the bar. He rubbed her butt through her short skirt, and she laughed.

"You can take off after dinner if you want," Pike said just before Parrish got there, stood beside Pike's chair, and said, "I hope you gentlemen will understand if I stay at the bar. The tab's mine, though." He looked down at me. "Get the lobster if they have any. Get a steak with it."

"Think I'll just drink another beer for now. I'll switch to imported."

"No other way, smart-ass."

"That's enough," Pike said. "This was supposed to be a celebration." He looked disgusted with both of us. "Hell, I'm going back to the base."

"I'll stay a while longer," Parrish said, nodding toward the young woman. She smiled and switched her legs, showing a flash of red panties. "I'll find my own way home."

"Ready?" Pike asked.

"I'll stick around a little, too, Captain. Drink my fill of Parrish's beer."

Parrish looked glad to get me alone. Pike wasn't happy but smiled anyway. "Careful, boys. Henry, I've left directions to your next duty station and a security clearance on Parrish's desk. Get them before you leave Lejeune."

"I will."

"Good luck."

"Thank you, sir."

"Jim will meet you up there."

I shot my eyes to Parrish, who smiled like he owned me. "That's right," Parrish said. "The instructor you start with stays with you throughout the program. I'll see you in Virginia."

"Great," I said, actually kind of glad for more chances at that horrible killer. "Bring plenty of beer money."

I stood as Pike left. Parrish said, "You're on my tab, kid. Drink up."

He took a step toward the bar and then stopped and waited for his girlfriend to notice him. He controlled her the same way he did his students. She responded to him instantly by reaching into her sleeveless blouse and playing with the strap of a very sheer bra. It was red, like her panties. She caught me looking and smiled, then looked at Parrish and giggled. She switched her beautiful legs again. Parrish noticed me staring at the red flash. She kept the show going, reaching around to rub her back, thrusting out her breasts. Her small nipples were pointy and mesmerizing. Her gauzy blouse and thin bra were similar to but less sophisticated than the outfit Shannon wore in New York.

Parrish's woman looked ready to leave with him, maybe with anyone. She adjusted her dress, tugged at the hem, and then smoothed it. Then she leaned back, propped her elbows on the bar, and looked like she was getting impatient. She was in her mid-twenties, with a style that was rural high school. She probably spent her days running a cash register or wearing a paper hat, but tonight she was the beauty queen of The County Line.

I always thought it was sexy when Shannon abandoned her career and acted easy, one hundred percent sexual. This woman was doing the same thing, but from the other end of the professional spectrum, putting herself and Shannon on the same middle ground. I thought of Steve and Shannon, probably in bed right now. My thinking might have been a little blurry from the beer, but I wondered if some kind of justice was at hand.

Parrish watched her little show and then he moved. I shook my head and laughed softly. "You think you're all set up with her, huh, Parrish?"

"None of your business."

I knew there was no way he could leave the challenge alone.

"What now, smart-ass?"

"Well," I said, the beer washing the crispness out of

the word. "I'm just thinking what you're thinking. She's pretty, and very sexy."

"And mine. She's been waiting for me. You stay out of it. Don't confuse her."

"Thought you liked competition."

"Some other time."

"When you've got nothing to lose?" I chuckled and reach for my beer, but before I got there Parrish grabbed my hand and slammed it to the table, hard and loud enough to make people jump. I tried to get free but couldn't.

"Okay, you little shit. I'll play your game. You beat me for the Luger, but I don't think you can beat me twice. If I get her before you do, we're square on the ten grand, right?"

I was a little drunk, I admit, but if Parrish could dazzle this small-town creature, I should be able to do it, too. Besides, he already had her thinking about sex. He'd talked enough trash earlier to get his hands on her body.

"You're on. You win, we're even. Deal."

He gave my hand a vicious squeeze and then let go. As we walked over together, I put all my pain behind me and dusted off my Indiana farm boy charm.

"Hey," I said as Parrish started to talk. "I'm H.T. And you are . . . ?"

"Bri-gitte. Accent on the last syllable, like Brigitte Bardot." She giggled and touched my arm. I thought she might be put off by my bites and wounds, but she actually seemed to admire them, staring with keen approval as she more or less ignored Parrish.

"Doggone, you are purty. Ain't she purty, Sergeant?"

"Yes, she's—"

"Purty. My goodness. I ain't seen a woman purty as you in a long time. Longer 'n a rat's tail, I do bleeve."

She wiggled a little, lifted her slinky skirt slightly, and pulled it down toward her knees. Then she caught it with the back of her arm and dragged it up to where it was before, maybe even a little higher. "Where were you hurt, H.T.? Overseas?"

Parrish pretended to choke as a way of ridiculing me. He started to speak, but at his first syllable I cut him off. "Oh, I can't tell you that. Leastways, not here. Might could whisper it in your ear in the morning, maybe. Whatcha think?"

And then, as if she'd been planning to leave with me all along, she slid off her stool and led me out. I smiled back at Parrish as I left to screw the woman he wanted, expecting to see anger or grudging admiration on his face. But it wasn't there.

We walked through the no-man's-land of the parking lot, the well-lit middle section that separated the Carolina locals from the Marine interlopers. Seniority entitled the locals to park on the asphalt remnants of the long-ago-closed, next-door gas station. They leaned against pickups and muscle cars and watched us walk down the gauntlet of light that ran from The County Line's windows to the road. One of the car hoods was open, and the owner reached over and throttled the engine as he looked at us. It was lame but loud, like a six-banger with straight pipes. The rednecks talked and laughed while they stared, mostly at Brigitte, but often enough at me to show they were ready to have some fun.

On the dusty gravel on the other side of the lot, Marines milled around crappy short-term cars, the kind you get from a "Buy Here, Pay Here" guy and drive until you get some maturity or some new orders. They could tell I was a fellow serviceman, even though not a Marine. They flared up and strutted enough to let me know I could be the catalyst if I wanted. They were ready to back me up against the locals.

"Hey Brigitte," said one of the rednecks. "Your old man still out of town? I could deal with an oil change."

I looked at him as she grabbed my arm and put her head down. "Let it go, okay?"

"Okay," I said, doing my best to sound disappointed, amazed she thought it might actually cross my mind to fight for her honor.

Her Cavalier was on the grass by the bar's sign, near the road and midway across the entrance so we never had to deal with either side. I held the door and she got in. She smiled back at the redneck when she thought I wasn't watching.

The engine barely turned over, but Brigitte didn't seem surprised when it finally caught, sputtered to life, and the radio started blasting. She put it in gear and grinned at me.

"Oh, I love this song," she gushed as we pulled out and bounced down the road in her Cavalier. "Don't you love this song?"

"Love it," I said, although I'd never heard it before. She turned it up and sang along as I looked around in the car. The floor was littered with fast-food bags and a pair of panty hose. There was a salesclerk's uniform of some kind balled up on the backseat and a pretty dress on a hanger.

"I sing sometimes at the bar," she said. "Won a karaoke contest there last year."

"Wow." She had pretty legs that spread apart as she worked the clutch, brake, and gas. "What did you sing?"

"I act, too. Had the lead in the senior class play."

"What part? What play?"

"I might go to Hollywood. I've got a friend . . . well, my friend Karen has a friend who thinks I'd be great."

"I'm sure you would be," I said, wondering if she didn't answer my questions because she was making this all up. Not that I cared. I wasn't with her for her honesty.

She looked for traffic over her left shoulder, exposing lots of red bra through her sleeveless blouse. She turned back and saw me looking. She laughed.

"You can touch them if you want."

I hesitated, and she giggled.

"Go ahead. See, I think you should, otherwise we'll be all awkward later. So now while I'm busy driving and all, go ahead. Touch me. Feel me."

I reached over and put my hand on her neck, touched it softly and caressed it slowly. She didn't like it at all. She made a face and grabbed my hand.

"I've got a boyfriend who loves me. This is just sex, okay? When he gets home, he'll do that. I just want you to—"

She jammed my hand against her right breast and held it there. Then she smiled.

"I can't stand it when he's gone. He's on a ship. That feels good."

I slipped my hand under her blouse and pushed up

165

her bra. She reached for my groin and then ran off the road and said oops when her eyes closed a little too long. I watched the road as I felt her bra and felt her breasts. I felt pretty darn good.

"Up my skirt. I love being touched there while I'm driving. It's so dangerous."

I did what I was told, and she stroked harder. I lifted her blouse and put my mouth on her nipple. The car stopped but she didn't speak. When I moved to the other breast, she pushed me away.

"We're home. Let's go inside."

We were in a crowded trailer park where I was sure we were being watched and were probably heard, but I didn't care. We got out and tumbled through the trailer door. Her roommate was watching television, and Brigitte said "hey" as we groped our way down the hall. Brigitte closed the door to her bedroom, turned and grabbed my hand, and pushed it up her short dress and against her panties, which were silky and stimulating and wonderful. We didn't hug, she didn't kiss me, and I didn't kiss her, obeying some kind of code where it was okay for me to have my hand in her panties but not okay to hug and kiss her.

She wrestled off my shirt, and the sight of my infected chest almost brought her off, making her shudder against my fingers inside her. She held my hand in place so I couldn't get it free, then lowered us to the floor, touching my bites with her other hand and smiling.

I was smiling too. I wasn't exactly sure why, and knew a little deeper inside myself that I shouldn't be. But Shannon was with Steve, so now we were even.

I'd just re-earned ten grand and beat Parrish once again. My hands were all over this young woman who actually might, in truth, have a shot in Hollywood. So screw 'em all, I figured. I was entitled to smile.

Nine

I rolled off Brigitte, and while I looked around in the dark for my clothes, I ran my fingers along her body and pretended I cared, as if I valued her and she meant something to me. In truth, I hated that I'd slept with her, but it wasn't her fault so I acted sweet as she fell back asleep. I wanted to leave her feeling good. At least I could appreciate her for having condoms. So much time had passed since I'd had sex with anyone but Shannon, I hadn't even thought about them.

Because I'd never cheated on Shannon, I never wondered what I would do afterward, whether I'd tell her or not. Instinctively—perhaps because I wanted to take my punishment and move on—I felt the need to confess. I didn't want to live a lie, but the popular argument went toward secrecy because confessions simply shifted the burden to another pair of shoulders, making victims of the innocent, often the person you loved most.

I never believed I'd make Shannon a victim, regardless of what she might have done or whom she

did it with. I loved her and never should have lost sight of that, no matter how jealous or lonely I was.

I took a cab back to the camp. One of the gate sentries was getting off work and gave me a lift to the outer perimeter of the Jaspers compound. He was intrigued by the bites on my face. Maybe that's why he offered to wait in the dark at the end of the diked road while I grabbed my stuff and picked up my orders from Parrish's barracks. Parrish wasn't there, but it wasn't really that late, just a little after midnight. He was probably still waiting for me back at the bar.

I had decided, almost instantly upon hearing I was free to leave, to drive to Washington instead of flying so Shannon and I would both have time to think. As I packed what little gear I had, it sounded like an even better idea now—more time to separate me from what I'd just done and a chance for Brigitte's scent to wear off completely.

It also gave me a little time to consider what Pike had just told me. I was one of the people he talked about, an American who assumed we'd always be the most powerful nation on earth. It had never crossed my mind that we were just taking our turn at the top spot, but history was clearly on his side so I wondered what I could do to help us extend. I couldn't imagine other nations' flags flying over my country the way they once did, but I could imagine our flag as a last symbol of something lost, almost like the monarchy of England—a largely useless remnant of the past.

But most of all, driving would give Shannon a chance to figure out how she wanted to handle the mess with Steve. I was about to call her and tell her I was coming. If she was out somewhere with Mister Wonderful, I'd leave a message.

No, of course she didn't call him that.

The sentry asked about Jaspers as we rode back to the main gate, but I didn't answer. We both knew he shouldn't have asked and that I couldn't answer, but in the darkness of night and the shadow of his favor, I guess he figured it wouldn't hurt. When I got out, he wished me luck. I did the same back. We both seemed to understand we were heading to different kinds of wars.

I rented a car outside the gate and then, since cell phones were a luxury we weren't allowed to have in training, I walked to some pay phones. Shannon's outgoing message had the same beautiful voice and sexual urgency, but it didn't quite sound the same to me.

"Hi, Shannon, it's me. I'm sorry . . . sorry about a lot of things. Look, I have a few days off and I'd like to see you. We need to talk. I'll be there tomorrow afternoon. If you have a conflict, I'll understand. Bye."

I drove to Raleigh and spent the rest of the night in a motel, then got to D.C. around three on Sunday. Summer had slipped into fall, but it was still sunny and fairly warm. Government offices were closed, so the suits and uniforms were gone. People played football on The Mall and lovers cuddled on the lawns of public buildings.

Out of habit I wound up in Georgetown, not far from her home. As I passed restaurants, I couldn't help looking for her and Steve at a table in the window or walking along the sidewalk in front. I turned up her street but felt too much like a spy, so I left.

When I crossed the Key Bridge and got to Virginia, I pulled into a parking lot and got out. I stretched, then walked to the phones of a convenience store. She wasn't home, so I tried her at work.

"Shannon Sullivan."

"Hi, it's me."

"Henry," she said. Her voice was a little chilly. "I got your message. Are you already in D.C.?"

"Yes. I'd like to see you."

"I thought you were mad about Steve."

"Can we talk about it when I get there?"

"I don't want to," she said. Her voice was more playful than it was the last couple of calls. It was a weekend kind of voice, almost the way it was before New York. "No questions about Steve."

"That's not fair."

"No questions. That's the rule. If you want to come by the White House, I'm here catching up on last week's work."

She hung up. Ever since I left for SEALs, most of our calls have ended in hang-ups. She was quick and hard to beat.

I never enjoyed going to the White House. When I worked there, I made the sad discovery that the folks who run our country are just like the rest of us. They don't like to be wrong, embarrassed, or challenged, and they make mistakes just as we do, except they are in a position to make some really big mistakes that impacted us all.

I preferred what I thought of them before working there, assuming that for some reason they were better and smarter than me.

Thirty minutes later, I was at the Pennsylvannia Avenue entrance. I remembered standing in the exact same spot once as a kid, but back then there were cars passing by on the street instead of barricades that prevented all traffic. They seemed to prove some of what Pike said, that our nation truly was under attack, but more from within than without. We were a society that proudly proclaimed our freedoms, yet gave them up freely, probably without even realizing it.

Security was tight and a uniformed Secret Service agent asked me for my name, for the name of my White House contact, the nature of my business there, and a slew of personal questions he pulled from a computer. He gave me a badge and told me, "This must be readily visible at all times or you'll be seized." The badge had a locator and was programmed to activate an alarm and change colors to bright red if I stayed overtime. In my case, that meant an hour.

Another agent escorted me to Shannon's office, moving us easily through security zones as if he had full run of the White House. Shannon blushed as I leaned against the wall and watched her talk on the phone. As soon as she hung up, she came over and kissed me.

"Hi," she said, lingering over the "i." "I'm glad you're here. What happened to your face?"

"Bees. God, look at you. So beautiful."

"And who is Jim Parrish?"

"What?"

"It's a simple question. Where did I lose you?"

"How do you know about Parrish?"

"He called me at home in the middle of the night from some bar. He sounded drunk and asked for you."

173

"Did he say what he wanted?"

"Not really. Just kidded around and said he felt like he knew me from talking to you. No message or . . . wait. He did say you had done well but that he would win next time. Something like that. Didn't sound urgent, though."

"Oh."

"Something you want to tell me?"

"What? No. I work with him is all. He's kind of the crazy uncle in the closet no one likes to talk about. You want to tell me about your date with Steve?"

"You're not supposed to ask."

"Too late."

"The truth?" She pouted. It was cute, and I was glad that she would have had more fun lying. "Yes, the truth."

"Okay. He called and all, just like I said. He tracked me down through some media people and invited me to J. Paul's for a drink. I didn't go."

I couldn't have been more relieved if I'd passed a kidney stone.

"Thanks a lot for the torture. You're so much fun."

"Hey, fella, you did it to yourself. I told you—"

She quickly looked me over again, and then her hand went to her mouth and covered it. "Oh, my God. You did this because of me, didn't you? You did something crazy because—"

"No, I didn't. I was careless in training and got hurt. It had nothing to do with you."

She didn't believe me.

"I told you the truth, Henry, every word of it. I even told you not to worry. Why didn't you trust me? Why did you hurt yourself over it?"

"I didn't. But I might have. After all, you did screw him once before."

"Are you sure?" Her worry went away and defensiveness took its place.

"Yes, I'm sure."

She glared.

"Okay, I'm not sure. But you took him to our room alone."

"I did do that. But you don't know what else I did because *you* didn't come up."

"And you didn't go out? Swear?"

"I won't swear. You should take my word for it."

We faced off like a couple of kids, standing there staring until she said, "President Devereau wants to see you, Henry, and I want you to promise me you won't criticize him like last time. This is just a social visit, because he told my folks he'd keep an eye on me and the men in my life." She shook her head like she hated the attention, but I knew she enjoyed being loved like that. "It has nothing to do with work, so no politics, none. Say, 'Hello, Mr. President. Fine job you're doing, Mr. President' and then we're out of there." She rubbed her fingers across the grain of my whiskers, as if deciding whether or not I should keep growing the beard. "Deal?"

"I guess. I thought we would go get something to eat, but if you want me to stop in and talk to him first, I will. Doesn't matter much to me what we talk about."

She looked at me suspiciously and then messed with my hair.

I expected the meeting to last about thirty seconds. "Hello, Lieutenant, good to see you again. Everything all right in the ranks? No coups d'état heading my way? Ha-ha. Come back when you have more time. Good-bye." Then a late lunch with the prettiest woman I'd ever known. My stomach was rumbling.

Devereau stood at a window of the Oval Office, staring out as if lost in thought. He was about six feet tall, lean and strong-looking, with a nice head of dark hair that usually looked a little tousled, Kennedy fashion. It was still wet from the shower he takes after his midday workout, his way of beating the stress of the job, Shannon always said. He didn't have a coat on, just a white shirt, rep tie, and black suspenders. I knew that this attire—no coat—signified a social visit, confirming what she'd told me in her office.

Shannon looked at him for a few seconds, then led me around the edge of the room. We stopped a few feet away from him. She waited and seemed willing to do it for as long as it took.

"Good afternoon, Mr. President," I said.

Shannon gave me a cute version of a dirty look, then stepped toward Devereau. "Mr. President, you remember—"

Devereau turned around and looked at her, then me.

"Henry," he said, as though we were old friends. "How in the world are you?"

"I'm fine, sir."

"What happened to your face?"

"Bees, sir."

"Bees?"

"Or wasps. It's a long story."

"And a painful one, I bet. You'll be all right?"

"Yes, sir. And how are you feeling?"

He laughed and glanced at Shannon. "I'm great,

and thanks for asking. Most visitors to this office are so worried about running out of time before telling me what they want, they don't ask how I am. You ought to hold on to a man like this, young lady."

Shannon looked tongue-tied, so I tried to *carpe momento* or something like that. My Latin has always been terrible. "You could make her, Mr. President, by signing something into law."

He laughed again.

Shannon looked as if she'd lost control of the meeting. She tensed up and then said, "Henry, President Devereau doesn't have time to—"

"To what? Of course I have the time. They give me a break around here every once in a while. Sit down. Relax. Please."

I was hungry, so I thought about asking him if he'd like to continue this conversation at the Capitol City Brewery. But I didn't have enough money to cover Shannon and me and Devereau and a dozen or more Secret Service agents.

"Now," Devereau said as he sat down, "tell me what's going on with you. Are you stationed back in Washington?"

"Close, sir. Just recently assigned near here, in Maryland."

"We've missed having you here. I wasn't in this office when you left, was I?"

"As a matter of fact you were, although the last time we actually spoke was in your vice-presidential office."

Devereau nodded his head solemnly. "It was a sad day when President Simons died so suddenly. Hell of a shocker, too."

"Yes, sir."

"And you were here then?"

"I was."

We sat in silence for a moment. I guessed that Devereau was paying tribute to the man America elected, but I was thinking it must be awkward to get this office by accident.

"So where are you now? What are you doing?"

"I'm in school, sir."

"That's right. SEALs, as I recall."

"No, sir. I left there."

He looked surprised, but it didn't look real. He glanced at Shannon as though they'd already talked about it.

"Well, I'm sure you gave it your best effort."

"I did."

"And now you're . . . where?"

I hesitated. I knew he was my ultimate boss and could order me to tell him, but still, I'd suffered a lot to prove I could keep my mouth shut.

"It's secret. I'm sure no one figured I'd be having this conversation with you, but orders are orders. I hope you understand."

Devereau looked stunned and glanced at the silver bar on my collar, probably realizing he would have had more influence if it were an admiral's star. And he was right. I figured I'd look good with a star on my collar, so I found myself thinking, *Field promotion*.

But it didn't happen. Darn. Instead, Shannon picked up my hand and held it lovingly. This, I knew, was a show, a chance to prove how serious we were about each other.

"See how difficult he can be, Mr. President? He's not the easiest person to get along with."

Devereau took it all in and then leaned back in his chair. "I don't know, Shannon. He's a man of conviction, and that's good. He was told to keep quiet, and he does. We need more loyalty these days. I admire it."

"Thank you." There was little to tell anyway. A camp, a field, a Luger. End of story.

"Just be careful, Henry."

"Sir?"

"These are interesting times. It was never the intent of the founding fathers to maintain a large military, especially in these days of terrorism, coalition fighting, and cyberwarfare. The nature of war has changed. Very few direct threats exist that can't be handled by a small military reinforced by the Guard and Reserve, working in partnership with our allies. It's no secret that's what I want. I know the Reserve is stretched thin right now, but that's only temporary. In the long term, I intend to bring the military budget under control, scale it down and put the savings into better security against terrorism. There are those who say I'm putting our nation at risk, that it's dangerous to rely so heavily on reserves and small units of special forces. I don't believe it, though. Do you?"

"With all due respect, sir, I do." I held back my other concerns, the ones about symmetrical warfare against foreign nations with lots of tanks, ships, and airplanes, something I'd never considered until Pike threw it in my face over beers at The County Line.

He looked at Shannon, surprised, I think, but then he laughed.

"He's honest, too. Well, I guess I knew that from your last visit, so I'll respect your opinion. But I'm the president, Henry. The Constitution puts me in charge and your uniform puts you under my command. Patriotism can take the form of disagreement, and occasionally it should, but under no circumstances can it tolerate dissidence."

"What are you trying to tell me?"

"That you should be careful. Be extremely vigilant when you do things that are secret. There are many opportunities to become lost or misguided. You've read about this David Green fellow? Killed for espionage in Africa? He was lost, Henry. Misguided."

"If you say so."

"Don't let it happen to you. Remember what my old friend Senator Moynihan said years ago: 'Secrecy is a disease. It causes hardening of the arteries of the mind and hides mistakes.'"

"I'll remember that."

Devereau didn't look at all tense, but I knew he was because he'd folded his arms across his stomach. Shannon told me he did this when he thought he might be about to say something he shouldn't, a way to remind himself to pay strict attention. "Be absolutely sure you're not making any mistakes in . . . well, wherever you are in school. Okay, Henry?"

"I don't think I am. At least I hope not, sir."

"So do I." Devereau stared for a second, not exactly at me, but kind of over my shoulder. His eyes were a little unfocused. Then he said, "So do I" again and stood up.

I stood too, and so did Shannon. She grabbed my

arm and gave Devereau her best "we're-a-serious-couple" look.

"Well, Henry, a pleasure seeing you again," he said. "Don't be a stranger."

"I won't, sir."

"Good luck with whatever you're doing. Keep working hard. We need devoted young people like you."

"Now more than ever."

"You're probably right," he said, as he reached out his hand and waited for me to step over to him. "We need to get people involved again and restore their confidence in the system."

He held my hand like a preacher, squeezing it with his right hand and shrouding it with his left. "But all of them don't have to be in uniform, do they?" He grinned. "Sorry. I couldn't resist the parting shot. Good-bye, my young friend. Come back when you have more time. Take care of this pretty woman, all right? She's a handful, but I know you can do it."

"I'll try. You're right, though, she is a handful."

Shannon tossed her head, making her hair swirl around her face. "Okay, gentlemen, that's enough of that. Thanks for your time, Mr. President."

As we left the room, we walked around the Great Seal of the United States that was woven into the carpet and were met in the hall by the Secret Service agent who'd escorted me to Shannon's office.

"It's been fifty minutes, sir," he said to me. "Please give me your badge and I'll add thirty minutes to it."

"Don't bother. I'm on my way out. Will you make sure the president gets the items he ordered from me? They'll arrive in about a week."

"Sir?"

"They'll come in a brown paper wrapper. Don't open them, because they're quite personal. Understand?"

"Sir?"

"Stop it, Henry." Shannon turned to the confused-looking man who was quickly getting angry. "He's kidding. We're leaving, so the time on his badge will be sufficient. Thank you, Mr. Stephens."

"Can I escort you out?"

"I know the way," Shannon said.

"Sorry, Miss Sullivan. I know you do." He frowned at me and left.

When we cleared the small gate on Pennsylvania Avenue, tourists on the sidewalk gawked as if trying to recognize us. Then Shannon said, "You can't help but be a smart-ass to Devereau, can you?"

"I can't help telling him the truth. Being a smart-ass is optional."

"The truth as *you* see it."

"Isn't that what all truth is? Hey, he asked me a question and I answered it. You know I don't *do* obsequious."

"Well," she said with a half-smile, as if leading me into a trap. "You're sure good at being obdurate."

Uh-oh. She wanted to fight the battle of big words again, a war that always had me on the losing side. I was thinking fast and coming up with some of my best weapons—*officious* and *remonstration*—but I was a little vague on their meanings. Besides, I knew them only from hearing Shannon use them.

"I wasn't being obdurate," I said. "It's not my time of the month to obdurate."

"That's funny. You know, he didn't need an argument from you. He's got plenty of stress already. It worries me."

"Aren't *you* the caring soul? Anyway, I only gave him an honest answer."

"And you're the authority, huh? Listen, Henry, I suppose some presidents make decisions based on knowledge that's only PowerPoint deep, but Devereau's not that kind of leader. He's a brilliant guy. He really studied the military before deciding it was too large and lockstepped into past ways of thinking. If he doesn't shift its focus to terrorism, it'll be ineffective against future threats spawned by extremists. He knows it and so should you."

"I'm not going to argue with you. What's the point? But I strongly disagree."

I thought she might whack me, but instead she threaded her arm into mine.

"Henry?"

"Yup?"

"Can you tell me anything about what you're doing? Anything that's not secret?"

"I haven't heard any secrets yet, Shannon. I'm just a new guy."

"I hate that it's secret."

"Secrets are a pretty normal part of government."

"Shouldn't be part of a relationship, though."

"That's a point."

"I want to ask you something that's bothering me about your conversation with Devereau."

I tried to keep things light as I raced her to the question. "Speaking of Devereau, that was weird."

"What was weird?"

"His speech about secrecy. Where did that come from? And who was that guy he mentioned? Green."

"You don't know who that is?"

We turned off Pennsylvania Avenue and walked beside the Old Executive Office Building. "Sounds kind of familiar, but I haven't been keeping up with the news."

"You don't know who Devereau was talking about, swear?"

"No. I told you his name sounds familiar, so I won't swear. What's the big deal?" I looked at her with what I hoped appeared to be confusion. It must have been convincing, because I saw her soften.

"I'm sorry, Henry. Just a problem at work."

"What do *you* know about the guy, Shannon?"

"I can't talk about it."

"Now who's being secretive?"

"Don't try to turn this around on me. I hate it when you do that." She bared her teeth. "Grrr, you absolutely infuriate me sometimes."

"For asking you the same thing that you asked me?"

She smiled, and it was a good smile. It could have been motivated by something bad, evasive, or controlling, but it was a good smile nevertheless. "No, silly. Because you haven't gotten us a cab. I want an orgasm. This is going to be a me-day, because I'm still mad at you."

"Is that right?"

I waved a cab over. Shannon watched me admire her legs as she got in.

"I'm not so sure I want to make love to an angry woman." I said this as if her legs hadn't excited me at all.

"Want to go for vengeful?"

"I'm not scared." I scooted in beside her, then massaged the back of her neck with my hand. She closed her eyes.

"Should be," she said, her eyes still closed. "You know you can't trust me."

"That knife's got two edges. Be careful not to get cut yourself." I tried not to think too much about Brigitte.

"Henry?" She picked up my hand.

"Yes?"

"You *are* all right. I mean, what President Devereau said about you is true."

"That my face will heal okay?"

She slapped my arm, and the driver looked back. "No, silly, that you're a good man. He's right, and I know it."

She turned away but came right back and studied my eyes. She seemed pleased with either herself or the effect she assumed her words had on me.

"Well, Devereau *is* a brilliant guy, then. You said so yourself."

"Very funny." She bit her lip and nodded. "So you're going to play it cool, huh."

"Cool? Me? No, I just—"

Before I saw her coming, Shannon moved into me and covered my mouth with hers, her hands against my shoulders. She grazed my lips from corner to corner, murmuring something I didn't bother trying to make out. She looked into my eyes, and I couldn't look away. She looked happy and loving and different, vulnerable and revealing like never before. She nibbled lightly, first on my lower lip, then the upper.

Then she kissed me. I kissed her back, pinned against the seat as she escalated, letting loose as if some barrier we'd always felt had just tumbled away. I couldn't be sure, but I thought she said she loved me.

She kissed harder, suddenly, almost painfully, her knees dug into the side of my leg, her tongue exploring me while her hands held my head in place.

Shannon took a deep breath and let out a sigh. "I've missed you so much for so long," she said as I held her.

"I wanted to see you," she said. "I missed you and wanted to see you. But you were in that secret school."

"Yeah. Wasn't much fun."

She glanced at the driver, then back at me. "Tell me about it," she whispered. "What did you do there?"

I could almost hear President Devereau asking a similar question, which made me wonder if she was doing this on his behalf. "Can't tell."

"I've got a right to worry."

"You were worried? You told me you were going out with Steve, so don't tell me you were worried."

"Let's not fight." She kissed me again, once, twice, three times, all over my mouth. Then she sat back and leaned against my shoulder. She rubbed my leg absentmindedly, as if contemplating her last move or her next one. I could sense she was changing gears.

"Henry," she said, still leaning against me. "I've wanted to tell you something for a while, and I hope you'll understand. The way I tease men?"

"And torture men?"

"That too, I suppose. I do it because it's easy and just a little bit cruel, which was more or less how my husband treated me. He was cruel in an easy way. He didn't beat me or anything like that, but he made me feel inferior. He teased me about my dream of working in the White House and made me think I couldn't do anything worthwhile, probably so he could get away with running around behind my back. Since our divorce, I've treated quite a few men the same way."

I hated her ex and always would. Not for who he was, but for what he did to Shannon. His unfaithfulness infected the entire first phase of our relationship and kept Shannon suspicious and cautious as she waited to see if I was just like him. It was hard living down an unearned reputation, but I hoped that one day she'd believe I was different.

Thinking back on our past fights about her suspicions doubled my self-hatred over Brigitte. I made sure I sounded relaxed as I said, "I don't mind too much," trying not to show my anger that the pain and itching I had from Parrish's field was her ex-husband's fault. Shannon drove me into that field because *he* drove her to act the way she did.

"It keeps me on my toes," I added to mask the way my mind was working.

She picked up my hand and held it. "You're sweet to understand."

"I didn't say I understood. I said it keeps me on my toes. Besides, I think you know better than to push the limits with me."

"I've always been faithful to you, Henry. Even with Steve, I kissed him and hugged him, but that was it. I wouldn't have even done that except I thought you were all right with it. But you didn't show up, so I left."

"There's been no one else since we've met?"

"No."

"Good."

She could have been lying to me. How would I know? There was plenty of deception going around, and although I hated what I'd done with Brigitte, I'd done it all the same. Lying seemed the best option. "This will be a good change for us, then. I'm excited. Let's celebrate."

"That's what I'm thinking, too," she said. Then she sat back and leaned against my shoulder. She rubbed my leg absentmindedly as we rode in silence. I tried to keep my hands off her just a little longer.

"This is it, driver. Stop here."

We got out, and as I paid the driver Shannon raced for her front door. I caught up and pushed aside her hair and kissed her neck. It tickled her and made her fumble with her keys. She giggled and scrunched her cheek to her shoulder, squeezing my face away. I moved around her and kissed the other side of her neck until both her shoulders were up around her ears.

She finally got the door open, pulled herself out of my arms, and ran for the stairs. I had to close the door and then catch her, or she would lock me out of the bedroom and make me wait.

I slammed into the bedroom door, and she shrieked as it flew open and I burst into the room. She backed away from me.

"Got ya," I said with pretend menace.

She backed to the dresser. I pinned her against it, pressing into her, using my hands to trace across her shoulders, down her arms to her fingers, then up her sides, gently touching her beautiful body. I was about to explode.

She fumbled around in the drawer next to her, then her face changed and she pulled away, out of my arms and into the bathroom. She laughed as the door clicked locked.

"Hurry!"

"Poor boy. Has to wait."

"This is a hollow door, easily busted. Don't tempt me."

"Okay, I'll hurry. Get in bed."

I stripped and looked at my body in her mirror. Long gouges and infected bites made me look like a zebra with measles, so I jumped into bed and pulled up the sheet. I waited five minutes, which felt like an hour, thinking of all the great lingerie Shannon has surprised me with in the past, the purple bra and thong panties being my favorite so far. But when Shannon finally came out, she was wearing a cream-colored slip, very silky, with a delicate lace covering her breasts.

I stared but didn't say anything. I'd never learned the words I needed right then.

"Don't you like it?" She was uneasy and embarrassed, not Shannon the seductress, but something else, something unfamiliar to me and probably to her, too.

I got out of bed and walked over to her. She saw the scars on my body and gasped.

"Oh my God. I *did* do this, didn't I?"

"No, of course not."

She took a step back from me. "I know you, Henry."

"Shh, don't worry. It was part of the school."

"No," she said, her voice trembling as it rose higher. "I don't believe you."

"It doesn't matter. I'm just glad to be with you now. Calm down."

I pulled her into bed and held her close, pressing her against the least damaged part of my chest. She resisted for a few seconds, then broke down and cried. I had no idea what was really bothering her. It wasn't Steve, I was sure, and I couldn't imagine it was my scratches. Then she stopped crying, locked away whatever was bothering her, and shook her head and smiled. It started out as a forced effort, but gradually took root and grew to look natural, then playful.

"You're incredible," I said, and that's all I could say. I noticed my hand trembling as it touched the thin straps of her slip. The straps ran between my fingers as I slid along them, back and forth across her shoulders. The lace of her slip brushed against her breasts.

I left the straps on her shoulders and moved to her breasts, gently tracing the pattern of the lace that still covered them. Her hands went to my shoulders, and I closed my eyes. I glided my fingertips down along her body, barely grazing the silk and savoring this feeling, then went onto my knees beside her, blindly following a seam to the hem of the slip. Shannon pulled me up by gently stroking her fingers against the whiskers on my chin, tilting my face upward, lifting me with it. I opened my eyes. She'd slipped a strap off her shoulder so that a breast was exposed, full and round and glorious, the nipple erect in competition with the shrouded nipple that also demanded my mouth.

190

I was intimidated by the beauty of her breasts, feeling the same way I did the first time I saw them, totally mystified by their power over me. I kissed one gently, licked it lovingly, and then moved to the other breast. I slipped off the strap and pulled it down. I could have come at the sight of that beautiful fabric giving way to her more beautiful breast. I gasped, and she moaned, stroking me with her hand, stretching her beautiful arm, directing me where she wanted me. I lifted her slip and brushed my fingers along her legs until she grabbed my back and pulled me to her, holding me tight, embracing me in exactly the right position to enter her. I did.

I fought against the explosion I instantly wanted to have, stayed perfectly still until the threat of eruption subsided. She waited without moving as I postponed the pleasure, realizing that life would never be better than it was right then. I felt like we were truly making love, as if that powerful yet indistinct element of life had finally found its way into our sex. It was nothing more than a subtle quietness during our rage of passion, but I felt certain somehow that a diamond-hard carbon would stay with us long after the roaring flames and screaming sirens died out.

She locked her arms behind my neck and hung on as we pounded our way up the bed, the headboard slamming into the wall until I expected drywall to start falling off. We slid sideways and worked our way across the bed until her head was aiming at the floor and her chest was arched out and I was supporting most of our weight with one hand pressing against the carpet. I came in this incredible, sweaty, awkward position. Her body spasmed and her legs clamped around my waist and my arm was no longer strong enough. We tumbled off the bed and onto the floor.

My blood stopped throbbing as she cuddled beside me, nibbling my ear and giggling because it made me ticklish, just as I did to her earlier. "Oh God, I love you, Henry."

"I love you, too, Shannon. I think I always have."

"I know," she whispered. "We should do something about that."

"Make you a married woman?"

She rolled her eyes, and I guessed at the meaning. I pulled her close and didn't let go. We lay motionless for a long time before we crawled back into bed and cozied up. The sun went down before she moved again, lifting her head from my shoulder and onto my chest.

"Henry, before we can talk about marriage and a family, I want you to tell me something."

"Sure. What?"

"What happened between you and your dad? Why did you leave your family?"

I shifted around a little. Some people were outside, closing car doors and talking too loudly. They went down the street. "Nothing worth talking about."

"I still want to know. It scares me a little as I think about our future."

"It wouldn't sound like much to you, I guarantee it. You would have had to be raised by the man to understand."

She lifted her head slightly. "I'm pretty good at understanding, Henry. Why don't you try me?"

I searched my mind for a word that could handle

the load, something solid enough to carry my disappointment and contempt, and expressive enough to convey those feelings to another person. I doubted the word existed.

"My dad . . . You'll think I'm being petty."

She waited without speaking.

"My dad," I said, and already felt my teeth clenching. "My dad used to say, 'When you're faced with two decisions and you don't know which way to go, take the hardest path. It's usually the right one.' So I grew up like that. I took the hard road all the time because of him."

I looked to see if she was getting it but couldn't see her eyes. She stroked her hand along my arm, and the touch reminded me of the greatest praise I ever got from my father, back when I told him I was valedictorian of my high school class. He gave me a pat on the back as though there'd never been any doubt. It was a small school, but still, it wasn't like every third kid got to go home and say that.

"Can you imagine how hard I tried all my life to make him proud? But no matter what I did, what enemy I faced, what award I won, I was just doing what I was supposed to do. Not being a coward. Not failing."

She reached up and drew her smooth hand down my cheek. I saw in her eyes for the first time that she pitied me in some sad form of understanding. "I'm so sorry."

I wanted to say something stupid and macho in an effort to prove I was too tough for him to hurt me. But Shannon made me feel safe in being honest, and so I was, even though it was hard. "I loved him so much. All I wanted was for him to like me back. To respect me. It was important."

She dug one hand under me and hugged my shoulders. "I'm sure he did, Henry, and still does. Any parent would be proud to have a son like you."

There wasn't one chance in hell I would ever let those words penetrate.

"So one day my father, this man among men as I saw him, tells me he's leaving the marshals because he's a failure and a coward and a quitter."

Shannon gasped and raised herself up. "He said that to you?"

"No, of course not. He could never have said those words about himself. He could call another man a coward easily enough, but never himself, so he said his partner had died because he'd failed to control a prisoner. But my father was afraid to shoot as the guy ran away, so that makes him a coward. He shamed me, Shannon. No, that's not it at all. What he really shamed was my effort to be like him."

She seemed as confused as I was that day in the yard with Dad, unable to find any good words to say.

"See, I said you wouldn't understand. Maybe I'm just being stupid."

I felt her shrug as she rubbed my chest. "You know, Devereau says that intelligence is often like a lonely walk in some foggy woods. You can only go so far before you're out of everyone else's vision. Then they start thinking you're lost and confused, at least until they catch up and see what you see and are no longer blinded to it. Then you're brilliant once more, at least until you get too far ahead again."

"You think I'm lost in the woods?"

"No. I just don't think it matters whether or not I understand. It didn't happen to me. You've never been back?"

"No."

I propped myself up so I could see her. She glanced at me and smiled. "We'll be all right, Henry." She leaned up and kissed my neck. "We've got plenty of time to work through this."

Plenty of time to work through this?

"We can work on your problems with your ex-husband at the same time."

She sat up and pulled the sheet around her. "Why did you say that?"

I sat up too. "Hey, you act like I'm the only damaged freight here. Sure, my old man and I had—"

"Damaged freight? You honestly think I'm damaged freight?"

"No, I didn't mean damaged, but just, you know . . . hurt, cautious because of the way he controlled and manipulated you."

"I'm not damaged."

"I know."

"I got past that long ago. I overcame whatever he—"

"Shannon, I know. I'm sorry. I didn't mean it."

"I can't believe you called me damaged."

"I said I was sorry."

She stared at me and then turned away.

"I need some water," she said, then got up and went to the bathroom. When she came out, she was wearing a cotton robe instead of the silky slip. She didn't even look at me as she left the room and closed the door.

I sat on the bed and listened to silence, to the memory of her words, the good ones and the hurt ones. I picked at a large scab. It was still tender, but I peeled it off anyway, tearing it away from the skin and watching the blood flood through the wound. I covered it and went into the bathroom and compressed it until it stopped, and then I dressed.

BOOK TWO

Ten

I was stuck in a crevice and couldn't move, my arms stretched over my head and my feet hanging the way they did when Fidel strung me up for torture. My shoulders were jammed in a painful position when I fell, my hips felt broken, and pieces of bone shifted in my rib cage and pinched my breath into shallow gasps. I couldn't even whisper, let alone scream. Rats scurried around me, and it was only a matter of time before they started nibbling.

Slowly, suspended in this lifeless position, I heard the sound of loving voices far off in the distance, and one of them was Dad's. They got close, calling me, pleading desperately for my reply, but I couldn't answer. I had no way to cry for help.

The voices got louder and louder and then faded away, retreating back to their dark origin as night covered the chasm like a coffin lid.

I jolted awake and my knees hit the tray table, sending the stupid plastic cup of Coke flying. The flight attendant leaned over me to pick up my empty glass and wipe the tray table with napkins. She looked frightened or angry with me, or possibly both. I didn't really know and certainly didn't care.

"Are you all right, sir?"

Everyone on the plane seemed to be staring at me.

"I'm fine," I said. "Had a cramp while I slept, that's all." Then, to the nosy guy across the aisle: "Is it any of your business?"

The little boy in the window seat next to him leaned forward and started to speak, but the man looked at his lap and shook his head, touched the boy's hand and squeezed.

The flight attendant put down my drink and walked away, muttering something that sounded like a bad name, and that made me laugh because I was so far beyond her reach and ability to understand. I had finally become a very proud and fully sworn Jasper, and as such had managed a miraculous but necessary change over the past few months. I was no longer the weak little bastard who had cried in Shannon's arms after great sex, blubbering like a sissy about my father, as if I really gave a damn about him in the first place.

I came to realize that I'd done nothing wrong with Brigitte and could even remember it now with pleasure—the feel of her flesh and the way she moved in bed. Along with those changes in my personal relationships, I'd made dramatic progress in hardening myself for the work I was born to do. I was on my way to find a despicable man named Randall Baker and looked forward to finally getting a check in the box: I would become a cold-blooded killer.

I smiled about the flight attendant calling me a

name as I closed my eyes, concentrating on the monotonous drone of the jet engines, drifting back to sleep as proof that I wasn't afraid or willing to be intimidated. I was far too dangerous to fear anything, especially a nightmare.

Those bastard rats were waiting for me, though, as they always did when I slept. Some of them chewed on my jacket while others gnawed near my ears and tried for my eyes. One or two were inside my shirt, and the feeling made me want to vomit, but I would never do it. I refused to wonder what they might chew up as I twisted what little I could in the chasm to try and get them off me.

The plane jolted in some turbulence and woke me slightly, just enough to remind me where my body really was while I went back mentally to the lab at the Jaspers' advance school—a highly secured area of Fort Belvoir. Sergeant Parrish was there, watching me sew poison-soaked buttons on a pretend victim's shirt. I had just asked him how effective Jaspers had been over the years, the easy sort of question I might ask someone I'd just met at a party.

He shrugged. "It's hard to get to the targets and do the job. Ours is a tough business that can backfire and make the leaders we execute martyrs. If we get caught, the United States will be perceived as inhumane and uncivilized." He frowned. "As if it's civilized to wait until we have to send thousands of people to their deaths over someone else's power play."

"I guess that makes sense."

"If a Jasper can be groomed to make one good assassination, that's a big success for the program and will probably save lots of lives on both sides. Most guys will fail. The others won't even get their chance."

I started cleaning up, putting the shirt in a biohazard container, nicely folded and ready to wear. If this had been a real-world scenario, my target would have infected and killed himself by buttoning it.

"Why not? Why won't they get their chance?"

"Their guy is never targeted."

I stopped what I was doing. I didn't look up, because I needed to concentrate on what I touched with my plastic gloves. Not a good time to absentmindedly scratch an itch.

"What do you mean?"

"I mean they were recruited to target a guy who never quite makes the elimination list."

"You're telling me that once we're assigned someone we just sit around and wait for his name to come up on some memo that says, 'Go get 'em'?"

"Pretty much. Hell, what did you expect, that you'd be flying around the world, killing this guy and that guy and drinking warm wine in Paris? This is real life, the real way it's done. And it's a *hard* thing to do. You get assigned someone, usually based on your experience or knowledge, and then spend the rest of your career learning about that guy and no one else. You study him, understand his habits and culture, get a handle on his motives, and look for ways to get close."

"There's one guy for everyone?"

"Well, usually." He grinned. "I get multiple targets. But one Jasper, one target, that's the norm. You should know that. Didn't Colonel Maddigan tell you he had a job for you?"

"Just in a vague way. Certainly nothing specific."

"Take my word for it that he recruited you because you were the best guy for one of our targets."

"So what happens after I do the job? I go back to the regular forces?"

"No, we sort of keep you around until another target that fits your background pops up. That's the idea, anyway."

"Who's my target?"

"Probably someone you've never heard of. We get special details from the Justice and State Departments about who might cause trouble for America. As names come up, Maddigan recruits Jaspers to stand ready to eliminate them if they start to pose a real threat. Assassination is the last possible option before war, although we tend to act a little more quickly these days. Whacking terrorists isn't against the law. They're not legitimate leaders, so that works to our advantage and gives us speed."

"So I might study my target intimately and still never get to use my training."

"Actually, Thompson, I hate to say it, but that's the most likely scenario. Assassinations are tricky and pose lots of risks. We've done a handful, but not many. We're here in a just-in-case capacity. If we even think a war's coming that we can't win, or a political firestorm threatens to disrupt our government, we resolve it by whatever means are possible."

"Is Colonel Maddigan in his office?"

Parrish was backing up as I walked toward him with my gloved hands in front of me.

"He cut out early. You want to talk to him?"

"I didn't come here to sit and grow old waiting."

"Fair enough. I'll let him know."

He opened the door, and Elvis was standing in the hall. The two of them hadn't got along well since Nicholas disappeared, but it had grown worse, and that scared Elvis. Parrish scowled at him as he walked out. Elvis came in, acting differently—with less confidence than he had at Camp Lejeune. His hair was straight back, as always, but the gun sights and the cockiness that powered them was completely missing from his eyes. They were a little fearful maybe, like a junkyard dog repeatedly whipped by its master.

"Hey," I said. "I'm tired of wondering—what is it between you and Parrish?"

He shrugged. It took a while for him to answer. "I asked him once more about Nicholas."

"That's not out of line."

"Yeah. I figured it was a fair question after I was sworn in as a graduate Jasper. So last week I went outside when he was smoking a cigarette and asked him."

"What'd he say?"

Elvis shook his head, troubled, as if he doubted his own memory. "Stupid stuff about my sisters. He said he'd had sex with both of them when they visited me in Jacksonville. He said he really enjoyed doing a number on Molly."

"He was just cracking on you."

"Hell, I know that," he said quickly. "Don't you think I know that? He was like some old-style drill sergeant trying to get a misfit recruit to quit."

"Sure."

"Anyway, because he was so pathetic I didn't get mad, for a while. But he kept it up, telling me what he'd done and how they'd be afraid to say a word about it or he'd kill them. It was pretty sick."

"And what did you do?"

"I kept saying, 'Sure, sure, but what about Nicholas?' After enough time, though, I got pissed off. I was tired of hearing him talk trash about my sisters, so I took a swing at him."

"That had to be a bad move."

Elvis started to tremble as he looked at me for understanding, I think.

"Man, I've got no idea what happened, but it didn't take any time at all before he had my face in the dirt. I was down on my knees with both arms aiming at the sky. I wouldn't have done it, H.T., but he would have broken my arms and dropped me from the rolls."

"Done what?"

"That son of a bitch made me lick his shoes." His lip trembled and he turned away. Then he turned back with more defiance than I'd ever seen. "You know, it's easy to say you'd die before you'd do something like that, but he didn't give me that choice."

"What did he say? Why did he do that to you?"

Elvis pinched his eyes and purged his tears. "He said the torture didn't end at Lejeune, and we had to constantly learn how to endure emotional pain. He said he was doing it for my own good."

"File charges, Elvis. That could never be construed as training or preparation. If you don't do something, you're going to want to quit. Don't let him make you quit."

Elvis shook his head. "I won't quit. And I won't file charges."

"Then tell Colonel Maddigan. He would never stand for that kind of behavior, I'm sure."

"You're probably right."

"Then you'll talk to him?"

"No. I'm going to kill Parrish. I'll use what he taught me and one of the chemical weapons. Maybe the one they gave you for your graduation assassination. That's where I got the idea. No one will know what hit him, except Parrish. I'll make sure he knows it's me."

I started to argue the subtle but important difference between assassination and murder, but Elvis turned and strode out the door. Vengeance was what he sought, and I wanted no part of it. I didn't go after him, largely because I didn't really give a damn about the distinction anymore myself so it would have been hard to convince him.

The pilot made an announcement and I woke again, but slowly this time, having enough experience with my nightmare to understand its painful lesson: that any killing, even Elvis's desire to kill Parrish, could be twisted to appear noble. Looking back now with the advantage of time, I'll admit that I was confused by that. It confused me that day in the lab and confused me even more as the frequency of the dream increased with the approach of my kill date. I didn't want to be the least bit confused, not when I had my own man to assassinate. I didn't have any doubts that killing Randall Baker was in the best interests of my country.

How could it not be? Baker was vermin by anyone's standards, the leader of one of many hate groups growing like kudzu on the American landscape; a fanatic who took the law into his own hands to defend what he saw as the best of America. As Jaspers saw it, Baker threatened the peace of the nation, the welfare of its citizens, and the freedoms of gays and Jews and blacks—including one black man in particular, a local civil rights leader he was planning to kill to damage race relations, fueling a local venue of violence he would use as a recruiting tool to expand his ranks.

Although Baker didn't graduate from high school, he apparently had a talent for rhetoric, for rallying his stupid troops into a frenzy and inciting them to violence toward minorities, especially those who were very rich or very poor. He was a primary suspect in eight murders, but his actual criminal record was unimpressive: disorderly conduct, unlawful assembly, abusive language, threatening bodily harm, and throwing objects at moving vehicles. Adolescent stuff that made me wonder how a grown man could do those things and think he was good for America.

Using all the brilliance of his ninth-grade education, Baker had somehow determined that Jews were descendants of Satan; therefore, Christians had the right to kill them. I knew very little about hate groups and was just beginning to learn how their members thought, but I couldn't help but wonder if it ever occurred to cross-burners like Baker that it wasn't Jews, blacks, and gays who were destroying businesses and reputations. If the devil had descendants on this earth, Baker should shake the branches of his own family tree and see if that horned critter didn't fall out.

Baker was my graduation exam, my last bit of work before I became mission-ready as a Jasper. I hoped he turned out to be a worthwhile challenge, because I wanted to show off my training. I still had bad memories of Parrish's field—I didn't want it to be that difficult, but I wanted it to be challenging. I had my doubts, though. Only because Maddigan had been so casual about the assignment. We were talking about different types of threats when he gave me Baker's photo with his name and address on the back.

"Here's your man, a creep who hates everyone—the poor and minorities the most. You'll feel good about helping them out."

"They're not my problem."

"They're your countrymen, Thompson, the people you've sworn to protect. Beyond that, it's pragmatic to help the poor because a country can't advance for long by leaving a large share of its population behind. It's my job to anticipate and eliminate threats, and poverty's huge ranks make it a much scarier threat than some hate-filled ruler I can assassinate. I never take my eyes off the people with pitchforks." He nodded for good measure. "Words to live by."

"I don't understand."

"In the old days, peasants rebelled against elitist policies with pitchforks. They were used to stabbing a hundred-pound pile of hay and throwing it over their shoulders. They did the same thing to military forces sent to quell their revolts. I never bought into the idea of giving the poor handouts, but we have to give them hope and opportunity, if only as a security matter. If we don't and they revolt, they'll have allies waiting in the wings, foreign governments who'll support them, as in the last two wars on American soil. So I never take my eye off the pitchforks, simple as that, although there's not much I can do about it. Good luck with Baker. See Parrish for the logistics."

I shifted in my seat and looked out the window as the plane made its approach. I scratched the beard I'd grown over the months since crawling through Parrish's field, and ran my hands through the longest hair I'd had since high school. I hardly remembered how to wear a uniform anymore and found myself ridiculing the men who did. Were they hiding behind it somehow? Had I? The patches and ribbons and decorations—even the SEAL trident—seemed more like props than validations, trinkets of patriotism to those weak enough to need them.

I no longer needed them, and had to laugh that they had meant so much to me at one time. Not only did I not need the uniform or ribbons, I no longer cared about the support of family—either the one I left behind in Indiana or could have started with Shannon. All of that was behind me now. It was the way things had to be.

The plane landed and I got off. I'd never been anywhere in Texas, so the size of Houston surprised me. I'd always thought Indianapolis was a sprawling city, but when I looked down on our final approach, hell, Houston was all over the place.

I left the airport in a taxi, orienting myself on a one-page map I swiped from a rental-car counter, jostling along on Interstate 45 in the backseat as we drove through the city toward Galveston. Admitting to a weakness in geography, I had no idea that Houston was so near the Gulf of Mexico.

The map helped me follow along as the cabbie drove southeast of downtown Houston. I got out at an old motel with a vacancy sign, complete with a drained swimming pool and a limping dog in the weed-and-grass yard. I checked in using my alias and easily answered the few questions the old woman asked as she watched a game show with more interest than she showed in me.

I went to my room and searched the phone book for Randall Baker's junkyard. I found a big ad: *Largest Inventory of Used Corvette Parts in Three States*. A locator map showed it was just down the road from my motel, maybe five miles.

I also looked up the nearest Goodwill store, then went outside to the curb and got another cab. I selected enough used but clean clothes for three or four days and picked up a decent pair of cowboy boots I liked a lot. I figured I'd fit in, judging from the men I'd seen at the bus stops and gas stations. I wanted to dress like Baker and his junkyard groupies. I didn't really care what the average law-abiding citizen in Houston thought about me.

I paid the clerk and walked out looking, I hoped, like a hardworking blue-collar guy, maybe a craftsman of some kind. I figured I'd work on that part of my cover—my employment—based on how things went. I had a broad enough background to be convincing in a few areas, from farming to machinery repair to guns, to just about anything I thought they'd believe.

The only paperwork I'd seen up to that point was a voucher Parrish had me sign. They'd given me twenty thousand dollars, which I carried in a small duffel bag along with several vials of a heat-specific toxin I planned to use killing Baker. It was formulated at ten-degree increments ranging from one hundred degrees to one hundred eighty.

I'd spent six hundred and twelve dollars on an airline ticket, twenty-eight dollars on food, seventy-two dollars on cabs, forty-six dollars on clothes, and the hotel room required a two-hundred-dollar cash deposit. Not once did I identify myself as a military man, which was good because no one would have believed it anyway. I looked more like a dope dealer than a soldier. My beard was thick and I was badly in need of a haircut.

So my white northern flesh wouldn't stand out, I'd darkened my skin with instant tanning cream, and ground dirt and grease under my fingernails and into the pores of my hands. When the old woman at the hotel asked about my employer, I said I inspected containerships for OSHA. I'd probably stick with that story.

No one paid attention to me at a Denny's restaurant near the interstate, which I took as an endorsement of my clothing. I bought the *Houston Chronicle* while waiting for my dinner. The headline read: "President Accused of Ignoring Threat of Nuclear Proliferation," but I didn't read the article. Instead, I looked for what would help me do my job.

Killing Baker was going to be a major footnote in my life, even if written with invisible ink. For the first time ever, I would be a warrior. I was finally going to engage an enemy in battle. There was nothing conventional about it, and if I allowed myself to think about it I would have confessed to a preference for guns over germs. But it was a dangerous time for America, and it was my job to take away some of the danger in whatever way worked best.

I remembered reading Emerson in college and being struck by the ferocious insight of his words: "The end of the human race will be that it will eventually die of civilization." Although it meant something entirely different to me then, it was pretty much the same thing Maddigan had been saying since we met at Coronado.

I trusted Maddigan, and so I didn't hesitate to sign the oath that first day at Jasperville, a week after starting a future with Shannon that quickly became impossible. The survival of civilization—*my* civilization— depended on soldiers shooting people, blowing them up, slitting their throats, and even poisoning them. I signed the Jaspers oath and left the classroom. I had no idea how long it would take the others to decide.

Maddigan was out in the hall, leaning against the wall and smoking a cigar, his tanned, weathered face with the horrible scar and iridescent eyes mute but powerful testimony to his past as a soldier, killer, patriot, and leader.

I went over and leaned against the wall, too, although I felt like a kid beside him. He wasn't big, but he was such an imposing presence. His raw and powerful energy extended a foot or so beyond his body.

"That didn't take you long, Thompson. Did you sign the secrecy oath?"

"Yes, sir. I'm not much for reading the fine print."

Maddigan chuckled and drew on his cigar. "There wasn't any fine print."

"Just as well."

He let the smoke drift out of his mouth, held the cigar in front of him in an admiring way. "Cigar?"

"No, thank you, sir. I . . . Colonel Maddigan?"

"Yes."

"Not that it matters, but are we breaking the law here at Jaspers? Or is it designed to circumvent the law, because that's sure how it feels."

"That's an interesting question. Which law do you mean?"

"How many choices do I have?"

"Dozens."

"Then let's keep it simple. Are we breaking any of them?"

Maddigan took another puff and let the smoke float out of his mouth. "I could argue that we aren't and I could argue that we are. Both arguments would be valid."

"I'm not following you."

"There's man's law, God's law, state, federal, and military law, with all kinds of subsets. Some civil, some criminal. I don't know how many types of laws exist, but having that many different sets creates a minefield of contradictions, a bullshit maze that gets trickier every day. What's right and what's wrong? What's good and what's bad? Who knows? The judges sure don't. Courts disagree and overturn each other with regularity. So it's far beyond my simple abilities to synthesize it all down to one basic truth."

He thrust back his shoulders and moved into the hallway in front of me.

"I answer to one law, Thompson. Now that you're officially a Jasper, you do, too. That law is simple and says you will do anything and everything necessary that is asked of you to protect and defend our country from any and all threats."

"But will there be situations—"

"Your father understood it. I'm a little surprised that you don't."

I choked on the question I wanted to ask, and instead I heard myself stammer, "Colonel, you know my father?"

Maddigan gave me "the grin of the better informed," as I always called it.

"I do. A good man."

"If you say so."

"You don't? Your dad served this country well. Shame on you for thinking otherwise."

"What . . . where did you two meet?"

"We worked together once."

"He was never in the service."

"He was a marshal. It had something to do with that."

"And you knew him? Know him?"

"I knew him. I've only spoken to him once since he got out."

"When was that? If you don't mind my asking?"

Sergeant Parrish stepped into the hall. "Excuse me, Colonel. We're ready here."

"Thank you, Jim."

Maddigan grinned, his scar bending out of line. "By the way, did you tell your father about Parrish's Luger? I'm sure he'd be proud. You've got my permission. Ready?"

I thought Maddigan might put his arm around me and lead me back into the classroom, but he didn't.

He flicked his ash into his palm and smudged out his cigar on the back of a silver money clip. Then he stuck the cigar into his shirt pocket and walked in without me, stopping at the trash can to dust the ash from his hand.

I stayed in the hall a few seconds longer, thinking about my dad, his failure, and Colonel Maddigan, who by all the accounts I've heard is the Great Defender. I even considered, just briefly, calling my dad and asking him about his association with this man I respected, perhaps exchanging a few bits of our lives, maybe even telling him that I succeeded where others had failed. That I had owned, for a short while, an historic German Luger. A short call, certainly, but long enough to ask about my sister and brother and how the farm was doing, if the clutch on the tractor was still slipping. For the first time in the four years since I left for OCS, I wanted to call and ring the old phone on the kitchen wall. I imagined Mom wiping her wet hands on her apron before she answered, saying hello and then recognizing my voice before starting to cry as she asked, right away, if I was okay. Then she would frantically call out to Dad in the barn, and maybe he would come to the phone and we'd have trouble staying disappointed in each other as he forced himself to make the old lame joke he always made when I came home late: Had I run away and joined the circus so I could date the bearded lady?

There was a pay phone down the hall and I was aching to make the call, absolutely torn up inside to admit, at least to myself, that Maddigan might be right about my dad and I might be wrong.

But I didn't make either one, the call or the admission.

I went back in the classroom and took my seat instead. Maddigan checked all the forms while Parrish signed them as a witness. Once satisfied, both of them looked at us differently than before. We were all the same now—Maddigan, Parrish, and the five of us facing them. We were all Jaspers. A quiver shook my body and evoked some deep desire to pray for forgiveness for whatever I was about to do.

I trusted that prayer all the way into the heat and crowds of Houston, where I was unconventionally armed and inordinately dangerous, standing ready to be wholly uncivilized and kill Randall Baker—no, assassinate him. In doing so, I would save the life of a civil rights leader, and perhaps some homeless people upon whom Baker had declared war. It would be a good thing for my country.

Instead of reading the *Chronicle*'s articles about national defense or the local articles about cats in trees, I turned to the automotive section and looked for a car that fit my plan. I found it in the form of a *1978 Silver Anniversary Corvette, 112K miles, new transmission, asking $8,200*. I went to the phones and called the number.

"Hey," the guy said, just like John Wayne, a two-syllable combination of "hey" and "yeah."

"Hey," I said back. "Calling about your 'Vette."

"Yeah?" That seemed to brighten his day. "She's a dandy."

"Run okay?"

I heard him slurp something that sounded like a beer or an oyster.

"Sure, sure. Could use a little work to make it cherry, but it runs. Yeah."

"Burn oil?"

"Naah. Man, you're talking 'bout a 'Vette, buddy. Finest car ever made."

"Rust?"

"Well . . . nothing major. You got to see it to appreciate it. Where you at?"

"Where *you* at?" I was starting to have fun with this.

"I'm up off a Antoine."

"Where?"

"You know 290?"

"Sure." I searched my map. There it was.

"Get off on Antoine and head north. Go way out— ten, twelve miles. The car's by itself in a parking lot, so you go on and take a look at it now."

"What color is it?"

"What? You stupid, man? You read the ad?"

"Yeah."

"*Well?* It's a Silver Anniversary edition. What the hell color you think it is?"

Got me. Wasn't thinking. "Silver?"

"You damned right. Silver. Where you from, Lubbock?" He laughed and repeated my error. " 'What *color* is a Silver Anniversary Corvette?' Damn, if that ain't funny."

"You got time to meet me there?"

"I ain't wasting my time on no tire-kicker. You got the money to buy a car like that?"

"You're asking $8,200?"

"I 'spect to get it, too. Might take some off if you're a little shy but a good guy." He laughed again. "Little shy but a good guy. Damn, I'm a poet."

"Walt Whitman?"

"Naah, I'm Chuck. Just call me Chuck. Bring cash, too, 'cause I don't want no checks."

"Most of your friends carry that much cash around?"

"Wouldn't know, but you ain't my friend, so it don't matter. What time you want to meet? It can wait till tomorrow if you need to go by the bank first."

"Let's do it this evening. How about two hours?" I looked at my watch.

He slurped again. Definitely beer. I heard a couple guys laughing in the background. "Yeah, two hours'll work. Be dark, but you'll be able to see her okay by the lights. You know where you're going, right?"

I traced my finger along the map. "Sure, of course—290 to Antoine, and then north for ten or twelve miles. Which side of the street?"

"Right," he said. "On your right."

"Two hours, then."

I ate and then got a cab to take me to Chuck. I found the Corvette without a problem, parked diagonally in the lot of a closed strip of stores. I got out to pay the driver. Thirty-seven bucks. I made it an even forty. What did I care, wasn't . . . *weren't* my money.

The Corvette was junk, as I'd expected.

Chuck walked over to me from a broken-down bar next door. I'd never seen a bar like it before, a long rectangle with garage doors as close together as possible. All the doors were open, allowing lots of air circulation, I guess, and not-too-pleasing views. The inside of the bar was stools, booths, pool tables, and cowboy hats.

"Hey. I'm Chuck."

"Start it up, please."

Chuck stared at me while he fished in his jeans pockets for the keys.

"I should tell you, it ain't been run in a while. Been sitting here nearly a month."

"But it runs, right?"

He found the keys and bent to the lock. "Huh? Oh, sure. Yeah, it runs. Might not turn over, though. Bat'ry."

He squeaked open the door, climbed in and turned the key, and to my surprise the car started. Chuck looked stunned, but only for a few seconds.

"See? Told you. A good machine."

"You have the title?"

He leaned away and tapped his back pocket. "Right 'chere."

"Okay, here's my deal. I'll give you what you're asking, but I need to use your plates for a few days, until I can get to the DMV."

"Okay," he said. "Hell, I'll live with that."

"Good. Then we got a deal." I counted out the money while Chuck filled in the title.

"I don't have nothing for a receipt," he said, making a show of searching his pockets.

"I've got the title."

"Sure, that's right you do. So, buy you a beer?" He flipped through the stack of bills I'd just given him. "On me."

"Some other time, Chuck. Where should I send your plates? The address on the title?"

"Nah. Just bend 'em up and toss 'em. You sure about the beer? Friends inside. Gonna be a big night."

"Some other time."

I nodded, and he stepped away. Then he hesitated. I watched his hands slip into the back pockets of his jeans, and then he leaned into the window. It was a hot night and I'd already discovered that the air conditioner didn't seem to work, so I was anxious to get going.

"Hey, you know it's been sitting here awhile. Might want to have someone go over it before . . . you know, before you go on any long trips. Which way you heading, anyway?"

"Home. Thanks. I'll get her checked out."

He stepped back and looked the car over again. Gave me that "I'm-sure-gonna-miss-her" look.

"She's a dandy," he said.

"Yeah. See ya."

I took off and drove through Houston, nursing the old car most of the way. I started slow and braked easy, cornered gently and watched for bumps, but the Corvette seemed okay. Close to the motel, I actually stuck my foot in it and the old girl blew a load of white smoke as she hurtled off the line.

It was impossible to guess what might go wrong the next day, but if Baker's death looked like a murder and ended up on the news, I couldn't risk the desk clerk calling the police: "Silver Corvette with a long-haired driver? I had someone in my motel just like that." I parked a half-mile away in the lot of a bar on Route 3. The joint was rocking, so anyone seeing my car before I came to get it in the morning would suspect its owner had drunk too much and rode home with a friend. I grabbed the bag that held everything but my Goodwill clothes and walked back toward the motel.

The next day was Thursday, as good a day as any to kill Randall Baker. Despite what Parrish told me, I doubted that a clean assassination was necessary for graduation from Jaspers. The fact was, since I was the only Jaspers candidate in my class who had never killed a man, they wanted to make sure I could really do it before sending me after someone who really counted. Or maybe they simply wanted to give me a taste of blood because I'd never really hurt anyone badly.

Either way, I didn't care. I was going to kill Baker. I would ignore my doubts and deny my confusion. I was finally going to separate myself from my father's failure and prove that I was better.

Eleven

My legs dangled in the abyss and the rats scurried past me, leaping from one side of the chasm to the other, my body a momentary landing zone, their claws digging into my flesh and puncturing the skin as they chattered to each other in the darkness below.

The voices came again, my dad's deep voice lingering the longest, searching the hardest, coming the closest. The sharp ends of broken bones pushed into my lungs and kept me from answering, but it no longer mattered. I'd given up, and listened with interest dulled by repetition, a curiosity so bland it no longer fit the definition. The noises below killed the voice from above and the pit became a grave.

Something moved to the side of my gaze out the Corvette window. I brought my eyes into focus and looked around until I saw the round, spike-sided lizard scoot away from my car and run to the other side of the dusty road. It darted through the culvert and into the weeds that defined the edge of Baker's property, the place where my nightmare and I were destined to meet and determine which of us was more powerful.

I'd slept badly if at all during the night, waiting until dawn for the day to get rolling. I had stopped for coffee at a Kroger supermarket, a suburban refuge of shiny floors and safe faces that seemed absurdly foreign to the way I felt. I sat by a window in their little eating area and watched the parking lot until after ten, hiding behind a newspaper from the flirty young deli clerk who didn't charge me for my coffee. I wanted some food but not the attention, so I sat there hungry and waited for the thermal strip on the glass beside me to reach eighty or eighty-five, which I figured would put the metal surface of my car at over a hundred.

When I went to bed the night before, I was ready to kill Baker, and I was ready when I woke up in the morning. But as I sat in my car on the shoulder across the road and stared at my battlefield, I didn't feel ready anymore. I guess I was stalling, hoping he would walk over and start a fight with me or come running out with a gun and holler how he was on his way to kill some Jew or Mexican—something to help me justify what I was about to do. I needed that, because the stew of emotions I was feeling made me weaker, not stronger. Emotions that had no part in a Jasper but were there anyway.

I couldn't quit thinking about Elvis and what he said. I didn't want to think about it, but I did anyway. Elvis's confusion between murder and assassination led me to question if killing Baker was any more noble. Would I really be better than my father after I succeeded? What would happen if I didn't feel quite as patriotic as I expected?

I pondered all this knowing it was too late—and yet too early—to find answers to elusive questions. I had a job to do, and the answers waited on the other side of that success. It wasn't any more complicated than that, and I couldn't allow it to be. I twisted around toward my battlefield and took a good look through the side window.

Baker's Used Auto Parts was a small shack of a building on the main road of an old industrial area. The parking lot was gravel and dirt with about a dozen used and dusty cars for sale along the west end. Behind the shack, junked cars were crowded together, casually protected by a rusted chain-link fence with green plastic strips woven through the mesh to hide the metal carnage. A rolling gate to a garage was wide open, which made me doubt the sign that warned of attack dogs.

I pulled in and got out, walked up to the screen door of the shack, and opened it with the inside joint of my index finger, not really worrying about fingerprints but just practicing good habits. I kind of expected to see Rebel battle flags and Nazi paraphernalia hanging around, but I didn't find any. In fact, I was surprised to find a black man shuffling around behind the counter, giving Mr. Randall Baker lots of room as he talked to a customer. He gave me a friendly smile and then glanced at Baker before going back to whatever he was working on.

It was a hot day, in the high eighties and sunny. Dusty fans churned like algae-covered propellers, the brown strands of scunge spinning with centrifugal force. In the back, the black man was soaked with sweat. There wasn't a fan where he was working.

Baker's face was the spitting image of his pictures, even if he was wearing gray overalls instead of a Nazi uniform. His hands were filthy and a smear of grease lined his bottom eyelid. In other respects—height, width, and weight—he was bigger than he appeared in the photo, and that worried me. I hoped the lab guys were right, that any dose of Heat Sync would be lethal.

Not only wasn't there a battle flag or poster of Hitler, there weren't any hooded Klansmen or uniformed white supremacists either. I'd expected them to be sitting around on old car seats, planning lynchings or building crosses or *heil*-ing Hitler, so their absence kind of disappointed me. I was in the enemy's camp. I expected them to show their colors.

There was, however, a little girl, maybe eleven, idly turning a handle that cranked a rebuilt engine block on display, its pistons pumping up and down in a boring rhythm with the girl's slow turning. Her red hair hung wild around her cute freckled face. She stopped turning the crank as I walked in, and almost seemed to know I didn't belong there, that I was trouble she could not stop.

She forced a smile and said "Hi" as though she was trying to set aside her reaction to me and make me feel welcome. It almost made me turn around and leave, but not quite. I still had to prove I could kill and that I had what it took to do a man's job—with or without the poisonous thoughts I felt so powerfully surging through my veins on the plane yesterday.

"Hey," I said back, trying to sound like I hated kids, especially little girls. She lowered her head and went back to turning the crank.

Hubcaps hung all over Baker's place. Doors and quarter panels leaned against the walls and the entire front clip of a late-model Mustang stood in the corner. Everything was ground-in dirty, especially the counter that was nothing more than a thick plank of wood too rough to write on.

The other customer left and I stepped up. Baker held up a finger that signaled me to wait, then walked to the back and spoke roughly to the black man. I waited with my doubts.

There were dozens of rats gnawing off big chunks of flesh as they ripped and tore me to pieces. It wasn't really happening, I told myself, it was only a dream, but the nightmare was far too vivid for me to believe the truth, causing the kind of terror that remained after waking up from a nightmare and turning on the light.

Parrish was enjoying my fascination with what he was saying.

"We've got some new stuff we want to try, Thompson. Test it when you go to Houston to kill Baker."

"New stuff? What kind of new stuff?"

"It's just out of the lab, a heat-sensitive nerve agent that can be handled casually most of the time. Heat Sync, they call it. A similar biotype, serotype, and phage type as trichothecene mycotoxin, Yellow Rain. It combines the ability to penetrate skin with a variable heat setting. Until it reaches that preset temperature, it's inert. The protein that protects the nucleic acid core allows only one target transfer, which helps protect innocent people like EMTs and hospital staff. Cleanup is easy with formaldehyde and potassium permanganate.

"Slick."

"In theory you could carry it on your bare palm and apply it to your target with a firm handshake. I wouldn't try that, but wouldn't be surprised if you did. It will absorb into their skin or hair or clothing and stay there harmlessly for four or five days, even through washings. The trick then is to raise the temperature around your victim and let that act as the catalyst."

He looked for my reaction. "You going to say something funny?"

I was staring at the vial in his hand and hardly heard him. "What?"

"You going to be a smart-ass—"

"So," I said, "I need to find something Baker does, like saunas or sunbathing, maybe even cooking. Hot showers would do it, I bet. Calibrate the toxin to that temperature, apply it by shaking hands or whatever, and be long gone when the nerve agent goes to work."

"That about sums it up, smart guy. We've also got those pyrogens, you know, that raise body temperature. You could use Heat Sync on Baker and then disperse a pyrogen over his group. They'd all get sick and go to the hospital, but only Baker would die. Just a thought."

"Using their own body heat against them. Man, is that clever."

"I thought it would intrigue you."

"Any drawbacks?"

"Makes you cry. Not cry, really, but tear up. It's colorless and odorless, but for some reason, yeah, tears. Nothing much, though."

I stood in the greasy heat and looked across the counter at Randall Baker, glad that I was going to make him cry before he died. I was sure he made some of his victims cry. There would be justice in that, for sure.

"Sorry 'bout the wait," Baker said as the little girl watched me. "Help you?"

"Yeah. Hope so. Just bought me a Corvette. Need some parts to make it cherry."

Baker walked around the counter and went right past me to the door. He opened it and looked at my car.

"That's Chuck's 'Vette."

I was surprised but didn't really see it as a problem. At least nothing I could foresee. "Used to be," I said. "Not no more, though."

He gave me a hard look. "When'd you say you bought it?"

"Last night."

"What you give for it?"

"Eighty-two," I said. "Figure I did all right."

He walked back behind the counter, turning so I couldn't see his face.

"Yeah. You did real good. So, what do you need for her?"

"Well, she runs fair—"

"Chuck kept her up."

"But the spoiler's got a bad crack. Makes the whole thing look bad."

"It'll do that, for sure," Baker said.

"Got one?"

He scratched the whiskers on his chin, maybe a day or two old. "Yeah. Got one that color exactly. Buck fifty and it's yours. Even two hundred and I'll cover the tax and have Leo put it on for you." He jerked his thumb back at Leo, who was already getting some wrenches together.

"I got the one-fifty," I said, "but I want to do the work myself. Mind showing me how it comes off?"

Baker leaned over the counter until his elbows touched it. "Tell you what. Make it one-seventy-five. Hell, I'll still throw in the tax, too. You can sit here where it's cool while Leo goes out there and—"

"I want to learn to work on the car, see? 'Cept I don't want to screw it up, so I'd appreciate you showing me how it comes off. You have Leo get the other spoiler, then I'll be on my way. Easy as that."

"Come on," he snapped as he headed toward the door, "Putting on a spoiler's 'bout as hard as picking your teeth. Leo, get that other spoiler off."

He marched to the back of my car and waited impatiently for me. His little girl followed us, running her little fingers along the car's side as she headed toward the back. Panic I couldn't control flooded through me, a horrible thought of killing that cute little girl by accident. Her hand ran over the door handle, and in another five seconds she would have touched the spoiler and died in a horribly painful way.

"I'd rather she didn't get fingerprints on my finish," I said.

She stopped with her hand still on the car. Baker glanced at my faded car and then looked at me like I must have been joking. He grit his teeth and said, "Hands off the car, Annie."

Annie quit. She looked just a little less bored than before. At least she got some attention. Good attention was better than bad, but bad was better than none. I knew this from my own family, my younger brother who butted heads with Dad. Especially over the rats. The barn was full of them because of the feed for the horses. Brian would leap in with his .410 shotgun and blast away at them. He did it so often that the wood was overshot with holes. Dad made him stop. The rats flourished. I've always been terrified of rats.

Baker hovered around the rear of my car, waiting to show me what I needed to do. I'd checked the car's surface temperature before I left the grocery store and it was well over a hundred degrees. It might have cooled down as I drove, but I'd been sitting across the road from Baker's long enough for it to heat back up. The entire spoiler was coated with Heat Sync 100, and Baker was going to infect himself right about . . .

"Now," he said, grabbing the spoiler and prying open the crack so he could see inside, which was just what I would have done and why I cracked it in the first place. By his sudden, thoughtless act I'd won my first contest and assassinated my first man.

Randall Baker gave the spoiler a vicious shake. "You need to crawl back here from the inside," he said, "loosen the nuts, then pull this spoiler off. Bolt the new one on, simple as that." He wiped his eyes as they started to water, same as mine did when I applied the chemical. "Screws are loose already. When'd you break this? It wasn't cracked before."

"Last night. Some boys at the bar got fighting and landed on my car."

"White boys?"

"One was white. Other was black. He kicked the holy crap out of that white guy."

Baker's small eyes carbonized. "You didn't help the white guy?"

"Hell no," I said with a laugh. "He had it coming. He was picking on the black guy for no reason I could tell."

Baker looked like he wanted to hit me as his dying act, fighting one last time over the stupidity of racism. I stepped away as he conjured up an evil face no kid should ever see. "Annie, get back inside."

"But, Daddy, I want to stay with you. You said—"

"I *said*, get back inside. Move."

Annie turned and shuffled to Baker's grimy office. She didn't lower her head or act afraid. I was willing to bet she expected a beating later, but she didn't seem one bit sorry or bothered by it. I couldn't help but watch Annie walk through the dust, already a little too callused, her natural innocence prodded out of her by an intolerant father. She opened the screen door, stepped in, and turned around. The door slammed an inch or so from her face.

"Go on," Baker said, and I turned to see why he was still giving the girl a hard time, but he was looking at me.

"Go on," he said again. "Get out of here. I'm not selling you nothing, you worthless white son of a bitch. Now get!"

Leo came through the open gate carrying a spoiler over his head.

"Hey, man, what's your problem? I just want that spoiler. What the hell's bugging you?"

His eyes were big and moist and angry. He flared up and reached toward my throat, stretching to his full size even as he had trouble breathing. The veins in his neck and arms pumped up, swelling like cords as his blood boiled.

I took a couple of steps back. Randall Baker's insides must have been bloating by then, but he kept coming, his toes scraping the ground and kicking up dust. Then his eyes washed over with agony or fear or surprise, I wasn't sure which, but maybe all three or some entirely different emotions I could only wonder about. He was still reaching for me as the toxin bubbled in his blood and inflated him with nitrogen. He grabbed his stomach and doubled over, and his mouth stretched open as if he was going to vomit. He staggered, then stopped and stared at me, his mouth open so wide I could see all the swelling inside it. Then he fell face first into the dirt of the parking lot and didn't move. Not a twitch anywhere.

Annie rushed out of the office and ran to her daddy and fell down beside him, crying and sobbing and begging him to wake up. She was barely holding on to her hysteria, shaking Baker as if trying to wake him.

Leo dropped the spoiler and ran to help. He looked down at the body and Annie sprawled across it. Then he dropped to his knees and rolled the body over, listened to his chest, and pushed Annie aside so he could give CPR. Annie screamed through her tears as Leo pumped his hands on Baker's chest and looked at his contorted face and probably decided against giving mouth-to-mouth. She tore at Leo's back, fighting him for his spot, and after twenty seconds or so he gave it to her. She went back to sobbing, stretching her tiny arms across Baker. Leo turned and looked at me with the same look of disbelief I saw on my dad's face when he found my graves of buried rats.

"What'd you do to him?"

"Nothing. He got pissed at me, but I didn't touch him. Maybe a heart attack, or a seizure?"

Leo rubbed his chin, thinking, and took a glance back at Baker. "Yeah, suppose that could be it. I saw you didn't touch him. I was watching."

"I didn't. Swear."

"All right. Mr. Baker's in tight with the local police, so 'less you got lots of time for answering questions, you ought to get moving. Where you live? In case they ask."

"Lariat Lane," I said, although Annie's crying made it hard to remember any of the lies I'd memorized as a cover story. I was stunned, in shock over what I'd done. I was ashamed and desperate to undo it. I thought about antidotes and remedies and critical-care procedures, but like hateful words spoken in haste, my poison had traveled its journey and done its damage. There was no calling it back.

I'd killed my first man and watched him die. I'd rid my country of a racist who loathed anyone who wasn't white and proud and hateful. I'd also killed the father of a freckle-faced little girl whose tears were staining the dirt. I felt the most powerful emotions of my life, but pride wasn't among them.

Leo kneeled down and put a hand on Annie's shoulder.

"He's gone on to the good Lord, sweetie. I'm sorry."

Her wet, dirty face looked at me for another opinion. I faltered in her helpless, begging stare.

"Is . . . is—" I said, and then stopped thinking like a fool. The weight of realization pulled my head down. Of course there wasn't a chance the doctors could save him.

"Go on, now," Leo said. "Get in your car and get out of here."

I moved to the car, sidestepping my way because I couldn't take my eyes off Annie. She didn't even notice me leaving. She hugged her father and then pounded on his chest in her best effort of what Leo had done. She held his dirty face and kissed it, crying and screaming at him to wake up.

I heard Leo say he would call an ambulance and that seemed to make Annie give up. She stretched out in the dirt beside the big corpse, put one arm around him, and cried with her face buried into his neck.

"Daddy," she sobbed, the words almost too soggy to understand. "I love you so much. Don't die, Daddy. Please don't die."

Annie's suffering was all I thought about as I sat in the parking lot and tried to remember which way to go on the main road. I could barely see through the dark haze of her grief, so the road was nearly impossible for me to find.

Concentrate, H.T. Think!

I nailed the accelerator and the rear tires spun, churning at the dirt until they reached hardpack, the dust filling the air and drifting like a burial shroud toward Baker's body. My car slid onto the road and I kept the pedal buried, building speed and passing two cars on the shoulder as I got as far away as I could.

I headed up the Gulf Freeway for a few miles. I was being careless and I knew it, but I couldn't think straight and wasn't worried about Houston cops. Just past an exit I stopped on the side of the road, got out and decontaminated the spoiler with formaldehyde and potassium permanganate, and stuffed the rags into a plastic bag in my suitcase. I wiped all prints from the car, then got back in and stomped on the gas while it was still in park. The torque tilted the car to the right as I roared past redline on the tachometer, winding out until the engine threw a rod and came apart under the hood. I killed the ignition and got out, and walked down the ramp toward the silence and sanctuary of my hotel room.

Twelve

I was forever wedged in the crevice, listening for voices but hearing nothing, alone and scared beyond my own comprehension that the voices had given up on rescuing me.

I woke up terrified, just after three in the morning. I'd gone back to the hotel to pack, but I couldn't leave. I didn't have the strength to force myself out of my sanctuary and back into the world where I'd killed a man.

I crawled out of bed in darkness, each movement a struggle to look past what I'd done to a future beyond it, but Randall Baker surrounded me, his bloating body trying to absorb mine.

I hadn't lived with much shame until then—none that I'd brought upon myself—so I didn't know how to handle the loathing I was feeling. I tried to redefine my shameful act in glory, but that required me to think back and find something good, something that would get me up and moving toward a future I now knew I had to change. But I could only think back on two things: Randall Baker and rats.

I'd been terrified of the rats. After Dad told Brian to stop shooting up the barn, that left the problem to me. Every morning before anyone woke up, I'd pull on coveralls and welder's gloves and go into the barn with a flashlight to search for their filthy bodies, crawling through the bins and tight places, squeezing under the chewed openings where they lived and died. I slithered through their feces, praying they'd eaten enough of the poison I'd left to kill them. If they only had a nibble, they would gnash at me as I dragged them by their hairless tails, the bastards. Then I buried them far out in the field where no one would find out what I'd done. My family would never have understood that my sanity and self-respect demanded that I confront the threat that frightened me so terribly.

Sanity, self-respect, and fear. Funny how those shapeless specters formed so much of my life and how people never seemed to understand. Those very motivators squeezed me into the rutted rat trails and forced me into Parrish's field. Everyone was sure I was the one who got Parrish's pistol, but no one understood the reason, any more than my dad understood my reasons for killing the rats.

"That was impressive but nuts," I remembered Colonel Maddigan saying, his lack of understanding declared by his choice of words.

I sat on my motel bed and tried to remember every word of that conversation. It was a powerful memory and I needed it now, anything to compete with the disgusting memory of killing Baker and the terrifying future it qualified me to do.

"But it has nothing to do with why you've been accelerated through the program. I'm sure you know that."

I did know it, but I just didn't want to believe it. I took a breath of the odor-laden laboratory air and then I laid it out, hoping to sound stronger than I felt.

"I think an enemy has caught you off guard, Colonel, creating a threat that's serious enough to justify assassination. I can do the job because of some special talent or access I have. This threat is so imminent, there isn't time for me to wander through the entire maze of training."

"That's right," said Maddigan. "So who do you think it is?"

I could barely say the words and felt like I was about to use God's name in vain. "It's Devereau, isn't it? President Devereau is the man you want me to kill."

Again, Colonel Maddigan took me straight on. "Yes," he said. His eyes cut toward the floor just enough to show how much he hated what we were talking about doing.

I felt my body square up with Maddigan, his face in front of me, his breath colliding with mine, but I couldn't see him. I was suddenly blind, seeing only the back of John Kennedy's head exploding, Robert Kennedy dying in a restaurant kitchen, Reagan ducking behind Secret Service agents, Ford backing away from Squeaky Fromme, horse-drawn caissons, buglers, flags at half-mast, a nation in mourning, a swearing-in and a shift of power. Then, almost as a sequel, I saw my own trial, the scorn of a nation, my family in shame, and Shannon persecuted for the part she would necessarily but unwittingly play.

"Sorry, Colonel. I'm not going to be part of a coup."

Maddigan seemed even surer now. He tilted his head as though he had just missed Bingo by one number. "Coups happen all the time."

"Not by me. You don't like President Devereau, then vote him out. That's the process. He only has a little more than a year to go anyway. How much damage can he do?"

"Plenty. And he *will* get reelected. He's got a grassroots machine from his years as a television evangelist. You remember Jim Bakker?"

"What? I mean, who?"

"The *Reverend* Jim Bakker. Wife with eyes like black dandelions?"

"Sure, yeah. Bilked his flock out of some money or something."

"Doesn't matter. The point is that Bakker's followers supported him without question, even as he went to trial and then to prison. They stood behind him because they loved the man who had visited their homes every evening for years."

"So?"

"Devereau's political flock is twenty times bigger. He's preached politics to them for years, used their support to bully Washington whenever he could, forcing his way into a bargaining seat on all kinds of issues. Since he's serving less than half of Simons's presidency, he'll be eligible for a second full term. He'll run for reelection and win. He could have nearly ten years to implement his agenda."

"It's up to the voters whether they want his politics or not."

"Stupid."

"Sir?"

"It's stupid to count on the handful of Americans who even bother to vote. They elect their leaders the same way they buy breakfast cereal—falling for slick packaging, clever ads, and the promise of a prize like entitlements or a sympathetic ear to their pet cause."

"That still doesn't make him an enemy."

"He's emasculating the military that keeps us safe. By relying on Spec Op units, the Reserve, Guard, and technology, he's accelerated a trend that's eliminated more troops and equipment than all of our enemies since World War II, selling everyone the flawed logic that the nature of war has permanently changed and large armies are no longer necessary. Give his narrow-minded policies enough time, Thompson, and then ask yourself who will be around to protect your family and nation when we discover he's wrong. You and I will no longer have our jobs. And what's left of the military—aside from those focused entirely on terrorists—will be little more than a paper force, a mothballed fleet, and some ceremonial units."

"I'm sorry, but you've always said we need to see a target as the enemy. I can't do that with Devereau."

"You're prejudiced in his favor because he's your

president. But you took an oath to protect this country from all enemies no matter where they lived, China or Pennsylvania Avenue. I admit it's a lot easier when we can call our enemies names that ridicule their cultural differences, easier still if they're a different color, language, and religion. Those are simple assignments, and this is a hard one. An enemy is an enemy, even if he lives next door."

I needed a minute, but Maddigan wouldn't give it to me.

"If you can't imagine killing a countryman, imagine how combatants felt in the Civil War. They worked or attended college with men who were close friends, some of them even brothers, but when the war started they went home and put on uniforms. They faced each other across a battlefield. It must have been the worst day of their lives, loving the person they were determined to kill, but they did it for their cause, for their vision of the future of this country."

I didn't say anything, and it frustrated him.

"Let me put it another way. If you had the cure for an epidemic raging through some African nation, wouldn't you use it in America if the same disease were spreading here?"

"Yes, I suppose—"

"This is the same thing. You're perfectly willing to go to some other country and kill their leader to keep us safe. You tell me the difference!"

"But, Colonel—"

"You want someone else to do it? Someone who might not care who else gets hurt, someone who might use an indiscriminate poison that kills Shannon too?"

"Are you threatening me with her?"

"I'm telling you Devereau has to die and a Jasper has to do it. If you don't want the job, don't come crying to me later if she gets hurt. I'll try to protect her, but you're the only one who can guarantee her safety. If Cameron had succeeded, she might be dead now. She's been lucky once."

"Cameron was tortured overseas. You said so to Commander Nance in Coronado."

"Cameron was caught and killed doing his graduation assassination. Parrish killed a neighboring king as a decoy, a murderous dictator whose country is still celebrating his death. He had to make this guy look like Cameron's target and draw suspicion away from the United States and Jaspers. Cameron was going after Devereau next, using Shannon as a conduit. I guess she never told you that he was a journalism classmate of hers at Columbia. She promised him an introduction and a brief interview with Devereau."

I thought back on Shannon talking about Cameron, but I didn't remember any love or loss in her voice. I did, however, feel stupid and angry for suffering at Coronado for this man who would have used her and possibly killed her.

"Damn it, Thompson, can't you see there's nothing noble or worthwhile about a doctor who practices without healing, a government that serves itself before its people, or a soldier who follows reason before orders, as you're doing? I'm giving you an order. You will follow it and take comfort in the fact that you are ensuring her survival and protecting the lives of those you love, maybe more than any other person in the history of this nation."

"Is that what they told John Wilkes Booth?"

Maddigan shook off his intensity but kept quiet.

"Let me think about it. Okay? But I won't use Shannon. I won't put her in jeopardy."

"Do it right and it'll look like the pressures of the job killed him. No one will suspect what happened, so no one will suspect Shannon. You'll have to gain access to the president through her, though. Unless you and the president have enough of a friendship without her."

"I know Devereau because I'm Shannon's boyfriend. I doubt he'd agree to a private meeting with me."

"Then Shannon will have to get you close to him, or whatever you choose as a delivery device, but that's all. Do a good job and there'll be no suspicion. Do a bad job and you might be tried and executed. Let's call that The Motivation Factor."

"Right. A little mistake and I get hung as a traitor."

He chuckled, then paused and lowered his head. "We spend most of our time around here doing contingency plans, just-in-case scenarios. Occasionally, one of those plans needs to be implemented, but rarely. Maybe once every five years or so.

"In Devereau's case, we planned to do it during his last year as Simon's vice president. But Simons died and that changed our plans."

"So that's it? You recruited me because I dated a woman who is friends with Devereau?"

"No. You're a damn fine officer and a good trooper. You did well at SEALs and outstanding at Lejeune. You're made from the kind of timber I respect."

"I'm a fir."

"What?"

"Fir. I'm a fir."

"I don't get it."

"It's something I do. I classify people as trees. My dad's an oak. I'm a fir. I'd say you're a maple, maybe walnut."

"Is that good?"

"Very good. Hard and straight and valued for lots of things."

"Then thanks. So you're a fir. Your dad's an oak?"

"A gray oak." I forced a little laugh.

"I can see that."

"That's right, you know my father."

"Yes, I do."

"He's the reason you found me in Coronado?"

"As a matter of fact, he is. He followed your career as best he could and called me after you got to SEALs. He said I should take a look at you if I needed a good man who wouldn't let me down."

"My dad knows about Jaspers?"

"No. But he figured we'd work well together."

"Where did you guys get to know each other?"

"It's a national secret, okay? Highest priority."

"What isn't these days?"

"In the late nineties, I was sent to Southeast Asia with orders to kill the remaining American POWs, twenty-three years after that war ended. They were a potential embarrassment our country couldn't face. At the last minute, the president negotiated a secret release and I brought them back, working with a select group of marshals who processed the POWs into the Witness Protection Program. That's where I met your dad."

"My dad worked with you to *hide* prisoners of war? They should have been heroes."

"No question. But it was part of the deal for their release, and better than killing them. We do a shameful, unpleasant job here, sometimes reluctantly. I know how you're feeling about Devereau because I didn't want to kill those POWs."

"But you'd have done it?"

"I would have, yes. I got lucky in the end, but it made your father sick. That's why he quit his job."

"He quit because he let a criminal kill his partner."

"That's part of the reason. He was devastated over losing his partner, but I doubt he would have quit over it, especially when it was Matt's fault."

"What do you mean?"

"Matt got careless and it cost him his life. Almost cost your dad's, too. Your father did the same things I would have done. I wouldn't have fired through that crowd, trying to thread a round through all those heads, so that wasn't why he quit. But this POW secret had him royally pissed at Washington. Of course, he couldn't tell you about it, yet he knew you'd demand an answer. He knew how proud you were that he was a marshal."

"How . . . how could that happen? The POWs, I mean."

"Because people don't stand up and do the right thing anymore. They put their careers and lives ahead of their country, just like you're trying to do right now."

"You really think killing Devereau is necessary, and possible?"

"If we were still strong militarily, we'd find a way to handle the shift toward terrorism. But we're forty percent smaller than we were ten years ago yet twenty-six percent busier, trapped in a death spiral of downsizing as if we never expect another country to declare war against us. We've had a twenty-year procurement holiday, so even if it changed today, right this second, we're years away from any next-generation weapons, other than a new fighter plane and a nuclear bunker-buster.

"But it won't change today, not with Devereau in control, so our situation is nothing short of desperate. We're already abandoning our commitments around the world as we re-deploy troops against Muslim extremists. Maybe we no longer needed troops in places like Germany, but that sure assumes a lot of stability that just isn't there. Hell, Putin has already taken over mass communications and convinced his people to trade freedom for safety. They're giving up rights so quickly, they'll revert back to communism before you even make commander. Now take a second to think about the abuses of the Patriot Act in this country and see if that doesn't sound familiar—our Constitutional rights, the cornerstones of our great nation, traded away for a better sense of safety."

"Is it really possible to kill Devereau?"

"If you can get the weapon in, it'll be easy."

"We're talking about the president, a man protected by Secret Service agents ready to take a bullet for him."

"But you and I both know Devereau resists their

247

protection in the inner sanctums of the White House. It annoys the hell out of him, the same way you'd feel about strangers in your home. In these days of microscopic weapons, by far the easiest place to assassinate a president is in the White House. If you can get in."

I thought all this through as I would any assignment, trying to tiptoe across a dizzying legal chasm.

I wanted to say I could do the job, basing my decision on the fact that Colonel Maddigan was a noble soldier and my trust in his orders. I tried to make President Devereau my enemy because he might very well be my country's enemy. I tried to give him no quarter or escape, and no options. I wanted the desire to kill him.

But I knew I couldn't do it.

"I'm sorry."

Maddigan's lips locked together, holding back whatever he really wanted to say and settling for these few last words: "Think about it. Remember, your girlfriend's already been lucky once."

That day, Maddigan had stood like a massive rock, frustrated and angry with me the same way Randall Baker acted in his parking lot as he seethed about the black guy beating a white guy just before my toxin killed him. For a few minutes as I sat on my bed, I was stuck with a vision of Jaspers as just another hate group, not unlike Randall Baker's, killing people with whom they disagreed. It was an ugly vision I only managed to blank out by determining never to join or stay in any group that hated.

I shuffled around the motel room like the oldest of

men, bending awkwardly and rising unsteadily. I eased into the shower and turned on the hot water and sat in the tub as water sprinkled down through the faulty showerhead. I didn't move for a long time, my eyes closed, my skin waking to the pattering massage. I crawled out of the shower a half hour later.

The mirror was steamed over, so I clipped my beard by feel, knowing my face well enough to do the job. Ten minutes later, the steam was gone and I lathered up, shaving my face to an innocent smoothness.

By eight-thirty, I started to think that maybe I could hide my sin of murder from the world. I wanted to make the effort, and so I started with what I most wanted to do since killing Baker yesterday.

"Hello, this is Shannon," said the answering machine. "Leave a message and I'll call you back. Thanks."

"Hi, it's me."

It seemed impossible to find any words that were worth a damn. I wanted to hang up but refused to quit on something so important.

"Look, Shannon, I really owe you an apology for letting my work get ahead of you. I'm out of town right now but will be heading home soon. I'd like to see you and hope you'll let me come over."

I left the motel without checking out, and walked to a gas station on the corner and called a cab that arrived in a few minutes. I tossed my bag onto the seat and slammed the door.

The driver was a fat man about forty-five years old, his pear-shaped body having evolved over time to give him support and cushioning where he needed it most. Amazing. Evolution. As I got in I noticed a large, stainless-steel revolver in a break-front holster on his belt.

"Where to?"

"The airport."

"Sure."

We rode in silence for several miles through downtown Houston. I was trying to think about home and Shannon, but the driver's gun was like Lucifer's sentry, preventing me from going to any place peaceful.

"What's with the gun?"

He glanced at me in his mirror, then smiled.

"Self-defense, buddy. I'm in a high-risk occupation and need to protect myself."

"From other people with guns, I guess."

"Them, sure. Anybody who gives me trouble."

I should have shut up and let it go. I know I should have, but I didn't really know who I was anymore, with no recollection of what I'd been and no idea of what I might become. So I went with my heart and trusted those feelings.

"You're kidding, right?"

He glanced over his shoulder and looked to see what my hands were doing, which was nothing. "Ain't kidding about none of that."

"So anybody gives you trouble, you pull your gun?"

He smiled. The idea obviously made him happy. "You're damn right."

"Even if they don't have a gun?"

"If they're going to give me trouble, friend, they better have a gun."

"So they might have a gun, and that means you've got to have a gun. I guess one day we'll all have to be armed, huh? Crazy."

He lifted off the seat and cranked his hefty chest around. "Hey, I ain't letting some no-good so-and-so get the drop on me." He went back to driving.

I couldn't seem to stop. I wanted to, I think, but I couldn't because his intolerance and his cavalier willingness to kill reminded me too much of Randall Baker, and maybe the person I was when I killed him. I didn't really have much of a chance to talk to Baker, so I hoped I'd find an answer by talking to this guy. I doubted it, but I was desperate.

"So, basically, you're afraid."

"Huh?"

"You're a coward." I tried to say it with as little offense as possible.

"What?" He jerked around so violently that he changed lanes as other drivers honked.

"I take care of myself, mister. I ain't no coward!"

"That's what you think, but you're living in fear that differences between you and someone else might get you hurt if you don't hurt them first. If that's not a coward, what is?"

"I got a right to defend myself."

"You couldn't."

"The hell I—"

"I'm telling you that you couldn't protect yourself. You just think you can, by sauntering around with a lethal weapon that makes everyone else think they should have a gun, too."

He pulled over to the curb and skidded to a stop. "Get out of my cab!"

251

I had no idea why I was arguing with him. I'd never picked a fight and I wasn't really trying to start one, but I couldn't seem to stop.

"See, that's just what I mean. If you really think I'm a threat to you, there's not a damned thing you can do to stop me. Shoot me and you'll go to prison. Fight me with your fists and I'll win. So go ahead and make your play. Let's see if you can make me get out. Come on, you've got a gun on your hip that gives you so much power. Make me get out of your cab, fat man. Do it."

He climbed out and opened my door, leaned in with his hand on the butt of his revolver. "Get . . . out!"

I slapped his face with the back of my hand. "No."

He didn't move. He just stood there stunned, half in and half out of the car.

"What's the matter? You've got a big bad gun. Well, use it. Isn't that why you carry it? Go ahead. Pull it out and stick it in my face and threaten me with it. See what happens." I rose in my seat. "Do it!"

His hand twitched on the gun butt. My hands fidgeted in the battleground between us.

"I want you out."

"Tough. I want you unarmed, so I guess we'll both be disappointed." I slapped him again, and this made his gun hand move a little, drawing the weapon an inch or so out of the holster.

"Draw it, coward. Big-man-with-a-gun coward. Draw it! Prove something, for God's sake. You're not going to take this crap from me, are you? You said you wouldn't let someone give you trouble, but isn't this trouble?" I moved a little more toward his big face. "Well, isn't it?"

I vibrated my hand, ready to slap him again. He looked at my face, and I knew what he saw. I'd totally lost it, gone way beyond any form of normal behavior. My emotions were right on the surface, raw and ready to fight this heavyweight who shook with outraged energy. He wanted to pull his gun and stick it between us, and I was suddenly amazed at how large a man can hide behind such a small weapon.

Suddenly, the familiar voices came back for me, their Pentecostal music descending quickly and forcefully, finally freeing me from the grasp of the chasm. The rats stopped chewing and scurried away in fear as a clean breeze caressed my face and calmed me.

"I'll tell you what, mister," I said in a strained attempt at civility, trying to do a little evolving myself. "Get on your radio and find another cab for me, a driver who isn't armed. A nice guy who might want to talk about art or literature or something. You have any drivers like that?"

He looked at me like I'd asked him to conjure up a stagecoach, but even in his anger he saw the solution, the escape for us both.

"Don't know. Yeah, probably. I guess." He spoke in a voice of stalemate, then hauled his big chest out of the backseat and stood up, apparently bewildered. He moved his hand away from his gun and pulled his shirttail out to conceal it.

"Let me check."

I knew I wasn't going to the airport with this guy, so I got out with my bag while he slid into his seat and spoke on the radio. When I slammed my door, he glanced back and then drove away.

I was thankful he was gone, glad to have some time to myself. I knew where the airport was because planes were taking off and landing in the distance, so I headed in that direction, not in any hurry or bothered by the heat. My boots felt good and broken in. It was only Friday and no one was expecting me for another week. "As long as it takes to get back," Parrish had said.

The airlines could get me to D.C. in a matter of hours. I had no idea how long it would really take me to get back to who I was, but at least I was on my way, understanding that my own deadly actions were no better than Baker's—intolerant and dangerous because he wasn't like me and didn't think the way I did. Randall Baker was different from me in exactly the same way that blacks and Jews were different from him, and I killed Baker for that difference, the same way he killed them.

I breathed deep and took my first step through Baker's ghost. He was so solidly alive in front of me that I flinched and closed my eyes as I passed through him.

"Sorry," I murmured, as I stood in his soul for a moment.

He stuck to me like a web, stretching and tingling as I moved. He kept stretching and I kept walking, the tension straining my back. I walked a mile, maybe more, but he kept sticking to me, sapping energy from my step and life from my heart. I dragged him all the way to the airport, through districts of commercialized nudity, neighborhoods built around churches, and unsigned landscapes of humanity's confusion. Baker was with me the whole time.

A flight through Atlanta to Washington was scheduled to leave in two hours. I bought my ticket, stubbornly refusing to think about buying one for Baker. I went to the restroom to change into some Goodwill clothes that were still clean, and washed under my arms and around my neck. Then I went in search of a barber.

"Who cuts your hair?" I asked the first barber, who wore his hair something like I did before I grew it long.

He pointed with his scissors. "He does," aiming at the guy reading *People* in the next chair, who looked at me.

"Cut mine like his, okay?"

The seated barber tilted his head to see the long hair over my ears and collar. Then he looked at the other barber. "He's got a narrower face, mister. You'd look better with less on the sides."

"Fine. Anything in that general style is fine."

I sat down and closed my eyes. I didn't open them until he was done, and even then I didn't look at the mirror. I paid and walked out, plopped down in a chair at the gate area and waited, trying to map the road that brought me here so I could trace it back to wherever I took the wrong turn.

When I was growing up, my dad used to ask if I was doing what I wanted or what was wanted from me. I realized that I'd been confused by the Jaspers program, thinking it was one of those instances where I was doing both. But it was suddenly clear that in being a Jasper I could do neither.

The simple fact was I wasn't a killer. I finally knew that. I guessed I'd always suspected it but didn't want to be honest about it, afraid I'd disappoint myself and discover I had inherited a reluctance to kill from my father, some kind of genetic deficiency that made me an unsuitable warrior.

I felt some relief that my country does have soldiers who can kill, because there are clearly times when someone needs to do it, to stand up for freedom against our enemies. I just wasn't one of them. I was missing some essential element or had too many contradictory ones.

Or maybe no one aside from nutcases killed easily the first time. Maybe it wrenched everyone's guts. Colonel Maddigan said something like that in his welcoming speech the first day at Fort Belvoir.

"Congratulations, men," he said on that day a lifetime ago. "From this moment on, everything you hear, do, or learn is secret.

"On December 4, 1981, President Ronald Reagan signed Executive Order 50, Section 401, outlawing assassinations of political leaders. This action, while politically expedient, seriously limited America's options against our enemies. It permitted Pol Pot to continue a reign of terror that exterminated twenty million people and allowed General Augusto Pinochet to commit his crimes against humanity. It forced us to stand by while Slobodan Milošević murdered thousands in his attempt at ethnic cleansing, and allowed Kim Jong-il to create a genuine nuclear threat to the United States.

"This personal-warfare school was conceived as a response to significant threats that will arise in the future, while those threats are still far out on the horizon and imperceptible to anyone else. If we anticipate an upcoming challenge, we will eliminate it long before it threatens us. We no longer have the manpower, matériel, or mind-set to wage full-scale war, so we will prevent war whenever possible by eliminating the leaders who might threaten us. Our job is to be like lightning, gentlemen, striking with ruthlessness and surprise."

Maddigan stopped and waited for questions. I was too spellbound back then to ask one.

"The name I gave this place is a euphemism implying personal warfare, one-on-one combat. It's not entirely inaccurate, but what are we really talking about? Anyone?"

I said the word slow, clear, and loud. "Assassination."

Elvis turned and looked at me. The others did too, but I didn't look at them. I just stared at Colonel Maddigan, at the strong, strained face of my very own future.

Maddigan nodded slowly. He didn't smile or seem proud, and in that instant I realized he did the job for one reason only: because it needed to be done.

"That's right, we assassinate people. You'll have a problem with it, I guarantee you. And you should. If I weren't certain the concept would make you sick, you would not be here."

He came out from behind his podium and sat on the edge of a desk. "I've killed my share of men in combat where it was life or death, and I felt pretty good about living even if the other guy died. But assassinations are different. You're killing a man or a woman who isn't trying to kill you. They can seem like innocent people, and it gets confusing because we swore to protect innocent people. How many of you have already killed someone?"

I was the only one who didn't raise his hand.

"You men already know that killing someone takes his life but puts his soul on your back for the rest of your life. It's worse if you don't perceive them as enemies. So that's your first lesson: See your target in a hostile, deadly light. Maybe he's not threatening you today, but five years from now he might kill your brothers-in-arms or take over your country. Think of Jaspers as a far-flung, isolated, almost forgotten outpost that engages threats before anyone else is even aware of them.

"Ours is a murky world, and you'll need to trust me and those around you to keep your heads on straight. We're not killers, we're assassins. If you start enjoying this work, I'll want you to leave. If you ever look forward to killing a person, I'll want you to leave. If you ever kill anyone not personally approved by me or one of my successors, you'll be out. Or worse.

"Gentlemen, you are here to learn how to sacrifice the few to save the many, to kill a single enemy before it's necessary for both sides to fight a bloody war neither nation wants. Work hard. Do well."

Work hard, he said, and I did. I studied my craft until I'd perfected new field-expedient procedures, learning to kill with a millionth of a gram instead of a bullet or missile.

Maybe with time I could have become comfortable with the job and learned to deal with the ghostly souls and gloaming shadows who would share my life because I'd taken theirs. But it no longer mattered. I had no intention of finding out if I could kill again. I wanted nothing more to do with Jaspers. It was an all-volunteer force, and I was going to quit.

They called my flight and I boarded, wondering if Randall Baker had ever been to Washington before.

BOOK THREE

BOOK THREE

Thirteen

I went straight to Fort Belvoir from the airport. What little good that remained in me desperately craved time with Shannon, but Jasperville called like a seductive, demanding mistress who had to be told the relationship was over. Otherwise, my life with Shannon would always be threatened by a wicked lover who could show up at her door and expose me for what I was capable of doing or, even worse, what I'd done to Baker in Houston.

I cleared security and entered the converted barracks where I'd learned how to kill efficiently. The building was quiet except for a class in session at the far end of the hall. I could barely hear the instructor and wandered toward his voice, not sure why. Looking, I guess, for Parrish.

The instructor was a guy named McCauley, a former field agent on loan from the Army Medical Research Institute of Infectious Diseases at Fort Detrick, Maryland. He was a short, frail-looking guy who was mostly bald and had pale, thin skin. I stood outside in the hallway and leaned against the wall, staring into the room. McCauley had a new class of five Jaspers, fresh faces brought up from Lejeune, each one recruited for some special skill or access and assigned to an unsuspecting person who had found their way onto Jaspers' list of potential targets. I was surprised to see Big Mouth, the guy I fought my first day in North Carolina, leaning against the back wall of the classroom watching his recruits. At least I finally knew he was an instructor at Lejeune, that the fight he started with me was a test after all.

I looked at his men and wondered if they knew whether or not they were killers. Then I had no choice but to consider that one of them might have been recruited to kill me if I refused to kill Devereau. I looked at each candidate for a sign, something familiar, for some reason I might let them get close enough to kill me once I left this place.

"Man, those were the days," McCauley said, giving his canned speech about the history of chemical assassinations. He was telling his favorite story about Vladimir Kostov and Georgi Markov, and the Bulgarian secret police using umbrellas to fire 1.7-millimeter metallic Whiffle balls, filled with ricin and sealed with wax that melted at body temperature.

McCauley noticed me and headed casually toward the doorway, talking as he navigated the desks. He was goofy and geeky, but at one time he'd been a proficient killer. For all I knew, he still was.

"Chemical warfare has evolved over the centuries, from catapulting plague-infected cadavers over fortress walls to sending Native Americans smallpox-infected blankets during the French and Indian Wars. Germany once infected the livestock of neutral trading partners, who later shipped the contaminated food to Allied troops. Japan had fleas feed on plague-infected rats and then air-dropped them over Chinese cities.

"In 1942, the game got more elaborate. America filled five thousand bombs with *B. anthracis* spores. We actually *used* a culture of plague bacilli in the Korean War. By 1954, we were fermenting, concentrating, storing, and weaponizing large-scale quantities of microorganisms in a new facility at Pine Bluff, Arkansas.

"By the late 1960s the U.S. military had a huge arsenal of bacterial pathogens, toxins, and fungal plant pathogens. The CIA, meanwhile, had developed its own stockpile of weapons for *covert* use. Their arsenal included cobra venom and saxitoxin. So there we were, ready to attack our enemies with Rift Valley fever, anthrax, encephalitis, typhus, brucellosis, Q fever, tularemia, and snake venom. Everybody was ready to fight wars with bugs."

I wanted to leave, to go to my room and pack. I didn't want to relearn anything about poisons or pathogens. But this first-day lecture was so simple and sanitary compared to what would follow that I felt slightly better listening to McCauley, going with him to a day of purer innocence.

"Massive biological weapons were eventually outlawed, even though eighteen nations never signed the 1993 convention that banned them—one of our reasons for invading Iraq, the nonexistent WMDs aside. But hell, we violated it, too, by making a first-strike use of chemical weapons in Bush 41's Gulf War.

"So why did most countries sign the ban? For this

simple reason: to keep out small, annoying little countries from the arms race, it needed to be prohibitively expensive, or . . . BANG!"

The new students jumped the same way I did.

"Nuclear. The big bang. Nuclear weapons cost billions, whereas biological weapons are cheap. If they weren't outlawed, too many countries could play the same game of dominance as the superpowers and wage a war of fear—the very war we're fighting today."

Once his stories got current, I had to leave. It was one thing to hear history, but I knew that soon he'd be mentioning things I was trained to do, the chemicals I'd learned to use proficiently but didn't want to ever again think about.

"Hello, Thompson," he said, as I took a step away. "Welcome back."

At the sound of my name, men shifted in their desks so they could get a look at me. They whispered to one another, then one of them stood and walked past McCauley, right up to me. Every group had a leader, it seemed, and I could tell this man led this group.

"You're the guy," he said.

He looked so innocent, so sparkling clean and thrilled to be a Jasper. I knew he'd endured pain and torture to get this far, but still, my God, he looked like a baby.

"What?"

"You're the guy who got the Luger from Parrish's field. Man, you're a legend."

I felt like an old man staring at a photo of when I was young and strong. He was almost twitching with excitement, ready with the same round of questions my own classmates asked me over and over. He looked back into the room to make sure everyone saw he was talking to me.

"I'm not that guy," I said, and then watched the disappointment cross his face. "Not anymore."

I walked away. As I moved down the hall he laughed at me with spite and embarrassment, that odd pairing of emotions that attacked and defended at the same time. "Sorry, bub," he shouted. "Thought you *were* somebody."

I went upstairs to my room and packed my stuff, even my notebooks of techniques and my idle doodlings about killing Devereau. I piled it by my door, then went to the cafeteria to wait for Parrish.

I was a little shocked, but not badly, to see two pictures of Randall Baker taped to the wall like semester grades. One showed him in his Nazi uniform, the same photo Maddigan gave me along with my assignment to kill him. The other showed him on a stainless-steel tray, his face still morbidly contorted and his chest hollowed out from the autopsy that removed his organs.

I walked over and looked at the coroner's photo, then at the ghost that leaned against me.

"You've looked better," I said.

Baker didn't answer.

I got a cup of coffee, sat down, and was still staring at the photos when the door opened and Parrish walked in with the rest of my class. Elvis brought up the rear. They had all changed over the few days I was gone. Three of them looked bigger, stronger, and more confident than I remembered. When I left I thought I carried those tough-guy banners with me,

but there was no way I could compete with the toughness I saw in them. What happened to make them so
powerful?

Elvis, looked . . . well, normal. More likable than
before I left and much more human. I caught his attention and nodded, but he didn't respond. He just
followed the group into the cafeteria and selected an
apple from the fruit tray.

They all sat together and acted as if I wasn't there
or wasn't welcome, I couldn't tell which. I walked to
their table and stood behind Parrish, looking down at
the birthmark on his scalp.

"Hello, Thompson," Parrish said, and then nudged
the guy next to him and laughed. He turned around
and looked up at me. "Nice haircut. Shave, too. How
was your trip?"

I stiffened up and drew a breath. I had forgotten
the smell of this place, the pharmacological cocktail
of odors that now nauseated me.

"Can I talk to you, Parrish? In private?"

"Why? We keeping secrets these days?"

I was in a room full of killers and preferred to think
I wasn't one, so I had a pretty good idea of where I
stood. But I hadn't yet got myself back to being a nice
guy, either, so it was impossible for me to predict
what I might do.

"I just want to talk to you in private. What's your
problem?"

He got serious and leaned back. He moved his leg
around to the side of his chair so he could shift
around and see me better. He seemed ready to jump.

"I don't have a problem." He glanced innocently

around the table. "Any of you guys have a problem?"

Bill and Dan and Felipe looked at me while Elvis studied the apple he was polishing on his sleeve. Parrish stood. They all did the same and gathered around me.

"Maybe we do have a problem, Thompson," Parrish said, and then everyone but Elvis started laughing as I realized I was the butt of their joke.

Parrish pushed my shoulder and looked like he just might hug me. "What the hell are you doing back so soon? We were indirectly routed copies of Baker's photos from the Houston PD after their rush-job autopsy. We didn't expect to see you for another week or so. Figured you'd use some excuse about covering your tracks in order to go to Mexico or the beach. Who knows?"

"I'd have gone to Vegas," said Felipe.

Dan and Bill stared at him. "You suck at gambling."

"No, man, for the girls. The girls!"

"That's probably what I'd have done, too," said Parrish. "I was surprised when security said you were on the grounds. Hell, we were planning a party. You've cheated us out of a good celebration drunk."

They were shaking my hand, patting my back, and yucking it up. Elvis reached through the crowd and quietly congratulated me, then sat back on the table and ate the apple.

"Well, how'd it go?" Parrish asked.

They stared as though I'd just come from a hot date with a movie star. I fidgeted, catching a glimpse of Randall Baker as I looked around. I didn't want to talk about the poor bastard and trivialize what I'd done for the amusement of these men. I was trying not to think about it at all.

Then I wondered if it might help me in some way to talk about it. Maybe getting it out into the open would help me heal from it. Shrinks always want their patients to talk about their problems. If I talked about killing Baker, maybe some psychological force would go to work and perform a miracle.

"It was strange."

"Strange, huh? How'd the new toxin work?"

"Good. Yeah, it worked really well. There's some kind of eye irritant in it, like you said, but it dropped him in fifteen seconds. He was dead when he hit the ground, at least as far as I could tell."

"You were there?"

"Standing right in front of him. I had to step back so he didn't hit me on the way down."

The other Jaspers laughed. Dan went stiff and fell into Felipe and Bill, who caught him just before he hit the table.

Parrish didn't laugh, though. He snapped his head to the side and scrutinized me.

"You were there?"

"Yes. I was there."

"That wasn't the plan."

"I know."

He turned around but didn't stop, and ended up making two about-faces.

"I didn't send you there to kill him in front of everyone. Any idiot could have done that, walked up to him with a gun and gone *bang*." He shot me in the head with his finger. "You're a Jasper, Thompson. We trained you to be an elite killer who doesn't leave evidence or hang around to watch the victim die. Never, ever are you to take the chance of being caught!"

"I didn't trust the toxin. I wanted to make sure—"

"You what?" His voice made the other Jaspers sober up. "You didn't trust the toxin? You some kind of quality-control guy now? Listen, if we give you a toxin or pathogen or virus or anything, you can trust it'll work."

"Yeah? Well, my mistake, then. What are you going to do, kill me?"

He looked like he considered this for a second before calming down.

"Always the smart-ass, aren't you?"

"No. But getting smarter. Let's go. We need to talk. Where's Maddigan?"

"The Pentagon. Why?"

"I need to talk to him, too."

I headed for the door, and Parrish followed. The room was mortuary-quiet as the other Jaspers watched us leave. Elvis sat on the table, taking it all in. As I opened the door, he snapped off a noisy bite of apple.

Parrish and I walked down the hall, up the steps, and into his office. I went in first and closed the door after us.

"I want out."

"What?"

"Out, I want out. Jaspers is volunteer. I just unvolunteered. What do I have to sign, an oath of nondisclosure or something?"

"You've already signed that."

"Fine. Then all I need are some new orders. Will you call my detailer?"

Parrish eased to his desk, moving as if I had a gun

aimed at him. All he needed to do in order to complete the picture was hold up his hands.

"Tell me what's wrong."

"You were right, okay? Your first reaction to me—that I didn't fit in—was right."

"You proved me wrong."

"I proved nothing! All I did was show that I could learn this stuff, the same way I could learn how to perform surgery, maybe. Whatever. It doesn't mean I should go out and do it. Understand?"

"No, I don't. You did a good job. Sure, it would have been better if you left before Baker died, but I was a little hard on you about that, considering it was your first time and all. I'm sorry, okay?"

"Not okay. Don't you get it? I don't care about you or those guys in the cafeteria. I don't belong here and I know it. How do I get out of here?"

I could see he was worried. He rubbed his face, maybe wondering how he was going to explain this to the colonel. But I'd said the hard words and didn't want to give up the momentum. "What is it? Are you thinking this will make you look bad? Just tell Maddigan the selection criteria were accurate, that you were right and he was wrong. I've got no business being here."

"That's not what I'm worried about."

"Then what? *Devereau?*"

He moved his hand from his face and leaned back against his desk. "I guess. Hell, I was pretty sure you'd feel differently after killing Baker. I thought you'd see that killing's not so hard a thing to do."

"Maybe not on a field of battle with bullets flying,

but the way I killed Baker? I could never do that again."

"Don't go soft on me. Jeez, boy, our whole country has gone soft and we can't afford to lose you. This has become a nation of lazy people who want everything to be free and easy—including national security— even if things *aren't* free and easy. I know how you feel. I still remember the first man I killed. The situation was different because it was open combat, but I struggled with it. You know, kind of wondered what right I had, what business I had being there in the first place. Lots of guys have those thoughts. But in the end they realize they killed an enemy, simple as that. Maybe I did a bad job of drilling that into you. It's combat, pure and simple. Only on a very small stage."

"It's *not* combat, and shame on you for pretending it is. It's murder. You sanitize it with a nice title like 'personal warfare,' but it is murder."

Parrish made a slow lap around his office. As he passed his locker, he let fly with a side kick that crushed the metal door, the sound hurting my ears like too-close thunder.

"Okay, maybe it is murder, like you say. So what? Our military is in crisis, and Devereau's pursuit of terrorists while disregarding other threats will escalate that crisis to the point where we won't be able to fight off the friggin' Boy Scouts. And that's exactly when China will attack Taiwan."

"What are you talking about now?"

"That's really why Devereau is a threat, Thompson. Maddigan didn't want to tell you unless it was necessary, but hell, everyone knows that China is going to take Taiwan back by force within the next three or four years. They've already put six hundred ballistic missiles across the Taiwan Straits. They're constantly rehearsing their air, sea, and ground assault on Dongshan Island, which is nearly identical to Taiwan in terrain and weather. Devereau has sworn to side with Taiwan, but guess what, we'll be too weak. So we'll go to their aid in a fool's move because of a treaty and a historical precedent of Truman and Clinton defending them from previous acts of Chinese aggression."

"If we said we'd defend them, then we should. No way does that make Devereau my enemy."

"We should go fight China, huh? Did you even stop to question if it's really our fight, something we can win—or if it's something that could cost us more than we're willing to pay? Haven't you learned anything from Iraq? We can no longer afford to police the world, Thompson, and with China heading toward our spot at the top of the pinnacle we sure as hell can't afford to police them."

"So now we're afraid of China beating us?"

"Oh, no, we're not afraid, and we don't have to be. They won't ever beat us, because we'll throw everything we've got left at them, and they'll do the same to us. Once both sides have ruined their countries and economies by spending and bleeding too much, once they've fired all their bullets and artillery rounds and sent all available men to slaughter, there will only be one remaining choice. Both leaders will have their fingers on nuclear buttons, and once the desperate reality of the situation sets in and the first missile leaves a silo, the world as we know it will end, poof. And for what? Long term, Thompson, will it really have been in our best interest to destroy our world and ourselves defending a tiny island ally?"

I didn't answer. I didn't know what to say.

"I wish Taiwan the best, I really do, but at the end of the day *this* is the country I want to survive. But Devereau's already promised to defend them at all costs, and he's got such a bullshit sense of keeping his word—as long as it's not his kids who are dying—he'll never back down. At that point it will be too late to kill him, to *murder* him to make him stop. The missiles will have already flown, Thompson, and it will be your fault the country is lost. You gonna let that happen?"

He might have been right. In fact, I believed he was right. But it was no longer my job.

"Thompson, you have to do it! We're all depending on you. If you don't . . . man, I don't want to see you jammed. Don't become the enemy. Don't get across the battlefield from me."

I stood there looking at Parrish, who was the razor-wire fence imprisoning me there at Jasperville. I was pretty sure I could leave, but there would certainly be a cost. I'd already been warned that Shannon might be the one to pay it.

Would Parrish kill her just for vengeance? I didn't think so, and had even greater doubts about Colonel Maddigan going along with anything so vicious. But I could easily imagine lots of scenarios where Shannon could be collateral damage. She'd already been targeted twice for access to the president.

"Okay," I said, while Parrish looked at me with the same menace as the snake in the field of ants and mines and lasers. "I'll do it."

"Never mind."

"What?"

"This is too important to trust to someone lacking conviction. You just want to keep Shannon alive and don't care squat about our country. I'll do it myself. I'll infect the photos Brigitte took for me the night after The County Line escapade. They turned out pretty nice, some great shots of your bare ass in bed. Shannon will take one look and go crying to *Uncle* Devereau. He'll look them over and touch some Heat Sync that she left behind and that'll be that. You idiot, you don't think I make contingency plans?"

I stood there speechless while the son of a bitch walked out the door and toward the lab. I was trying to think faster than my options were closing. I heard him punch in the code to the lab door. It opened and closed.

I rushed to the lab, where Parrish was already mixing up something I hadn't seen before. He grinned when I entered, and put everything down when he heard me approaching. I guess he knew I'd grab him, which is exactly what I did.

"Doesn't matter what motivates me."

He looked hard at me until I lowered my hands, and then in quiet contrast to the raging of my emotions he said, "I say it does matter."

"I heard you killed a king in Africa after Cameron was captured. Why? Were you *motivated* to kill him?"

"It was a necessary and pragmatic move to protect

Jaspers, essential to defending something I valued. I . . . okay, I get your point, smart guy."

"That's right. I'm motivated to protect something important to me, same as you did over there. And love is a stronger motive than patriotism, I'll tell you that."

"Wouldn't know."

"But I want to do it now, right away, so Shannon and I can get on with our lives."

"You're really leaving Jaspers after you do it?"

"Yes."

"We'll see." He smiled. "There's a seductive satisfaction in controlling the future. It gets kind of addictive."

"It won't for me."

I said it, but I didn't really believe it, mostly because I was already planning to control the future in ways Parrish couldn't imagine.

I had to admit he was right. It was seductive.

Fourteen

"How do you want to do it, Thompson?"

I wanted to stall, but Parrish already had doubts that I was serious. He eyeballed me to see if I understood it's either showtime or go time.

"Remember when we studied the way folks mailed germs to newspapers and politicians after 9/11? How they'd botched the job so badly?"

"They were too indiscriminate," he said. "And they used viruses ill-designed for the purpose."

"After studying those cases, I thought up new uses for stronger pathogens and surer ways of hitting my target."

"Good."

"I need something important, though. Something President Devereau will want to read personally. Either that or—"

Parrish's face lit up like I'd finally asked the right question. He grabbed me by the arm. "Got just the thing. Come on."

He led me to a security vault I had never seen

opened. Parrish seemed to have it for his stuff alone. I had to believe Colonel Maddigan had access, but Parrish was the only one ever seen entering it. He placed his right hand in a biometric scanner and tapped a code I managed to see. Five seconds later, his access was approved and the door clicked open.

It was a messy room inside, with files scattered around or in messy stacks. Parrish was a soldier, not a clerk, and it showed. He seemed to know where everything was, though, and went right to the file he wanted and picked it up. It had red-slashed tape on the tab, along with David Green's name and code name: Cameron. When Parrish opened it, I got a glance at the top page and saw the *RD—Crypto-Top Secret* stamp over Devereau and Shannon's names and what appeared to be an outline of Cameron's strategy to kill him. Parrish saw me peeking, pulled out one of several photos, then flipped it closed.

"You a snoop, Thompson?"

I gave him the "aw shucks" look that worked so well on Brigitte in the bar. "Cool room. Lot of history here, I bet."

"None you'll ever know about. Wait outside."

I left the vault, and a minute later Parrish joined me and secured the room.

"Devereau's been having an affair. Maddigan has a source in the White House."

"Devereau? The moral conservative? Hard to believe."

"Go figure. Here's a photo of the two of them from last week. It's not as good as the ones of you with Brigitte in her bedroom, but look where his hand is."

I choked back the anger I could not use. "He's pretty familiar with her, no doubt."

"He won't want anyone else to see it. Tell him you got it from a reporter or something. Make it look like you're protecting him by telling him about it. Don't threaten him with it."

"I can only see legs and a hand on them. Not very incriminating. Could be anybody."

"Think the First Lady's got legs like those? Devereau will recognize his ring. Let him know there are other photos that show their faces." He snickered. "I better not show those to you. You might lose your objectivity."

I was pretty sure those legs were Shannon's, which would mean the problems between us hadn't been all my doing. It would explain a lot about the way she'd been acting. The bottom of my stomach almost fell out, but I wouldn't let it, not with Parrish standing there cackling about Brigitte and enjoying my pain.

Affair or not, I was still going to protect her. That's what you do for people you love, even when they break your heart.

Besides, whatever else I'd become, I was never going to be the kind of guy who lied to myself. I admitted that whatever she'd done with Devereau was no worse than my screwing Brigitte. In truth, her actions were far better than mine, because she cared about him and I know he cared about her. Brigitte and I meant nothing to each other.

Still hurt like hell, though.

"Parrish, it's just a wild thought here, but couldn't you just blackmail Devereau into not running again, or destroy his followers' faith in him so he's beatable?"

"Probably, except someone else is already playing that card."

And that was the moment when the whole operation made sense to me. "So that's really what earned him a place on Maddigan's list. He might be bad for the military and the country, willing to annihilate us in defense of Taiwan, but he's a security risk because he's subject to blackmail. That's what really has your knickers in a twist."

"Hey, not just any old security risk, but one with the highest security clearance in the world. If he could wink this away like Kennedy or Clinton, it wouldn't be a problem. But he's determined to protect his reputation and will do anything—and I mean anything—to keep it quiet."

I reached to take the photo, but Parrish pulled it away.

"You nuts, Thompson? What about my fingerprints?"

"Sorry. Wasn't thinking."

"Better start," he said, and then went to the copying machine and put the photo on the glass. He stretched on surgical gloves and put a new pack of photography-grade paper in the tray and made a copy. Then he opened a new box of manila envelopes, took one out, and carried it and the photocopy to the lab with gloved hands. He infected the copy with whatever he was mixing when I first came in, then slid it into the envelope.

"If Devereau got this through the mail, it would be inspected seven times before he saw it, if he saw it at all. If you give it to him, he'll open it personally. Even if an aide opens it first, he'll know Devereau will want it right away, so he'll touch it before the aide shows any symptoms of being infected."

"No limit on chemical transfers?"

"Nope, so be careful."

He handed it to me. I hesitated before taking it and putting my prints on the envelope. "Thanks."

"Good luck," he said, as though I were off to a job interview or something. Then he started cleaning up the lab.

I went to my room and pulled out the folder that once held Parrish's orders for me to kill Baker. He'd taken back the orders after I read them, but I kept the envelope for class papers. I tapped the envelope Parrish just gave me until the infected photocopy slid into the old one with Parrish's fingerprints on it and wrote Devereau's name and "very personal" on the outside.

I called Shannon from the car. She was cool, but warmer than if I hadn't left the message from Houston. I was actually glad we were at odds. Otherwise, she'd know something was up if I sounded hurt.

"Can I see you?"

"I'll get home about six, maybe seven. We can talk then."

"No, now. Can I see you now?"

"Not at work, Henry. It's going to be awkward enough for us at home."

"It's urgent. I'm anxious to see you, first off, but I've also got something you need to give Devereau."

"It has to go through security and his staff."

"He wouldn't want that to happen. I'm trying to hide his affair."

She said "oh" as if she knew exactly what I was talking about, which confirmed what I already knew. "How did you . . . ? I'll meet you outside by the Old Executive Office Building. Too hard for you to get in here."

It took a little more than an hour to get there. Traffic was bad, and so was my luck. I caught all the lights and got behind lots of slow-moving tourists. I took the first parking spot I saw and ran the last few blocks. Shannon was standing by the fence, and I slowed as I approached, not quite sure how to say hello to her anymore.

When she saw me, she smiled and took a step in my direction. I wasn't going to risk embarrassing her so near work, but I could see she wanted a hug. It was nice to see, almost surprising, so I hugged her briefly and kissed her lightly, then separated immediately. It wasn't an easy thing to do with the confusion I felt.

"You look tired, Henry. I almost didn't recognize you clean-shaven with short hair."

She touched my cheek, the first time since I left for SEALs that she'd seen it without whiskers. Had I been on this ride that long?

"You look great, Shannon."

We had so much to say that we couldn't say any of it. Some other place and some other time. We stood there as awkward as kids on a first date until she asked, "How did you find out?"

"My commanding officer, Colonel Maddigan, gave me a photo."

I didn't mention Parrish or follow his suggestion that a reporter dug it up. I was changing the rules of this game I'd been forced to play.

She looked worried.

"Shannon, I'm just trying to help. This is only a copy of the photo, but at least he can start putting together a plausible story if it ever comes up."

I had to force myself to give her this lethal tool, a photo laced with an invisible weapon that would kill her if her curiosity got the better of her. My hand to Shannon's.

"Listen carefully. I haven't opened the envelope and you shouldn't either, but Colonel Maddigan has obviously got something against Devereau or he wouldn't have archived this shot."

"The president has his share of enemies."

"I don't trust Maddigan and don't want to be responsible for whatever's inside, so have the contents examined just like United States mail delivered to the White House. Tell Devereau what's inside, and then let him pick an agent he trusts to walk it through every step of the normal analysis. Okay?"

Without realizing what she was doing, Shannon shifted the envelope until she was barely gripping it between the tips of her thumb and a finger. "You're scaring me, Henry."

"Just being cautious. All kinds of kooks out there, you know. I carried it here, so I'm not really worried. I just don't want to imply it's from a trusted source. I'm probably just cynical."

"You're not. If anything, you're a naive guy, and that makes me even more scared."

Naive? Me? God, that would have been beautiful if true.

"I've got to go," I said. "I don't know if I'll come home—"

The word hit me like laughter in hell. Home was so far away from where I was, but I truly believed I was going in the right direction to get there. "I'll get back to you soon. Jammed for another day or so, but then I'm all yours."

She eyed me skeptically. "Be sure, Henry. I don't want to be hurt again. If we're starting over, we're *really* starting over, leaving all the hurt behind."

"Last-minute details to get us there, that's all. A day or two, tops."

She smiled and scrunched her shoulders like an excited kid. "Maybe we can get away this weekend."

"Sure. One last thing. Have Devereau call me after he sees the photo. I've got some other stuff for his ears only."

She gave me a quick kiss and left.

I watched her clear the gate and disappear into the building. As I jogged to my car, I called Colonel Maddigan, who agreed to meet me in a garage in Crystal City. He parked beside me, and I jumped in as he turned off the engine and shifted in his seat to face me. It was amazing how much he reminded me of my dad, with that same uncomfortable look of apology when I last saw him.

"I talked to Parrish. He said you wanted to quit but that he pressured you into doing the job."

"That's right."

"You gave the envelope to Ms. Sullivan?"

"Just before I called you."

"I'm not completely on board with the plan. There's not enough distance separating it from Jaspers, and no contingency plan. Did you say it was from a reporter?"

"I did."

"Do you have someone in mind to give up when they ask?"

"No."

"I'll get you a name. Hell, there's a long roster of reporters and bloggers who hate Devereau. I'll set up one of them."

"Let me know." I reached for the door handle, then hesitated for what I thought was an appropriate amount of time.

"Parrish screwed up, Colonel. He handled the envelope I gave to Shannon. I'm sure he didn't realize it was the same one he'd picked up before he had gloves on."

"Parrish isn't that careless."

"Fine, if you think he can't make a mistake. But after Devereau dies, they'll find both my fingerprints and Parrish's on the envelope. I'm cool, I think, but the investigation will take them to Parrish. From there it's even a shorter leap to Jaspers than you ever feared."

Maddigan squeezed the steering wheel. "Why didn't you tell him?"

"Because I was pissed, that's why. The son of a bitch threatened to kill Shannon, and I saw my chance to get even. I'm trying to protect you now because I don't think you knew what he was doing."

Maddigan balled his fists together under his chin. The muscles of his forearms bundled up beneath his shirt.

"Very smart of you, Thompson. Clever as hell." He said these words quietly, like praise for a worthy adversary.

"Sir?"

"You've managed to make your enemy my liability. Am I supposed to destroy him for you now?"

"Colonel, all I did was put you in the same situation Parrish put me. How you handle it is up to you, but he made me do something I hated to protect something I loved. Now that same decision is yours."

"You had no right."

"That is *so* pompous, Colonel. Jaspers has never been about what's right! It's about what's expedient. What's the expedient thing for you to do now, Colonel?"

He refused to give his emotions a toehold. "Exactly as you say, I'm afraid. I'll have to destroy Parrish. Beyond that, there's no official record of him serving with Jaspers. Just like you."

I was shocked at the ease with which Maddigan accepted this. His quiet acquiescence screamed of command, of hard decisions made in battles where soldiers like Parrish were sacrificed by the thousands for a greater cause. He stared into space as if reading his options off some faraway menu, as though I was no longer in the car. I was scared to break the silence, but I did it anyway.

"Listen, Colonel, Elvis hates Parrish. He's already sworn to kill him. There's a tool for you."

Maddigan didn't answer, and I found myself thinking back on the first day I met Elvis, traipsing along in front of me, yucking it up with Nicholas and the rest of the candidates until Parrish made his impressive appearance. And where had they all gone? Dwayne's legs and pelvis had been sent home to Alabama and the rest of him was in the bellies of little fishes. Nicholas was dead too, probably because Parrish considered him a traitor or a threat or maybe because he just didn't like him. And Parrish would soon be dead. Elvis was still alive, but even if he managed to kill Parrish he was sure to start dying. I could only hope he would recognize the disease that was destined to destroy him and try to find a cure, an escape of his own.

"Elvis can't take him," Maddigan said. "I'd better do it myself."

"What if I helped him?"

"Why would you do that?"

"I hate him. Always have. It has nothing to do with you."

Maddigan didn't look like he could believe me, but he seemed relieved to have an option besides killing Parrish himself. I didn't wait for an answer. "Tell Elvis to meet me at Jasperville in two hours, just inside the compound gate." I opened the door and stepped out.

"Thompson."

There was warning in his voice that made me stop.

"You've completed your mission, so leave Jaspers after dealing with Parrish. Don't let our paths cross again."

I leaned into the car and stared at him. "I'm tired of being threatened, Colonel. Stay out of my crosshairs or I'll hurt you."

He looked stunned, probably for the first time in his life.

Fifteen

I left the garage angry, not just at Maddigan's threat but with myself. As I learned my way around that world of deception and death and became confident in my skills, I was pissed that I'd let Parrish and Maddigan manipulate me in the first place. But until I was sure my mission was complete or I died trying, I would not give in to it, and forced myself to shut down all but the essential elements of who I was, all traces of anger, guilt, sympathy, love, and hope. They were weaknesses that could be preyed upon and make me hesitate or fail.

I found myself entering the abyss I had left behind in Houston, but I wasn't slipping into it, I was charging. I knew the way in and how to get out. I'd become smarter since my first descent and was going to do whatever was necessary and deal with the consequences later, the way Rutger dealt with Dwayne's death in the swamp. It sure seemed to work for him.

I had no choice if I was to survive. Despite all the talk about becoming an instructor after completing my mission, I'd noticed over the weeks and months that there weren't any post-mission Jaspers around. They weren't even carried on duty rosters. Someone was keeping track of them in their head or, more likely, they no longer existed. Parrish, Pike, and Nance were the only ones who hadn't been murdered after completing their assignments, I bet, probably because they were the original team of Jaspers. The men and women who'd followed their lead had become liabilities as soon as they succeeded, security risks the colonel could not tolerate. Since I had delivered the infected photo I was Maddigan's enemy now, a threat instead of an ally. Good thing to keep in mind as I went back to his command center—now my enemy's camp—to get my notebooks and samples and any other evidence that would help me prove his guilt and my innocence.

I threaded through the force-protection barricades at the secondary gate of Fort Belvoir and presented my military ID card. The guards examined it carefully and eyed me suspiciously. They'd seen me in my car several times during the last few months, but I'd been a long-haired guy with a civilian contractor's pass. I expected them to direct me to the side for a search and inspection, but they didn't. That made me suspicious, because they certainly should have. Had they been told to let me onto the base but never let me out again? Would they alert someone down the road who might slam into me at an intersection or shoot me from a window? I'd made myself Maddigan's enemy, and there was no way to predict what he might do other than expect him to do *something*.

I got back to Jasperville, a small, highly secured compound deep in the bowels of the base, but Elvis wasn't waiting inside the gate, as I'd instructed Maddigan. In fact, there didn't seem to be anyone around, but I wasn't surprised by that. The facility was too large for the handful of men who used it, so it could easily look deserted.

My cell phone rang as I parked, and I wasn't surprised to hear Devereau's voice.

"Henry," he said. "I'm disturbed by what you left with Shannon."

"I haven't seen the photo, sir, but I hope you were careful."

"I've only seen a copy. The actual picture was poisoned."

"I'm not surprised. That's why I told Shannon to make sure it was inspected."

"Hmm."

There was a silence I hadn't expected, as if Devereau was wondering what to say.

"The envelope has the fingerprints of the man who infected it," I said. "Staff Sergeant Jim Parrish."

"I see."

"He works for Colonel Maddigan, my commanding officer."

"I know."

I stopped talking. I couldn't figure out what was going on, so I forced myself to be quiet. Neither of us spoke for most of a minute.

Finally, Devereau said, "I'm disappointed in you, Henry. Colonel Maddigan warned me that you might try to kill me."

"What?"

"He said you were a rogue soldier out for vengeance."

"That's ridiculous."

"Come on, Henry, you're far too intelligent to play dumb with me. Colonel Maddigan is on his way over here right now to give me a complete situation report."

I was shocked and then afraid as I realized that Maddigan never intended to trust me with a mission as important as killing Devereau. All along, my role was never anything more than to provide him access.

"I don't know what you're talking about," I said. "Can't you tell I'm trying to protect you?"

Devereau was confused, I could hear it. Colonel Maddigan had a bird on his collar and an impressive war record, but Devereau knew and trusted me. At least he was inclined to trust me.

"Tell you what, Henry. Why don't you join our little meeting and we'll sort through this without a lot of fanfare. Nothing good can be gained by attracting attention to any of this, especially your assassination attempt."

Clearly, it wasn't me he was trying to protect. His voice carried fear, not of death but of embarrassment over his affair. It was a powerful motive for anyone, but even more for a strict and public moralist. I wondered how many important decisions he'd already made to cover it up, which made me think he might need to die after all, assuming there was no other way to stop the blackmail. But I wasn't convinced enough to take the fall for it.

"Wait for me before you meet with Maddigan," I

demanded, reversing our roles of who was in charge. "And arrange access to your office."

I hung up and got out of the car, wondering how long before we met at SEALs Maddigan had planned that moment, anticipating my actions so far down the path he motivated me to travel. For more than a year, I bet, even to the final stage when I would become the scapegoat.

And he was about to succeed. I'd played perfectly into his hands by giving Devereau the poisoned photo. Now Maddigan had his excuse to meet with the president, and I had no doubt he'd already armed himself with some plausible motive for why I poisoned the photo.

On my way to the lab, I grabbed a fire ax that hung in the hall. I needed more proof than just my notebooks and handouts from different classes, and that meant I'd have to have some toxins the president could trace back to whatever lab produced them and then verify their purpose. I hoped that information, along with my notes, would be enough, although I couldn't help but doubt it.

I slammed the ax into the lab's door three times before it opened. The noise had me a little panicked, I guess, because I ran over to the cabinet of toxins and swung so hard I accidentally shattered it. Some vials broke on impact, and others shattered as they hit the floor. I jumped back and ran to the hall, hitting the panic button for the evacuation fan as I left the room and pulled closed the busted remains of the door.

Gravity would force the poisons to the floor, so I ran upstairs. At the top of the stairs I heard a moan from Parrish's office. If he was still there, then maybe I could get other evidence against Maddigan, perhaps even forcing him to open the vault so I could get the assassination plans. I rushed down the stairs and smashed my shoulder into his door. It wasn't locked, and opened without a problem.

Parrish was a horrible mess on the floor, stripped to his shorts, his right hand cuffed and hanging from the handle to the vault. He looked like he'd been attacked by a pack of wild dogs. There was little left of him that wasn't bleeding, and several bones were broken. His ribs stabbed against his stretched skin, and bones protruded from a compound fracture of his right wrist. A bloody piece of pipe lay on the floor nearby. His mouth was open and some teeth were missing. He looked at me with one good eye, his face covered with blood. He looked a little like me in my nightmare.

I felt sorry for him in an odd sort of way. Although I'd wanted to kill him almost from the moment I met him, that vengeful part of me died in Houston after Randall Baker. Walking to the Houston Airport, I'd vowed never to hurt anyone again, for any reason. I was relieved the fight between Elvis and Parrish took place without me there. I wouldn't have been able to watch Elvis beat him up and mutilate him, and would have hated myself if I did.

It took a while before I could take my eyes off Parrish and look around for Elvis, who was on the floor at the other side of the office, leaning against the wall and holding his side, bleeding almost as much as Parrish. I looked at him and then back at Parrish. The two of them were savages, men who fought and killed and felt good about doing it, and I suddenly realized how estranged and isolated I felt from them.

"Son of a bitch bit me," Elvis said.

"Let me see."

"What kind of an animal bites like this?" He moved his shirt from a hole where a chunk of meat the size of a baseball was missing from his side. He was so full of adrenaline, victory, or shock that he seemed almost immune to his injuries.

"You need a doctor."

"No kidding. You come up with that all by yourself?"

"You fought him alone?"

"Had to be this way. Now I'm going to torture him to death. I've even got orders from Maddigan to do it."

"Elvis, I need him first. I need him to scan his hand and open the security vault."

"You want me to uncuff him?"

"Yes."

"No."

As I wrestled with bad options, I heard Parrish say something. He was hard to understand, so I got close, but not too close. He was still dangerous, and always would be as long as he lived.

"Go to hell, Thompson," he mumbled, almost unintelligibly because of his missing teeth. It took us a moment to decipher his next words: "Ain't opening no vault."

"There you have it," said Elvis as he crawled away from the wall and struggled onto his feet. "He 'ain't opening no vault.' That is what you said, right, Parrish?"

"Screw you."

"I think that's what he said, H.T." Elvis straightened up and breathed deeply. "Whew. Son of a bitch bit me," he repeated, as if that's all Parrish did to him. I guess Elvis expected the other damage he sustained, but the biting came as an interesting surprise.

I was trying to think, but Elvis was moving around, gaining strength from God knows where and moving toward Parrish. Then he grabbed the bone protruding from Parrish's wrist and pulled it like a stuck lever. Parrish's eyes lit up, but he didn't scream. I couldn't believe it. Then his eyes closed and he slumped over as he passed out.

"Elvis, I need to get into the vault. For you and me both. I'm taking Maddigan down, and Jaspers will come with it. You need to get whatever they have on you and walk away. If you kill Parrish now, we won't get in."

He let go of the bone and thought about it. "I haven't done anything. I trained, just like you and everyone else, but I haven't broken any laws."

"You're murdering a man!"

"No, I'm not. I'm protecting the president. Maddigan said he tried to kill Devereau."

"You caught him, fine. But from this point on, it's excessive."

He leaned toward his damaged side and looked frustrated with me. "Who's going to testify against me? You? Come on, whatever I do will look justified. Jeez, just look at my side! The bastard," he said, and took a swing at Parrish's busted ribs.

Parrish was only pretending to have passed out, because he tightened his muscles in anticipation, which probably caused him more pain than the blow. Elvis's fist hit right on the tip of a busted rib that punched through Parrish's skin and stabbed Elvis between the knuckles. Elvis leaped back and grabbed his hand, cussing and hopping around the room. His side started bleeding hard again. I looked at Parrish, who had to be hurting from the blow, but all he showed was delight in Elvis's pain.

"I'll save you, Parrish," I said, too quiet for Elvis to hear as he cursed his way around the room holding his hand. "But you've got to open the vault."

"No."

"You'll open the damned vault!"

Elvis started in with a long stream of promises about the torture he planned to inflict, but Parrish only grinned. I stood there trying to make smart decisions, trying desperately to keep my vengeful instincts under control. I could have easily killed him right then, but it might have set off a headlong tumble into the abyss.

I took aim at the handcuff chain with the ax, swinging it in an awkward maneuver with its head parallel to the floor.

"Don't do it, H.T.!"

"He can't beat the two of us."

"Damn you," Elvis shouted as the ax arced around me. Parrish moved so that his head was right where the blade was going to impact, trying to protect the handcuff chain from the ax. I jerked my shoulders up, the ax followed, and I missed his head, although just barely. He grinned as the ax head slammed into the steel door and reverberated up my arm.

"Don't make me kill you, Parrish."

"Screw you."

"Pull his head away, Elvis."

"No."

Parrish checked to make sure his head was still protecting the handcuff chain.

I repositioned the ax and prepared to swing again. "Last chance, Parrish. I'll go right through your head if I have to, no different than splitting logs back home."

I meant those words. In my mind, the rats heard them, too. I could hear them chattering as I lowered myself into the abyss, knowing what I had to do and hoping to find a way of dealing with it later. Promises and oaths meant only what they could afford to mean in times of desperation. With the chemicals spoiled downstairs and Maddigan so close to success with me so well-placed to take the fall, my oath had to take a backseat to my duty as Parrish kept his head against the handcuffs and I swung hard. As the ax flew around, he could see I wasn't swinging at the chain this time, that I was doing something I swore I'd never do again. He jerked his head lower, but there wasn't time. The ax blade hit hard, sliced through his forearm at the compound fracture just below the handcuffs, and lopped off Parrish's hand.

We all stared at the hand on the floor. Then Parrish looked at his free wrist. In the next instant, he was up on his feet.

"Damn it!" Elvis said as he dove in and tackled Parrish. They crashed together across the desk, blood from Parrish's stump spraying the room like a hose.

As they banged around, I grabbed the hand and stuck it in the scanner, then punched in the code I'd watched Parrish enter that day. Nothing happened. I repositioned the hand, but still nothing. I moved the hand a little more and took my time entering the number, making sure I got it right. This time the lock to the vault clicked. I grabbed the big handle and pulled it open.

I went in and took the files Parrish showed me earlier, the ones with the photos of Shannon and Devereau and the orders for Cameron and me to kill him. I didn't look at the photos to make sure it was Shannon. I didn't have time for the pain.

When I came out, Parrish was on the floor, still. Either he had bled to death or Elvis had killed him. I couldn't tell which and didn't want to know. I didn't want to look at Elvis, who stood over Parrish waiting for me to leave so he could desecrate his enemy further, getting his vengeance for Nicholas and, to a far lesser degree, his own humiliation. I looked in every direction but his as I told him to destroy anything in the vault that pertained to either of us, but nothing else.

I rushed to my room and jumped into uniform. It felt strange after so many months of long hair and civilian clothes. For the first time since the SEALs I actually felt like a patriot, doing what needed to be done to protect my country, bringing down an organization that circumvented the law by training soldiers to be assassins and then murdering them after their mission.

I was afraid Maddigan had anticipated my every possible move, including Devereau's request that I sit in on their meeting. I was sure he would have a contingency plan in the event Parrish didn't kill me, which was why he let me slip back into the sanctity of Jasperville, I now realized. Getting off Fort Belvoir was going to be tricky. I would be too obvious in my car, so I walked through the Jaspers security gate and joined a group of soldiers walking outside the Jasper compound. Although they were in Army uniforms and mine was Navy, there was enough diversity on the base that I didn't stand out much.

As we approached Tulley Gate, I saw they'd added force-protection barricades and additional sentries since my arrival, at the exit as well as the entrance, which meant that Maddigan wasn't taking any chances. I was sure all the guards had my photo, so I turned around and walked back the way I'd come, past the entrance to the exchange and down the sidewalk behind it. At the rear of the building was a tractor-trailer idling noisily, waiting to be off-loaded, I guessed. I didn't see a driver, so I jumped into the cab and studied the gears and panel. It was surprisingly similar to a lot of the farm equipment I'd driven back home, at least close enough for me to figure it out.

I revved the engine and pulled away as a guy came running from the loading dock. Instead of Tulley Gate, I drove to Pence Gate, the one Jaspers seldom used because it was far from our compound and less convenient. As I'd hoped, it wasn't nearly as heavily fortified, although there were two Hummers that exiting cars had to pass at very slow speed. There was a line of cars waiting to go through the checkpoint as Big Mouth helped the sentries look for me, even though those young MPs couldn't have known what was really going on or why they had orders to arrest me, assuming that was the extent of their orders.

I idled a few seconds while deciding my best strategy, then downshifted and accelerated as I bounced the semi over the curb, roaring down the sidewalk toward the gate. Sentries aimed but didn't fire, at least not until Big Mouth did. I saw his pistol come up, and almost instantly the windshield shattered. I took a last look to make sure I was aimed toward the exit and then flattened out on the seat, holding the wheel firm and keeping the pedal down as bullets splattered all over the cab. One whistled close to my ear as all the glass shattered and bullets ricocheted around in the cab.

When they started shooting through the doors I knew I was passing them, so I popped up and took a quick look as I clipped the fence and my trailer dragged a Saab at the front of the line into the Hummers. They tangled in a pile that blocked most of the exit as I got up behind the wheel and bounced back onto the road, the trailer swaying and whipping around while I ground gears, built up speed, and headed down Richmond Highway.

Two Hummers came after me. I could see them in my mirrors and knew I wouldn't stand a chance when they pulled beside me and started shooting. I demanded everything from the tractor and probably could have outrun the Hummers on an open road, but there was too much traffic. I-95 was five miles away. I wouldn't make it. I had to brake and accelerate too often, and my slow acceleration was their best advantage. Cars were slowing down up ahead, and from my high vantage point I could see an accident. Damn it!

I jerked the wheel and almost flipped as I drove onto the shoulder in order to pass the wreck. Just as I

Wes DeMott

did, a Virginia state trooper rolled down an onramp and into the outside lane of Richmond Highway, obviously not expecting a huge tractor-trailer to be blistering along the outside edge of the road. The lady trooper looked back at me with shock as I pulled up to her car's rear quarter panel, gravel flying off my wheels and dust filling the sky behind me.

She was trying to get away from me as I lined up my bumper just behind her rear tires and then turned my front wheels into her, forcing her to lose control. As soon as she did, I slammed on the brakes so I wouldn't crash into her when she slid to a stop in front of me.

The air was full of dust and tire smoke, and the trooper was still sliding sideways as I ground to a stop and reached for the handle to get out. Just as I jumped from the cab one of the Hummers slid into the back of my trailer, hitting with enough force to throw me onto the ground. Blood splattered the gravel, but I didn't know where it came from and really didn't have time to care. I ran for the trooper's car, needing to get there before she oriented herself. Soldiers shouted behind me and someone fired a couple of shots. I waited for a string of three-burst rounds from the M-16s, but when none came I figured only Big Mouth was shooting. He wouldn't hesitate to kill a civilian to stop me, but the others were probably having trouble blasting away while I ran beside cars carrying their friends and neighbors.

One of the bullets hit the trooper's car with a loud ping, and as she got out she drew her weapon and aimed at me. She was obviously confused, but also had to make a quick decision of which target presented the greatest threat—a Navy guy running empty-handed or some Army guys with rifles and Big Mouth shooting.

"Wasn't me who shot at you. You gotta help me!" I jerked my thumb behind me as I ran like hell, although I hadn't looked back since leaving the cab and could only guess what she might see.

"Get down," she shouted, as she aimed past me.

I acted like I was going for cover behind her car, but when I got close I hit her as hard as I could. She dropped like a stone and I jumped into her car, backed up in order to straighten out, then dropped it into drive and hauled ass out of there, spinning the tires and spraying a ton of rocks at Big Mouth as I put as much dust in the air as I could.

Almost as soon as I roared onto I-95 I heard sirens behind me. Then I saw a southbound trooper drive off the interstate and slide into the median, his lights flashing and siren wailing as he turned in my direction and accelerated after me. I hit 100. 120. And then 140, passing cars on the left and right, going faster than I'd ever driven before, quickly learning how easy it was to change lanes or lose control just as quickly.

I searched around for my seat belt and found it, buckled up as I moved to the inside shoulder, and passed a line of cars in the HOV lane. The trooper behind me followed. As I bumped back onto the highway my rear tires lost traction just for a second, but enough time for the momentum to throw my back end a little bit forward so that when the tires hit I was almost perpendicular to the road. I had no idea how to recover from my spin at that speed. I slammed into a car and then another, but it happened so fast I never saw them. I felt the collisions almost as incidental events as I spun my way down the interstate, slowing a little, glancing off another car, then another, losing speed and hearing sirens until I slammed into the guardrail and stopped instantly.

I hit my head on the glass. It shattered at the same time, but I think it broke from the accident, not my head. Almost in slow motion, I watched the glass spray across the car, saw the dashboard crumble, watched the roof bend and the steering column collapse.

Everything was quiet. I was still alive. I must have been hurt, because there was blood everywhere, but I didn't feel it until I tried to crawl out of the window and over the guardrail. I collapsed back onto the seat, wanting so badly to give up and rest, accept that I'd done my best but it wasn't good enough. Then I thought about Maddigan and Shannon and Devereau and forced myself to try again. This time I made it out the window and down onto the ground, face first.

I lay on the ground and looked under the guardrail and saw that the interstate traffic had stopped, so I got to my feet and climbed over the rail, started limping toward the cars. Then I managed to run. The sirens were just getting there. It must not have been more than a few seconds since I'd spun out of control, although it felt like much longer.

A young kid rushed over to help me, leaving his car running. I ran past the kid and was almost inside his car when a trooper tackled me. I tried to fight but couldn't do much good, and in less than a minute he had his handcuffs on me.

I stayed on the ground and heard him request an

ambulance. I hoped it was for me—not because I wanted it, but because I didn't want to believe I'd seriously hurt anyone else. More sirens arrived and then stopped, then some shiny shoes stepped up beside me.

"You're Thompson?"

I nodded my head slowly, scraping the road with my cheek but not caring anymore.

"Damn if this feels right to me, but I've been instructed to take you to the White House."

I looked up and saw the flash of lieutenant bars on his uniform, the Smokey the Bear hat on his head, and the total confusion on his face.

I jumped up, sort of, although my entire body hurt. I would probably be sore for months, but I didn't think I was badly hurt. It was hard to tell with all the adrenaline, but I was going to proceed under that assumption.

"What are we waiting for? Which car is yours?"

As the lieutenant put me in his car, the trooper who'd tackled me aimed his finger and gave an "I'm gonna get you" look.

We took off and sped toward Washington, picking up two state police escorts along the way.

Sixteen

"Have a seat, Lieutenant," President Devereau commanded as he dismissed the agents, who were reluctant to unlock my handcuffs and even more reluctant to leave a bloody, beaten man with the president.

I sat down and glanced at Shannon, who must have been warned how I looked, because she bit her lip and looked horrified but said nothing. Then she looked at Devereau, confused or worried or both. None of us spoke. Then Colonel Maddigan came in escorted by another agent. He was surprised to see me but hid it well, and I doubted Devereau saw it. He walked to Devereau's desk and saluted, then held out his hand. "A pleasure, Mr. President."

Devereau didn't shake hands, even after Maddigan thrust it closer. He just pointed at me and asked, "Is that the man you warned me about, Colonel?"

Maddigan didn't turn my way. "Yes, sir."

"I see."

"A bit of a misfit, Mr. President. Not sure how he slipped through our screening process, but I must take responsibility for that."

I sat there watching Maddigan, trying to figure out how he was going to kill Devereau and me and make it look like a suicidal assassination attempt on my part. That had to be his plan, the only way he could get away clean.

"During a routine security check we found these, sir." Maddigan opened his briefcase and took out my notebooks of lethal formulas and strategies, things I'd figured out how to do but never intended to carry out. "Here are his notes on how he was going to kill you."

"I was never going to—"

"Be quiet," ordered Devereau.

I looked at the notebooks and couldn't have been more ashamed if they had been child pornography. I was sure Maddigan had infected them and would somehow tie in my murder of Randall Baker as additional proof. He might even infect himself to validate that none of the events were his doing, although I was sure he'd dilute his exposure in order to survive.

"What's going on here?" demanded Shannon.

"That's pitiful," I mumbled.

"What?"

"You! You're pitiful. You know very well what's going on. I could tell when you climbed all over me in the cab. You were trying to get information about this for Devereau."

"What are you talking about?"

"Here." I threw the file of photos on Devereau's desk. "Tell me it's not you in those pictures."

"Don't touch them until they're tested," said Devereau.

Maddigan looked surprised to see them. A lot of worry crept onto his face, but only for a second. It was immediately replaced by an even higher level of determination.

I flipped the file open and put my hand all over the photos. "I didn't poison them. I'm not the guy trying to kill you."

Shannon looked down at the photos and then at Devereau. There was a look of shame on her face for a secret that was entirely too personal, a look of sadness that showed she'd given up completely and wanted to confess to a sin that was exposed prematurely. She kept looking at the photos, unable to resist staring at my evidence of her affair with him. She picked up one of the photos and held it carefully, then grabbed the entire stack of them. She turned them so Devereau could see. "It's what I told you would happen."

Then she looked at me, but not with the look I'd expected to see. Instead, she was angry.

"*This* woman is my mother. I started to tell you that on the phone, but it was really none of your business."

I looked at the photos again, but quickly, because I couldn't afford to waste time worrying about being wrong or rejoicing in her fidelity. If I'd relied on Parrish's lie as the truth, I was even more vulnerable than I'd expected. Everything I'd planned, all the information I'd relied upon, was suddenly in doubt as Maddigan took a step forward and said, "Doesn't matter, sir. The fact is Lieutenant Thompson *thought* Miss Sullivan was the woman with whom you were having an affair."

He was right; it didn't matter. He was there, I was there, and so was Devereau. The excuses and pretenses that brought us together no longer mattered. Maddigan may actually have killed us already; he could have left poisonous residue anywhere he stepped, breathed, or touched.

"I'm convinced he volunteered for Jaspers with the intent of killing you, sir. Jealousy is only part of his motive, I'm afraid. I can't speculate on the rest."

"What? That's ridiculous. Henry, tell him . . ."

"It was Colonel Maddigan who ordered me to kill you, sir."

Maddigan looked like he'd been shamed by a misfit recruit.

I pulled out the files that proved my innocence and Maddigan's guilt, but he must have known I'd been in the vault, leaving him no other option but to attack, his only chance to kill Devereau, then Shannon and me, and somehow make himself look like a victim in the process. He had to succeed in killing us and in recovering the files I'd brought with me, the evidence that proved he was a liar and a criminal.

He dove for Devereau, his right hand out and straining to touch the president's skin, but I intercepted him, ignoring all my soreness and pain, knocking Shannon down as I slid across the desk and grabbed hold of Maddigan's wrist, hanging on to it at all costs and not letting his infected hand near Devereau or me as the two of us crashed around the room.

Devereau hit a panic alarm that summoned a cadre of Secret Service agents. They were everywhere at once, like cockroaches in a cheap motel. Two agents wrestled Maddigan while another pulled me off him with a poorly executed carotid artery hold that became a suffocating chokehold. Three other agents rushed President Devereau out of the office as more agents spilled in. Too many of them were in the room at that point, creating a confusion that Maddigan converted into opportunity as two of the agents holding him suddenly bloated and died just like Randall Baker in Houston. That left Maddigan's left arm free, and he used it to smack the agent who stood between him and Shannon, who was just getting up from the floor. He grabbed her by the neck and threatened to break it.

I was hoping he had infected only his right hand, expecting to shake hands with the president. That's what I would have done so I'd have a clean hand for my keys and personal items. But it was hard to count on that with Shannon so firmly in his grip. I could only hope. If I'd had an extra second or two, I definitely would have prayed.

Maddigan edged toward the door, dragging Shannon with him as a shield. There was no chance of his getting away, but I knew him well enough to understand that he wanted to be cut down in battle. Capture was an ignoble option for a man like him, so he kept his right hand in front of Shannon's face, threatening her until he got away or was killed. I'd seen three men die from the stuff he held so near her beautiful face. I didn't think Maddigan wanted to kill her, but if he was the least bit careless she would die that same horrible death.

The agent strangling me moved, trying to see through the crowd of agents who trained their guns on Maddigan but didn't shoot because his face was too close to Shannon's and his body too well hidden behind her. I was hoping another agent would come up behind him, but the area must have been isolated and locked down once Devereau was evacuated.

Blood from my face ran down my neck and made it hard for the agent who dragged me around to keep a tight grip. At one point, he let go in order to grab a new spot. As he did I dropped an inch or two, and as soon as my feet planted on the floor I swung my legs behind him and snapped up. He had no choice but to let go and fall back, and as he dropped away I ran my hand up to his waist and dragged the pistol out of his holster. I raised it to fire, barely able to see through the drawn guns and anxious faces, looking for Maddigan's head in the crowd, seeing it so awfully close to Shannon's, aiming, seeing other people about to cross my line of sight, wondering who I'd hit, knowing that killing an agent or Shannon would be murder. Thinking I didn't want to be a murderer, remembering my vow never to kill again and wanting so badly to keep it, being confused and yet totally committed to saving the woman I loved. It was a tall, fast-moving crowd with lots of interference. I had too many doubts. It would be hard to hit a target that small with a handgun. I wished someone would come up behind him. I wanted . . .

I fired.

The noise deafened me. At first I didn't know what I hit, because everyone dropped except Shannon. But then, in that frozen slice of time, I saw a corona of blood haloing around Maddigan's wobbling head.

Shannon watched me as he fell away and hit the floor. Her face was tilted forward and her mouth was open. A half-instant later, gun barrels the size of soup cans swung my way. Slow motion. Amazing.

I dropped the gun and fell to my knees, threw my hands up as high as I could, and knelt there praying that no one shot me before they could stop their trigger finger. Two seconds passed. Three. Four.

I thought I might live.

An agent marched over to me. He didn't have a gun in his hand, but I wished he had. I heard Shannon scream "No" as I closed my eyes and took the hit, a nose-busting blow into my face. The crackle of shattering cartilage rattled its way through my brain and into my ears, drowning out Shannon's screams as my head slammed into Devereau's desk.

Thirty minutes later, the president's physician was taking care of my wounds and packing my nose with cotton while agents cleaned away the mess, and a plausible story was concocted by Devereau and his staff, something that would keep the whole thing out of the papers. After they all left, I looked at Shannon, who was even more bewildered than I was.

"Well, that was interesting," said Devereau, as he got some coffee. I noticed his hand trembling, but only a little.

I felt my left ear, where Big Mouth's bullet tore a ragged hole. "How . . . how did you know about Jaspers? When did you find out?"

"Coffee?" He was buying time as he tried to calm down.

"No, but thanks."

He turned with the cup in his hand, slowly stirring in the milk. Then his hand trembled again and he set the coffee on the table, took a deep breath that helped him a lot.

"Months ago."

"But how?"

"Cameron—David Green—gave up the information when he was tortured. Those terrible men who killed him offered to trade us that information in exchange for one of their spies."

"So you've known all along? Even last time I was here?"

"I knew. That's why I wanted to see you. I needed to know which side you were on. I certainly couldn't take an enemy's word as gospel that there was an assassination heading my way. When Colonel Maddigan said he needed to see me, it was easy enough to guess his intentions."

I thought about my last visit here, Devereau's firm handshake, his proximity to me and his trust. "You, sir, were careless."

"Henry, I'm the president of the United States. That makes me a target, not an idiot. I've got good insight into people and could never see you as a killer. I don't think I was careless."

"You bet your life on your trust in me?"

"Never really doubted you."

"Will I make things worse if I tell you you're still not safe, that there will be others?"

He laughed. There was a lot of nervousness in it, but it was a damned courageous laugh. "I'm three threats behind the average for presidents at this point in their term. I'd be disappointed if there weren't more threats. But they won't come from Jaspers. They will come, I'm sure, but not from them." He looked at me hard. "Don't go back there looking for anything, Henry. General Krueger is already in the process of dismantling Maddigan's organization."

Shannon walked over to me, easing her way, unsure but wanting to help. "Is Henry under arrest or something? What are you—"

"What do you think? He planned to kill me."

"But he didn't! You can't prosecute a person for planning." The edge went out of her voice and she was suddenly pleading. "Can you?"

"Hmm," said Devereau. "I guess you're right." He kissed her cheek and then walked over and shook my hand. He took a long look at our hands pressed together. "I will always trust good men, Henry. That's how I'm made. Thanks for not letting me down."

He let go, and I stood there, still confused over what to do.

"Let's go, Shannon. Okay?" I was talking to her, but the question was for Devereau.

He nodded and went back to his desk, sat down, and picked up some papers. I was sure he wasn't reading them, just using them as a tool to help him move on.

I stopped at the door, and Devereau looked up.

"The reason Colonel Maddigan wanted you dead, sir? Well . . . I think he's right. You are a security risk, you're bad for the military, and therefore you're bad for the country."

He took off his glasses and stared at his desk. Shannon weaved her hand into mine as we both watched him. A half-minute passed.

"I'll give all of my actions some more thought, Henry. I promise. Fair enough?"

I snapped to attention and saluted—actually, the first time I'd rendered that honor to Devereau. He looked me over like a proud father and saluted back. "Don't be strangers."

Seventeen

"So this is Indianapolis," Shannon said as she walked and I hobbled up the jetway from the plane.

"No," I said, forcing myself to try being silly, wanting very much to be that kind of person again. "This is just the airport. Indianapolis is much bigger." I looked around the jetway. "Much bigger."

"Been a long flight, Henry."

I was almost giddy with the excitement of going back to where I lost myself, when I turned my back on my family without ever considering how many ways it would make me different. The hard work of being alone, of making decisions without trusted counsel and choosing actions that took only myself into account, had changed me mightily, and in the previous evening's solitude I'd made it my goal to reverse every one of those changes. "Not for me. Like the saying goes, it's never a long way home."

"Then next time, we'll drive. See if that's really true." She squeezed my hand and smiled as if everything was going her way.

"I'm looking forward to meeting your parents. I'm proud of you for calling them."

"Had no choice. If I'd shown up without a warning, they might have had heart attacks."

"Hmm," she said as if she didn't want to think about death, even accidental ones. Certainly, nothing that had to do with Colonel Maddigan, or the world of killing from which I'd escaped. She tried to pretend that none of it ever happened.

And that was fine with me. Other than my phone call to my mother a few hours after I left the White House and Shannon leaving D.C. with me the next morning, nothing else I'd done since Coronado seemed real anymore. It was almost like I'd been dreaming, maybe while suffering from some slow-growth sickness I didn't know I had until I killed Baker. A sickness that healed almost instantly after I pulled the trigger on Maddigan.

"Henry," she said, and then gently lifted my hand in hers, touching my fingers to her face.

"Yes?"

"While you were so busy with work . . ." She drew a deep breath of courage, tilted up her chin, and looked me straight in the eyes. I saw it all in slow motion, and it caused a curious mixture of pain over the past and passion for the future—if I could just hold on to her and the future I now desperately wanted us to have together. "Were you ever with another woman while you were gone from me?"

I so badly wished I could do something, anything, to earn back a clear conscience, but that was impossible. Brigitte was a piece of my history I would never forget, a shameful mistake I would not burden on

Shannon. That left me no choice but to be a liar all the way to my grave. Sadly, unlike the government secrets I'd also take there, I didn't expect the self-loathing this secret caused me to fade with time, although I truly hoped I was wrong.

As I stood there staring at Shannon, I briefly thought about her teasing me with Steve. That would give me a reasonable excuse. It would force her to live with some of the blame, and that would make my conscience a little clearer.

But that would be a lie, too. Shannon played no part in what I did, so there was no way to shuck off my feelings without hurting her. It was my mistake, and therefore my burden to carry. I hated myself for doing so poorly when Shannon deserved so much more, but there was only one thing I could do about it: be as good a man as possible from that moment forward.

"No, Shannon, there was never another woman and never will be. As long as I have you, there'll never be room in my heart for anyone else."

She leaned up to kiss me, and I heard some guy passing behind me say, "Wow." He looked back as he passed and was shocked she'd kissed a guy with such a ravaged face.

We stopped at the car-rental counter and got keys to a car. As we walked toward baggage claim, I saw Colonel Maddigan's picture pop up on the airport televisions. It showed him in full dress uniform with all the glory of his past pinned to it. I glanced up and down the corridor and saw his face a dozen more times, sitting proudly with his chest of medals and his eyes full of the same resolve that stared me down as I aimed the agent's pistol. I'd tried to aim at the center of his face, but his eyes were so intense that they drew all my attention until the bullet splattered through his left eye and obliterated the image.

"Hang on a minute, Shannon."

The television reporter said, "Military investigators in Washington last night shot and killed this man believed to be a foreign spy. He is identified as Colonel Walter H. Maddigan, United States Army, a highly decorated veteran of several conflicts. Unsubstantiated rumors link Colonel Maddigan with the military's elite Delta Force and an unnamed Central Intelligence Agency paramilitary unit operating out of Fort Belvoir, Maryland. But as we noted, those reports cannot be confirmed at this time."

Then a smiling picture of Devereau flashed onto the screen and the reporter continued. "In other news from our nation's capital, President Devereau has vetoed a bill to continue funding for the anti–missile defense system that was initiated under President Simons's administration and widely supported by the Pentagon as a strategic piece of American security. Critics of the president say his veto will increase the risk of attack to the United States, suggesting that America has no defense for the nuclear warheads aimed at the U.S. by a dozen countries. However, strong voter support for Devereau's position seems to have kept both sides of the House at bay. In other news—"

The programming shifted to sports. There was no mention of the assassination attempt or Parrish's death or Jaspers, other than the vague mention of a CIA army at Belvoir. I stopped listening and wandered to a seat, trying to think how I would put all this behind me and move forward with my life.

"Need a little time?" Shannon asked. "Want to meet me in baggage claim?"

"Maybe a good idea. I'll be right behind you."

She rubbed my back. "Take your time. I'll go see if our suitcases made the trip." She walked away.

She was worried about me, but I knew I'd be fine. For some reason, though, I couldn't stop feeling bad for Maddigan, for his life and his death. In truth, I still respected the man. For everything I could have held against him, for every misguided move I believe he made, I still respected him as a patriot.

Patriot has always sounded like a funny title with a vintage ring to it, an old-fashioned word that fell out of use and style with businessmen's hats. If it sounded funny to someone as gung-ho as me, I wondered how weird it must sound to civilians. But as I thought about the news segment, the talk of missiles and enemies and national defense, I wondered if Maddigan wasn't right to worry and to make such terrible demands on me. "Defend your nation," he said, "against all enemies, foreign *and* domestic."

That was his dream. That was his life. He was more than willing to sacrifice himself to kill Devereau and protect his country's future. He would have done so gladly. I didn't have any idea what else to call that if not patriotism.

I breathed deeply and hoisted myself out of the chair, trying to leave my worries behind as I headed for Shannon, the woman of my dreams and the hope of my future. My life belonged to her from that moment on, and I couldn't have been more thrilled. The next day or the one after that, we would come back into town and buy her a ring, probably bringing my folks along to ooh and aah at the choices if Shannon didn't mind them tagging along. I doubted she would.

I had the rental-car papers and Shannon had located the bags, so we walked outside and boarded the bus that took us to the off-site parking lot. Shannon marveled at how flat everything was while I told her the Indianapolis Motor Speedway was just up the road and that my home wasn't far away.

I took the Loop north for two exits, got off at State Road 36, and headed west toward Danville. If Shannon had asked me a week ago what there was to see there, I'd have said "corn." But as we rode along I became a one-man chamber of commerce, spouting facts and details and historical information I'd long ago tried to forget, telling her about things we would do, the treats my mother loved to make, horses we were going to ride, and so much other stuff.

I also told her about my father, for the first time in years speaking of him with respect. What an unfaithful son I was to walk away from him without giving him an instant's worth of credit for his decades of honor, and for my own lifetime of benefiting from his firm and faithful guidance. Not once had I even considered that something else might have happened to make him quit the Marshals, something, as Maddigan said about the returning POWs, that made my dad's decision a noble protest.

As I turned onto the last road before my dad's driveway, I got scared. I'd called them in the middle of the night, sure, but only asked if I could stop by. I said nothing about where I'd been or Shannon or what she meant to me, nothing about what I wanted to say to them. I still had a backup plan of checking into a hotel in town if the situation got too tense.

I slowed down when I saw my dad's barn in the distance. It was surrounded by empty fields of cut-down crops and soil turned over in reverence for the death that winter was about to bring. Shannon looked at me and then at the barn. "Is that it?"

I drove another quarter-mile and stopped on the shoulder. "Yes. Looks nice, huh?"

"Pretty. Red."

"All barns are red."

"Why?"

"I don't know," I confessed. "Doesn't show the dirt?"

"Black wouldn't either."

"Black's not a pretty color for a barn."

"Oh."

My hands trembled, and Shannon noticed. She leaned over and hugged my neck, then picked up my hand and rubbed it vigorously. "Let's go, Henry."

"Okay."

I didn't move.

"Henry?"

"Yeah?"

"Come on," she said gently. "Let's go."

"Okay."

I stared at the big red barn, not really afraid of facing my dad or my mom or anything else except the terrible sin of my walking out, of being too weak to let my dad be human. I looked down at the road and studied the pocks in the asphalt, remembering the last time I traveled it, heading toward town and never planning to come back. Yet here I sat with a woman who loved me, scared to go back to the family I hoped still loved me. Was I pathetic or what?

"You want me to drive?"

"No, I can do it."

"You sure?"

"Sure. It's just a couple hundred yards. I've driven farther than that before."

"You know what I mean."

"Oh."

I bit my lip and then took a deep breath. "Let's go."

I pulled back onto the road, and a car I hadn't seen coming blew its horn and swerved around me.

"Sorry. Didn't look back."

Shannon giggled, or smirked. I was way too busy to figure out which.

I pulled into the drive, which went about three hundred feet to a wide gravel area we called The Yard, not to be confused with the grass surrounding the house we called The Garden.

With the house on the left side of the yard and the silo directly across from it, the red barn was straight ahead, with the pig barn and garage on either side of it. It would sound stupid to say that it was just like I remembered it, but it was, well, just like I remembered it.

My dad was sitting on an overturned bucket in front of the barn with his back to the drive. From where I sat it looked like he was lubricating the grease fittings of the yard tractor. I knew he heard my tires crunching on the gravel, but he didn't stand up. He just kept working.

My mother stepped through the screen door and

onto the porch, holding the wooden door open on this cool day. Then she took two steps off the porch and stopped, her hand balled up and pressed against her lips. She was still dainty and thin as she leaned this way and that, her anxious eyes trying to glimpse me through the windshield, her thin face confused over who might be with me and my reasons for coming home.

When I lived here, I always parked in front of the house under the big elm shade tree, and I saw no reason not to do that again. I turned off the ignition and sat there staring at my mom, who kept staring at the two of us.

"Henry?" Shannon said.

"Yeah?"

"This is getting a little embarrassing."

"Yeah?"

Another minute went by.

Then Shannon turned and looked out her window at my father. I did, too. He finished whatever he was doing to the tractor and stood up. He was bigger than I remembered and stronger-looking. The farm work, I guessed.

He turned toward us but didn't really move at first, leaning for a couple of seconds until he had to either take a step or fall forward. He threw out a foot and then another.

"Come on," I said. "Let's get out of the car."

"Dying to."

I climbed out and walked slowly around the car, my dad and I both moving cautiously. I stepped beside Shannon and closed her door.

Dad's hair had gone from movie-star gold to dirty

blond. His face was still handsome, but with more curves than angles. He was darker, more weathered than I'd ever seen him, and the deep color added an intensity to the quickness of his blue eyes.

"Hello," he said to Shannon, and the sound of his voice made me happy and sad at the same time. "I'm Henry's father, Howard."

"Shannon Sullivan. Nice to meet you." She reached out and accepted his hand.

"My pleasure. Mother's been baking all day. I would've made my special candy if I'd known Henry was bringing home such a pretty lady."

"Cookies?"

Dad rolled his head and chuckled. "Sure, cookies, all right. And cakes. You'd think Mother was getting ready for a bake sale."

"I love cookies."

"That's good," he said. "Plenty of 'em."

We all stood there a minute. I was so nervous, I was sweating in the cool breeze. A bead rolled down my back and gave me a shiver. My dad noticed but still didn't look at me.

"Well," Shannon said slowly as she looked to me, then my dad, then back to me, "I think I'll meet Henry's mother, if you'll excuse me."

"Sure," my dad said. "Sure."

"Very nice to meet you, Howard."

"The pleasure was mine, Miss Sullivan."

What a charmer.

Shannon smiled at me as she walked between us. Then she was through the gate and up the steps. She introduced herself to my mom and they went into the house. Thirty seconds later, I heard laughter. My dad and I both looked at the house, and I bet the sound had washed him over with some of the same memories I was having.

I cleared my throat, or at least tried to. There was a big clod of dust back there, I thought, and it took a pretty serious effort to break it up. My dad stole a glance or two at me but said nothing.

"How . . . how's the farm doing?"

He looked down, and then around, studying the buildings as if he were about to describe them to a blind person. "Good, sure. Decent year. Not much money in farming, you know, but I like it. We do okay."

"That's good."

"Yeah."

Another minute went by, and then the screen door slammed. Shannon and my mom stepped out and were walking around the house.

"Having some trouble with the yard tractor," my dad said. "Needs a bearing, I think."

"Oh? That's too bad."

"Well, it's old. Things wear out."

"Sure. They sure do."

My dad's eyes met mine for the first time, holding them gently and with great care. He seemed to ignore all my injuries, as if only interested in whatever my eyes might say. "You run off and join the circus, Henry?"

I could have guessed he'd say that. One side of his mouth turned up.

"I suppose, Dad. A circus. That's exactly what it was."

He rubbed his face like he was wondering if he needed a new blade in his razor. "Enjoy it?"

"No. Not really."

"I was kind of hoping to hear from you."

"Sorry."

"What happened to your face?"

I reached down and grabbed a rock, then threw it at the silo, trying as I always did to hit it from here. My muscles cramped and rebelled, and I didn't even come close.

"Fight, Dad. I got in a fight."

"Yeah? That's what I figured. You okay?"

I didn't even need to think about that. I picked up another rock and threw again, wrapping myself in the memories of that place and the power of that man. Remembering how I lived there and who I was there, and then appreciating how good it felt to get some of those feelings back.

"More than okay, Dad. You have no idea."

Dad turned from me and picked up a rock, then hurled it against the silo, dinging off it with a tinny sound. "That's good."

I was feeling good and bad at the same time. I wanted more of the good feelings, so I made the best effort I could to shake the bad ones. "Dad?"

"Yes, son?"

"Dad, I'm sorry."

My lip trembled, and I bit it. My dad turned to me. He was biting his lip, too. And he was crying.

"It's okay, son. I was just worried about you, that's all." His voice cracked, which broke me down even more.

"No, Dad. That's not it. I mean, I'm *really sorry*."

He studied my eyes, and I knew he saw the same thing he saw the last time we spoke, in just about this very same spot, all those long and painful years ago. Something in them that was wild and strong, careless and wonderful, both his son and himself. But with so many hard lessons behind me, it was more grown up than before.

"I know you are, son. I'm sorry, too. Forgiven?"

He stuck his callused hand between us, and I shook it until he grabbed my forearm and pulled me into him. I let go and threw my arms around him like I was ten years old, hugging his neck and squeezing his back. Which was just what he did to me.

"There's nothing to be forgiven, Dad," I said, my face feeling the rasp of my father's whiskers for the first time since I was small.

He squeezed me so hard, I came off the ground. "Welcome home, Henry."

I heard my mom calling us to join them.

"Glad to be home," I whispered in his ear. "You can't even imagine."

Eighteen

After an hour of visiting, I walked outside and found myself drawn to my dad's barn, wandering through it while the rest of them got to know each other in the house. He had repaired the damage from my brother's shotgun and no longer boarded any animals. I didn't see any evidence of rats, so he must have found a way to get rid of those filthy creatures. I kept looking for them, though, as I thought about what I'd done to kill them, realizing only at that moment the similarity to what I'd trained to do as a Jasper.

I discovered some important things about myself in the barn that day, things I finally knew for sure about my own nature. I was equally sure there were other mysteries still hidden inside me, fears perhaps, that might lie buried for years, waiting for a shifting wind or another life-changing moment to expose them.

I was more than willing to wait for those revelations, though. At that moment, I didn't have the strength to explore them anyway, although I knew it would be both fulfilling and painful to pursue an understanding of the person I really was. It could take decades, perhaps a lifetime, to get there. But Jaspers had taught me a lot in a short time, so I felt content with that for the time being.

I'd learned that the power to kill another human being resides at a very distant locale in the finite geography of my mind, and maybe in most people's. Despite roll-off-the-tongue slogans about duty, flag, and honor, it had become impossible for me to believe in killing over political rhetoric. Yet it was natural and automatic in support of the simplest of loyalties— keeping a loved one out of danger, or protecting a president when given a chance.

As I look back now on all that happened to me my year as a Jasper, I realize it was somewhere on my trip back home that I managed to look beyond the hackneyed rhetoric and understand with a little less mystery and a lot more clarity some truths about America. As I leaned against the barn's timbers, I found myself questioning much of the way we do things as a country, pretty sure that public apathy and political inefficiency are major culprits. I just didn't know what to do about it, understanding that right and wrong were difficult concepts to apply to politics, leaving large areas primed for the gray paint of pragmatism.

God, I'd changed a lot since I last walked through that barn. I knew I had because it didn't seem at all demeaning to quit the Navy or to have walked away from Jaspers after identifying it as something I no longer wanted. At the same time, I realized that quitting was seductive, like making excuses or failing. It wasn't something you wanted to do often, but on occasion, the right occasion, it was acceptable. It felt good to have that choice, really for the first time in my life.

It felt good to have my family back, too. They seemed the same as when I left them, proving that love is truly a mirror. It reflects what it sees in you, the love you give or withhold bouncing back at you like a beach ball or a BB. It's your choice, always your choice.

And I learned that I loved Shannon so much for so many things. But on that crisp, forgiving fall day I loved her most for accepting me back after our ordeal at the White House. She had hugged me as soon as I regained consciousness and never questioned me about the things Maddigan said, as if unconcerned about which crevice of hell might have swallowed me. Amazing. Truly amazing.

A winter wind was moving down from Canada, and the barn seemed to creak in anticipation. The noises and sights and smells of my dad's farm played back the song of my youth, as unchanged over the years as the land my father worked. Because the song *was* the same, it highlighted how much my country had changed in ways that were hard to see. I was sure it would continue to change whether I was a part of it or not. If Maddigan was right, the changes would either ensure us several more decades as the greatest nation on earth, or end the most noble experiment ever attempted.

That's pretty much the end of my story, one I could hardly believe myself if I hadn't lived through it.

Shannon suggested I commit it to paper in hopes of moving on with my life, and so, like a phone number recited over and over again so it's not forgotten, I'm hoping that writing down these facts will someday allow me to forget that I finally became the killer I once wanted desperately to be, although I always expect to look back with regret.

When I wasn't writing, I threw myself into the hard work of helping Dad get this place ready for winter, and the spring and summer that will surely follow. Working alone in the fields made me a little frightened of the fact that farms are tiny, isolated communities, nearly self-sufficient and therefore removed from the events that tease the rest of the world into conflicts of lust or necessity. Out here in the great flatness of Indiana, it's easy to define the world by visual horizons—the farthest fields where the sun rises and sets and all the crops growing in between. That makes it easy, almost natural, for farmers to ignore what occurs beyond those borders.

I now know, more than ever before, that a maze of unsolved problems threatens this great nation as it tries to adapt and survive in an ever more complex world. None of the challenges are really that much different from the resolved problems of our past— those vanquished threats that could have brought us to ruin the other times we fought for survival. There will always be problems, and they will always require real solutions, even extreme ones on occasion. Although newspaper and television reporters will expose many of them, not all of my countrymen will choose to see. Not every man will want to know.

Some men will make a point of looking away, as if they don't care about such foolishness. I once thought these men to be saints, but now I'm sure they're just too scared to follow the natural instinct that helps us survive. I will never trust them.

Other men will steal a glance and then look away. These men will always be cowards.

My greatest hope for this country is that there will always be the few who take a steady, interested look, which is what every damn one of them should want to do. Those people, in my opinion, have the courage it takes to protect my country.

From this glorious day forward, I pledge to be one of those people. I will love my country the way I intend to love my children, encouraging them to be strong but ready to correct them when they're wrong. I will be an informed voter, as trite as that sounds, ignoring partisanship and rhetoric and voting for what's best for America and not just me. I will expect honorable actions from politicians and demand accountability from those who fail to give it, refusing to accept the self-serving politics of the past because we can no longer afford to do so. I will protest if necessary, railing against decisions of big egos or small minds because protests are far less destructive than war. I will always remember that freedom is neither free nor easy, and so if this government I envision— the glorious government of our past—requires me to fight, I will once again stand ready to die for my country.

And when it comes to both Shannon and America, I swear to God that I will never again be a liar.

NOWHERE TO RUN
CHRISTOPHER BELTON

It's too much to be a coincidence. A series of computer-related crimes from different countries, all linked somehow to Japan. Some are minor. Some are deadly. But they are just enough to catch the eye of a young UN investigator. As he digs deeper he can't believe what he finds. Extortion. Torture. Murder. And ties to the most ruthless crime organization in the world.

It's a perfect plan, beautiful in its design, daring in its execution, and extremely profitable. No one in the Japanese underworld has ever conceived of such a plan and the organization isn't about to let anything stand in its way. Anyone who tries to interfere will soon find that there is no escape, no defense, and...nowhere to run.

TARGET
ACQUIRED
JOEL NARLOCK

It's the perfect weapon. It's small, with a wingspan of less than two feet and weighing less than two pounds. It can go anywhere, flying silently past all defenses. It's controlled remotely, so no pilot is endangered in even the most hazardous mission. It has incredible accuracy, able to effectively strike any target at great distances. It's a UAV, or Unmanned Aerial Vehicle, sometimes called a drone. The U.S. government has been perfecting it as the latest tool of war. But now a prototype has fallen into the wrong hands . . . and it's aimed at Washington. The government and the military are racing to stop the threat, but are they already too late?

- -

An Execution of Honor
Thomas L. Muldoon

They were a Marine Force Recon unit under the CIA's control, directed to maintain the power of a Latin American dictator, despite his involvement in the drug trade and a partnership with Fidel Castro. When rebel forces drove the dictator into the jungles, the unit led the holding action while his army was evacuated. But before he left, he tortured and killed two of the Marines. Now the unit wants justice—but Washington wants to return the dictator to power. So the surviving Force Recon unit members set out on their own to make the dictator pay. Both the United States and Cuba want the surviving unit members stopped at all costs. But who will be able to stop an elite group of Marines trained to be the most effective warriors alive?

ABDUCTED
BRIAN PINKERTON

Just a second. That was all it took. In that second Anita Sherwood sees the face of the young boy in the window of the bus as it stops at the curb—and she knows it is her son. The son who had been kidnapped two years before. The son who had never been found and who had been declared legally dead.

But now her son is alive. Anita knows it in her heart. She is certain that the boy is her son, but how can she get anyone to believe her? She'd given the police leads before that ended up going nowhere, so they're not exactly eager to waste much time on another dead end on a dead case. It's going to be up to Anita, and she'll stop at nothing to get her son back.

BODY PARTS
VICKI STIEFEL

They call it the Grief Shop. It's the Office of the Chief Medical Examiner for Massachusetts, and Tally Whyte is the director of its Grief Assistance Program. She lives with death every day, counseling families of homicide victims. But now death is striking close to home. In fact, the next death Tally deals with may be her own.

Boston is in the grip of a serial killer known as the Harvester, due to his fondness for keeping bloody souvenirs of his victims. But many of those victims are people that Tally knew, through her work or as friends. Tally realizes there's a connection, a link that only she can find. But she'd better find it fast. The Harvester is getting closer.
